SIDNEY SHELDON

Are You Afraid of the Dark?

HarperCollins*Publishers*

This novel is entirely a work of fiction.
The names, characters and incidents portrayed in it are
the work of the author's imagination. Any resemblance to
actual persons, living or dead, events or localities
is entirely coincidental.

HarperCollins*Publishers*
77–85 Fulham Palace Road,
Hammersmith, London W6 8JB

www.harpercollins.co.uk

Published by HarperCollins*Publishers* 2004
1 3 5 7 9 8 6 4 2

Sidney Sheldon asserts the moral right to
be identified as the author of this work

A catalogue record for this book
is available from the British Library

ISBN 0-00-716515-3

Set in Sabon by Palimpsest Book Production Ltd,
Polmont, Stirlingshire

Printed and bound in Great Britain by
Clays Limited, St Ives plc

For Atanas and Vera
with love

My special thanks go to my assistant
Mary Langford
whose contribution was invaluable

ARE YOU AFRAID
OF THE DARK?

PROLOGUE

Berlin, Germany

Sonja Verbrugge had no idea that this was going to be her last day on earth. She was pushing her way through the sea of summer tourists overflowing the busy sidewalks of Unter den Linden. Don't panic, she told herself. You must keep calm.

The instant message on her computer from Franz had been terrifying. *Run, Sonja! Go to the Artemisia Hotel. You will be safe there. Wait until you hear from –*

The message had ended suddenly. Why had Franz not finished it? What could be happening?

Frau Verbrugge was nearing Brandenburgische Strasse, where the Artemisia was located, a hotel which catered to women only. I will wait for Franz there and he will explain to me what this is all about, she thought.

* * *

When Sonja Verbrugge reached the next corner, the traffic light had turned to red, and as she stopped at the kerb, someone in the crowd bumped against her and she stumbled into the street. *Verdammt Touristen!* A limousine that had been double-parked suddenly moved toward her, grazing her just hard enough to knock her down. People began to gather around the woman.

'Is she all right?'

'Ist ihr etwas passiert?'

'Peut-elle marcher?'

At that moment, a passing ambulance stopped. Two attendants from the ambulance hurried over and took charge. 'We will take care of her.'

Sonja Verbrugge found herself being lifted into the ambulance. The door closed and a moment later, the vehicle sped away.

She was strapped to a stretcher, trying to sit up. 'I am fine,' she protested. 'It was nothing. I –'

One of the attendants was leaning over her. 'It is all right, Frau Verbrugge. Just relax.'

She looked up at him, suddenly alarmed. 'How do you know my –?'

She felt the sharp sting of a hypodermic needle in her arm and a moment later, she gave herself up to the waiting darkness.

Paris, France
Mark Harris was alone on the observation deck of the Eiffel Tower, oblivious to the driving rain swirling

around him. From time to time a streak of lightning shattered the raindrops into dazzling diamond waterfalls.

Across the River Seine stood the familiar Palais de Chaillot, and the Trocadéro Gardens, but he was unaware of them. His mind was focused on the astonishing news that was about to be released to the world.

The wind had begun to whip the rain into a frenzied maelstrom. Mark Harris shielded his wrist with his sleeve and looked at his watch. They were late. And why had they insisted on meeting here, at midnight? he wondered. Even as he was wondering, he heard the door to the tower lift open. Two men were moving toward him, fighting against the fierce wet wind.

As Mark Harris recognised them, he felt a sense of relief. 'You're late.'

'It's this damn weather, Mark. Sorry.'

'Well, you're here. The meeting in Washington is all set, isn't it?'

'That's what we need to talk to you about. As a matter of fact we had a long discussion this morning about the best way to handle this, and we decided –'

As they were speaking, the second man had moved behind Mark Harris and two things happened almost simultaneously. A heavy, blunt instrument slammed into his skull, and an instant later he felt himself being lifted and tossed over the parapet into the cold driving rain, his body plunging toward the unforgiving pavement thirty-eight storeys below.

Denver, Colorado

Gary Reynolds had grown up in rugged Kelowna, Canada, near Vancouver, and had had his flight training there, so he was accustomed to flying in treacherous mountainous terrain. He was piloting a Cessna Citation II, keeping a wary eye on the snow-capped peaks surrounding him.

The plane was commissioned to carry a cockpit crew of two, but today there was no co-pilot. Not this trip, Reynolds thought, grimly.

He had filed a false flight plan for Kennedy Airport. No one would think of looking for him in Denver. He would spend the night at his sister's home, and in the morning he would be on his way east, to meet the others. All the arrangements were complete, and –

A voice on the radio interrupted his thoughts. 'Citation One One One Lima Foxtrot, this is the approach control tower at Denver International Airport. Come in, please.'

Gary Reynolds pressed the radio button. 'This is Citation One One One Lima Foxtrot. I am requesting a clearance to land.'

'One Lima Foxtrot, say your position.'

'One Lima Foxtrot. I am fifteen miles north-east of the Denver Airport. Altitude 15,000 feet.'

He saw Pike's Peak looming up on his right side. The sky was bright blue, the weather clear. A good omen, he thought.

There was a brief silence. The voice from the tower came through again. 'One Lima Foxtrot, you are cleared to land at Runway Two-Six. Repeat, Runway Two-Six.'

'One Lima Foxtrot, roger.'

Without warning, Gary Reynolds felt the plane give a sudden, high bounce. Surprised, he looked out of the cockpit window. A strong wind had come up and within seconds, the Cessna was caught in a violent turbulence that began to toss the plane around. He pulled back the wheel to try to gain altitude. It was useless. He was trapped in a raging vortex. The plane was completely out of control. He slammed down the radio button.

'This is One Lima Foxtrot. I have an emergency.'

'One Lima Foxtrot, what is the nature of your emergency?'

Gary Reynolds was shouting into the microphone. 'I'm caught in a wind shear. Extreme turbulence! I'm in the middle of a goddamn hurricane!'

'One Lima Foxtrot, you are only four-and-a-half minutes from the Denver Airport and there is no sign of air turbulence on our screens.'

'I don't give a damn what's on your screens! I'm telling you –' The pitch of his voice suddenly rose. 'Mayday! May –'

In the control tower, they watched in shock as the blip on the radar screen disappeared.

Manhattan, New York
At dawn, at an area under the Manhattan Bridge of the East River next to Pier 17, half a dozen uniformed policemen and plain-clothes detectives were gathered

around a fully-dressed corpse lying on the gritty sand at the river's edge. The body had been carelessly tossed down, so its head was eerily bobbing back and forth in the water, following the vagaries of the tide.

The man in charge, Detective Earl Greenburg, from the Manhattan South Homicide Squad, had finished the official prescribed procedures. No one was allowed to approach the body until photographs had been taken, and he made notes of the scene while the officers looked for any evidence that might be lying around. The victim's hands had been wrapped in clean plastic bags.

Carl Ward, the medical examiner, finished his examination, stood up and brushed the dirt from his trousers. He looked at the two senior detectives. Detective Earl Greenburg was a professional, capable-looking man with an impressive record. Detective Robert Praegitzer was grey-haired and grizzled, with the laid-back manner of someone who had seen it all before.

Ward turned to Greenburg. 'He's all yours, Earl.'

'What have we got?'

'The obvious cause of death is a slashed throat, right through the carotid artery. He has two busted kneecaps, and it feels like a few ribs are broken. Someone worked him over pretty good.'

'What about the time of death?'

Ward looked down at the water lapping at the victim's head. 'Hard to say. My guess is that they dumped him here some time after midnight. I'll give you a full report when we get him to the morgue.'

Greenburg turned his attention to the body. Gray jacket, dark blue trousers, light blue tie, an expensive watch on the left wrist. Greenburg knelt down and started going through the victim's jacket pockets. His fingers found a note. He pulled it out, holding it by its edge.

'It's in Italian.' He glanced around. 'Gianelli!'

One of the uniformed policemen hurried up to him. 'Yes, sir?'

Greenburg handed him the note. 'Can you read this?'

Gianelli read it aloud, slowly. '"Last chance. Meet me at Pier 17 with the rest of the dope or swim with the fishes."' He handed it back.

Robert Praegitzer looked surprised. 'A Mafia hit? Why would they leave him out here like this, in the open?'

'Good question.' Greenburg was going through the corpse's other pockets. He pulled out a wallet and opened it. It was heavy with cash. 'They sure as hell weren't after his money.' He took a card from the wallet. 'The victim's name is Richard Stevens.'

Praegitzer frowned. 'Richard Stevens . . . Didn't we read something about him in the papers recently?'

Greenburg said, 'His *wife*. Diane Stevens. She's in court, in the Tony Altieri murder trial.'

Praegitzer said, 'That's right. She's testifying against the capo di capos.'

And they both turned to look at Richard Stevens' body.

ONE

In downtown Manhattan, in Courtroom 37 of the Supreme Court Criminal Term building at 180 Centre Street, the trial of Anthony (Tony) Altieri was in session. The large, venerable courtroom was filled to capacity with press and spectators.

At the defendant's table sat Anthony Altieri, slouched in a wheelchair, looking like a pale, fat frog folding in on itself. Only his eyes were alive, and every time he looked at Diane Stevens in the witness chair, she could literally feel the pulse of his hatred.

Next to Altieri sat Jake Rubenstein, Altieri's defence attorney. Rubenstein was famous for two things: his high-profile clientele, consisting mostly of mobsters, and the fact that nearly all of his clients were acquitted.

Rubenstein was a small, dapper man with a quick mind and vivid imagination. He was never the same in his courtroom appearances. Courtroom histrionics were his stock-in-trade, and he was highly skilled. He was brilliant at sizing up his opponents, with a feral instinct for finding their weaknesses. Sometimes Rubenstein imagined he was a lion, slowly closing in on his unsuspecting prey, ready to pounce . . . or a cunning spider, spinning a web that would eventually entrap them and leave them helpless . . . Sometimes he was a patient fisherman, gently tossing a line into the water and slowly moving it back and forth until the gullible witness took the bait.

The lawyer was carefully studying the witness on the stand. Diane Stevens was in her early thirties. An aura of elegance. Patrician features. Soft, blonde flowing hair. Green eyes. Lovely figure. A girl-next-door kind of wholesomeness. She was dressed in a chic, tailored, black suit. Jake Rubenstein knew that the day before, she had made a favourable impression on the jury. He had to be careful how he handled her. *Fisherman*, he decided.

Rubenstein took his time approaching the witness box, and when he spoke, his voice was gentle. 'Mrs Stevens, yesterday you testified that on the date in question, October 14, you were driving south on the Henry Hudson Parkway, when you got a flat tyre and pulled off the highway at the 158th Street exit, onto a service road into Fort Washington Park?'

'Yes.' Her voice was soft and cultured.

'What made you stop at that particular place?'

'Because of the flat tyre, I knew I had to get off the main road, and I could see the roof of a cabin through

10

the trees. I thought there might be someone there who could help me. I didn't have a spare.'

'Do you belong to an auto club?'

'Yes.'

'And do you have a phone in your car?'

'Yes.'

'Then why didn't you call the auto club?'

'I thought that might have taken too long.'

Rubenstein said, sympathetically, 'Of course. And the cabin was right there.'

'Yes.'

'So, you approached the cabin to get help?'

'That's right.'

'Was it still light outside?'

'Yes. It was about five o'clock in the afternoon.'

'And so, you could see clearly?'

'I could.'

'What did you see, Mrs Stevens?'

'I saw Anthony Altieri –'

'Oh. You had met him before?'

'No.'

'What made you sure it was Anthony Altieri?'

'I had seen his picture in the newspaper and –'

'So, you had seen pictures that resembled the defendant?'

'Well, it –'

'What did you see in that cabin?'

Diane Stevens took a shuddering breath. She spoke slowly, visualising the scene in her mind. 'There were four men in the room. One of them was in a chair, tied up. Mr Altieri seemed to be questioning him while the two other men stood next to him.' Her voice shook. 'Mr Altieri pulled out a gun, yelled something, and – and shot the man in the back of the head.'

Jake Rubenstein cast a sidelong glance at the jury. They were absorbed in her testimony.

'What did you do then, Mrs Stevens?'

'I ran back to my car and dialled 911 on my cell phone.'

'And then?'

'I drove away.'

'With a flat tyre?'

'Yes.'

Time for a little ripple in the water. 'Why didn't you wait for the police?'

Diane glanced toward the defence table. Altieri was watching her with naked malevolence.

She looked away. 'I couldn't stay there because I – I was afraid that the men might come out of the cabin and see me.'

'That's very understandable.' Rubenstein's voice hardened. 'What is *not* understandable is that when the police responded to your 911 call, they went into the cabin, and not only was no one there, Mrs Stevens, but they could find no sign that anyone had *been* there, let alone been murdered there.'

'I can't help that. I –'

'You're an artist, aren't you?'

She was taken aback by the question. 'Yes, I –'

'Are you successful?'

'I suppose so, but what does –?'

It was time to yank the hook.

'A little extra publicity never hurts, does it? The whole country watches you on the nightly news report on television, and on the front pages of –'

Diane looked at him, furious. 'I didn't do this for publicity. I would never send an innocent man to –'

'The key word is *innocent*, Mrs Stevens. And I will prove beyond a reasonable doubt that Mr Altieri *is* innocent. Thank you. You're finished.'

Diane Stevens ignored the *double entendre*. When she stepped down to return to her seat, she was seething. She whispered something to the prosecuting attorney, headed for the door, and walked out to the parking lot, the words of the defence attorney ringing in her ears. 'You're an artist, aren't you? . . . A little extra publicity never hurts, does it?' It was degrading. Still, all in all, she was satisfied with the way her testimony had gone. She had told the jury exactly what she had seen and they had no reason to doubt her. Anthony Altieri was going to be convicted and sent to prison for the rest of his life, and yet Diane could not help thinking of the venomous looks he had given her, and she felt a little shiver.

Diane handed the parking attendant her ticket and he went to get her car.

Two minutes later, Diane was driving onto the street, heading north, on her way home.

There was a stop sign at the corner. As Diane braked to a halt, a well-dressed young man standing at the kerb approached the car. 'Excuse me. I'm lost. Could you –?'

Diane lowered her window.

'Could you tell me how to get to the Holland Tunnel?' He spoke with an Italian accent.

'Yes. It's very simple. Go down to the first –'

The man raised his arm and there was a gun with a silencer in his hand. 'Out of the car, lady. Fast!'

Diane turned pale. 'All right. Please don't –' As she started to open the door, and the man stepped back, Diane slammed her foot down on the accelerator and the car sped away. She heard the rear window smash as a bullet went through it, and then a crack as another bullet hit the back of the car. Her heart was pounding so hard that it was difficult to breathe.

Diane Stevens had read about car jackings, but they had always been remote, something that happened to other people. And the man had tried to kill her. Did car jackers do that? Diane reached for her mobile phone and dialled 911. It took almost two minutes before an operator answered.

'911. What is your emergency?'

Even as Diane was explaining what had happened, she knew it was hopeless. The man would be long gone by now.

'I'll send an officer to the location. May I have your name, address, and phone number?'

Diane gave them to her. Useless, she thought. She glanced back at the shattered window and shuddered. She desperately wanted to call Richard at work and tell him what had happened, but she knew he was working on an urgent project. If she called him and told him what had just occurred, he would get upset and rush to her side – and she did not want him to miss his deadline. She would tell him what had happened when he got back to the apartment later.

And suddenly a chilling thought occurred to her: had the man been waiting for her, or was this just a coincidence? She remembered the conversation she had had with Richard when the trial began: 'I don't think you should testify, Diane. It could be dangerous.'

'Don't worry, darling. Altieri will be convicted. They'll lock him away for ever.'

'But he has friends and –'

'Richard, if I don't do this, I couldn't live with myself.'

What just happened had to be a coincidence, Diane decided. Altieri wouldn't be crazy enough to do anything to me, especially now, during his trial, she concluded.

Diane turned off the highway, and drove west until she reached her apartment building on East Seventy-fifth Street. Before she pulled into the underground garage, she took a last careful look in the rear-view mirror. Everything seemed normal.

The apartment was an airy, ground-floor duplex, with a spacious living room, floor-to-ceiling windows and a large, marble fireplace. There were upholstered floral sofas, armchairs, a built-in bookcase, and a large television screen. The walls were rainbowed with colourful paintings. There was a Childe Hassam, a Jules Pascin, a Thomas Birch, a George Hitchcock, and in one area, a group of Diane's paintings.

On the next floor was a master bedroom and bathroom, a second guest bedroom, and a sunny atelier where Diane painted. Several of her paintings were hanging on the walls. On an easel in the centre of the room was a half-finished portrait.

The first thing Diane did when she arrived home was to hurry into the atelier. She removed the half-finished portrait from the easel, and replaced it with a blank canvas. She began to sketch the face of the man who had tried to kill her, but her hands were trembling so hard that she had to stop.

Driving to Diane Stevens's apartment, Detective Earl Greenburg complained, 'This is the part of the job I hate most.'

Robert Praegitzer said, 'It's better that we tell them than have them hear about it on the evening news.' He looked at Greenburg. 'You going to tell her?'

Earl Greenburg nodded, unhappily. He found himself remembering the story of the detective who had gone to inform a Mrs Adams, the wife of a patrolman, that her husband had been killed.

'She's very sensitive,' the chief had cautioned the detective. 'You'll have to break the news carefully.'

'Don't worry. I can handle it.'

The detective had knocked on the door of the Adams' home, and when it was opened by Adams's wife, the detective had asked, 'Are you the widow Adams?'

Diane was startled by the sound of the front doorbell. She was not expecting anyone. She went to the intercom. 'Who is it?'

'Detective Earl Greenburg. I'd like to speak to you, Mrs Stevens.'

It's about the car jacking, Diane thought. The police got here fast.

She pressed the buzzer and Greenburg entered the hallway and walked to her door.

'Hello.'

'Mrs Stevens?'

'Yes. Thank you for coming so quickly. I started to draw a sketch of the man, but I . . .' She took a deep breath. 'He was swarthy, with deep-set light brown eyes and a little mole on his cheek. His gun had a silencer on it, and –'

Greenburg was looking at her in confusion. 'I'm sorry. I don't understand what –'

'The car jacker. I called 911 and –' She saw the expression on the detective's face. 'This isn't about the car jacking, is it?'

'No, ma'am, it's not.' Greenburg paused for a moment. 'May I come in?'

'Please.'

Greenburg walked into the apartment.

She was looking at him, frowning. 'What is it? Is something wrong?'

The words would not seem to come. 'Yes. I'm sorry. I – I'm afraid I have some bad news. It's about your husband.'

'What's happened?' Her voice was shaky.

'He's had an accident.'

Diane felt a sudden chill. 'What kind of accident?'

Greenburg took a deep breath. 'He was killed last night, Mrs Stevens. We found his body under a bridge along the East River this morning.'

Diane stared at him for a long moment, then slowly shook her head. 'You have the wrong person, Lieutenant. My husband is at work, in his laboratory.'

This was going to be even more difficult than he had anticipated. 'Mrs Stevens, did your husband come home last night?'

'No, but Richard frequently works all night. He's a scientist.' She was becoming more and more agitated.

'Mrs Stevens, were you aware that your husband was involved with the Mafia?'

Diane blanched. 'The Mafia? Are you insane?'

'We found –'

Diane was beginning to hyperventilate. 'Let me see your identification.'

'Certainly.' Detective Greenburg pulled out his ID card and showed it to her.

Diane glanced at it, handed it back, and then slapped Greenburg hard across his face. 'Does the city pay you to go around trying to scare honest citizens? My husband is not dead! He's at work.' She was shouting.

Greenburg looked into her eyes and saw the shock

and denial there. 'Mrs Stevens, would you like me to send someone over to look after you and –?'

'*You're* the one who needs someone to look after you. Now get out of here.'

'Mrs Stevens –'

'Now!'

Greenburg took out a business card and put it on a nearby table. 'In case you need to talk to me, here's my number.'

As he walked out of the door, Greenburg thought, Well, I handled that brilliantly. I might as well have said, 'Are you the widow Stevens?'

After Detective Earl Greenburg had gone, Diane locked the front door and took a deep, shivering breath.

The idiot! Coming to the wrong apartment and trying to scare me. I should report him, she thought as she looked at her watch. Richard will be coming home soon. It's time to start getting dinner ready, she told herself. She was making paella, his favourite dish. She went into the kitchen and started to prepare it.

Because of the secrecy of Richard's work, Diane never disturbed him at the laboratory, and if he did not call her, she knew it was a signal that he was going to be late. At eight o'clock, the paella was ready. She tasted it and smiled, satisfied. It was made just the way Richard liked it. At ten o'clock, when he still had not arrived, Diane put the paella in the refrigerator, and put a Post-it note on the refrigerator door: *Darling, supper is in the fridge. Come and wake me up.* Richard would be hungry when he came home.

Diane felt suddenly drained. She undressed, put on a nightgown, brushed her teeth, and got into bed. In a few minutes, she fell sound asleep.

At three o'clock in the morning, she woke up screaming.

TWO

It was dawn before Diane could stop trembling. The chill she felt was bone-deep. Richard was dead. She would never see him again, hear his voice, feel him hold her close. She kept thinking, It's my fault. I should never have gone into that courtroom. Oh, Richard, forgive me . . . please forgive me . . . I don't think I can go on without you. You were my life, my reason to live, and now I have none.

She wanted to curl up into a tiny ball.

She wanted to disappear.

She wanted to die.

She lay there, desolate, thinking about the past, how Richard had transformed her life . . .

Diane West had grown up in Sands Point, New York, an area of quiet affluence. Her father was a surgeon and her mother an artist, and Diane had begun to draw when she was three. She attended St Paul's boarding school, and when she was a freshman in college, had a brief relationship with her charismatic mathematics teacher. He told her he wanted to marry her because she was the only woman in the world for him. When Diane learned that he had a wife and three children, she decided that either his maths or his memory were defective, and transferred to Wellesley College.

She was obsessed with art, and spent every spare moment painting. By the time Diane was graduated, she had begun selling her paintings and was acquiring a reputation as an artist of promise.

That autumn, a prominent Fifth Avenue gallery gave Diane her own art show, and it was a huge success. The owner of the gallery, Paul Deacon, was a wealthy, erudite African-American who had helped nurture Diane's career.

Opening night, the salon was crowded. Deacon hurried up to Diane, a big smile on his face. 'Congratulations! We've already sold most of the paintings! I'm going to set up another exhibition in a few months, as soon as you're ready.'

Diane was thrilled. 'That's wonderful, Paul.'

'You deserve it.' He patted her on the shoulder and bustled off.

Diane was signing an autograph when a man came up behind her and said, 'I like your curves.'

Diane stiffened. Furious, she spun around and opened her mouth to make a sharp retort, when he went on:

'They have the delicacy of a Rosetti or a Manet.' He was studying one of her paintings as he spoke.

Diane caught herself just in time. 'Oh.' She took a closer look at the man. He appeared to be in his mid-thirties. He was about six feet tall, with an athletic build, blond hair, and bright blue eyes. He was dressed in a soft tan suit, a white shirt, and a brown tie.

'I – thank you.'

'When did you begin painting?'

'When I was a child. My mother was a painter.'

He smiled. 'My mother was a cook, but I can't cook. I know *your* name. I'm Richard Stevens.'

At that moment, Paul Deacon approached with three packages. 'Here are your paintings, Mr Stevens. Enjoy them.' He handed them to Richard Stevens, and walked away.

Diane looked at him in surprise. 'You bought three of my paintings?'

'I have two more in my apartment.'

'I'm – I'm flattered.'

'I appreciate talent.'

'Thank you.'

He hesitated. 'Well, you're probably busy, so I'll run –'

Diane heard herself saying, 'No. I'm fine.'

He smiled. 'Good.' He hesitated again. 'You could do me a big favour, Miss West.'

Diane looked at his left hand. He was not wearing a wedding band. 'Yes?'

'I happen to have two tickets for the opening of a

revival of Noël Coward's *Blithe Spirit* tomorrow night, and I have no one to go with. If you're free –?'

Diane studied him a moment. He seemed nice and was very attractive, but, after all, he was a total stranger. Too dangerous. Much too dangerous, she thought, as she heard herself say, 'I would love to go.'

The following evening turned out to be delightful. Richard Stevens was an amusing companion, and there was an instant compatibility. They shared an interest in art and music, and much more. She felt attracted to him, but she was not sure whether he felt the same way about her.

At the end of the evening, Richard asked, 'Are you free tomorrow night?'

Diane's answer was an unhesitating 'Yes.'

The following evening they had dinner at a quiet restaurant in Soho.

'Tell me about you, Richard.'

'Not much to tell. I was born in Chicago. My father was an architect and designed buildings all over the world, and my mother and I travelled with him. I went to about a dozen different foreign schools, and learned to speak a few languages in self-defence.'

'What do you do? For a living?'

'I work at KIG – Kingsley International Group. It's a large think-tank.'

'That sounds exciting.'

'It's fascinating. We do cutting-edge technology

research. If we had a motto, it would be something like, "If we don't have the answer now, wait until tomorrow."'

After dinner, Richard took Diane home. At her door, he took her hand and said, 'I enjoyed the evening. Thank you.'

And he was gone.

Diane stood there, watching him walk away, thinking, I'm glad he's a gentleman and not a wolf. I'm really glad. Damn!

They were together every night after that, and each time Diane saw Richard, she felt the same warm glow.

One Friday evening, Richard said, 'I coach a little league team on Saturdays. Would you like to come along and watch?'

Diane nodded. 'I'd love to, Coach.'

The following morning, Diane watched Richard working with the eager young ball players. He was gentle and caring and patient, screaming with joy when ten-year-old Tim Holm caught a fly ball, and it was obvious that the kids adored him.

Diane thought, I'm falling in love. I'm falling in love.

A few days later, Diane met up for lunch with a few women friends, and, as they left the restaurant, they passed a gypsy fortune telling parlour.

On an impulse Diane said, 'Let's have our fortunes told.'

'I can't, Diane. I have to get back to work.'

'So do I.'

'I have to pick up Johnny.'

'Why don't you go, tell us what she said.'

'All right. I will.'

Five minutes later, Diane found herself sitting opposite a sunken-faced crone with a mouth full of gold teeth and a dirty shawl over her head.

This is nonsense, Diane thought, why am I doing this? But she knew why she was doing it. She wanted to ask if she and Richard had a future together. It's just for the fun of it, she told herself.

Diane watched as the old woman picked up a tarot deck and began to shuffle the cards, never looking up.

'I would like to know if –'

'Shhh.' The woman turned up a card. It was the picture of the Fool, colourfully dressed and carrying a satchel. The woman studied it a moment. 'There are many secrets for you to learn.' She turned up another tarot card. 'This is the Moon. You have desires you are uncertain about.'

Diane hesitated and nodded.

'Does this involve a man?'

'Yes.'

The old woman turned up the next card. 'This is the Lovers' card.'

Diane smiled. 'Is that a good omen?'

'We will see. The next three cards will tell us.' She turned over another card. 'The Hanged Man.' She frowned, hesitated, and turned up the next card. 'The Devil,' she muttered.

'Is that bad?' Diane asked lightly.

The gypsy fortune teller did not answer.

Diane watched as the old woman turned up the next card. She shook her head. Her voice was eerily quiet. 'The Death card.'

Diane got to her feet. 'I don't believe in any of this,' she said, angrily.

The old woman looked up, and when she spoke, her voice was hollow. 'It does not matter what you believe. Death is all around you.'

THREE

Berlin, Germany

The *Polizeikommandant*, Otto Schiffer, two uniformed police officers, and the superintendent of the apartment building, Herr Karl Goetz, were staring at the naked, shrivelled body lying at the bottom of the overflowing bathtub. A faint bruise circled her neck.

The *Polizeikommandant* held a finger under the dripping tap. 'Cold.' He sniffed at the empty liquor bottle on the side of the tub, and turned to the building superintendent. 'Her name?'

'Sonja Verbrugge. Her husband is Franz Verbrugge. He is some kind of scientist.'

'She lived in this apartment with her husband?'

'Seven years. They were wonderful tenants. Always paid their rent on time. Never any trouble. Everyone loved –' He realised what he was about to say, and stopped.

'Did Frau Verbrugge have a job?'

'Yes, at one of those Internet cafés, where people pay to use the computers for –'

'What led you to discover the body?'

'It was because of the cold water tap in the bathtub. I tried to fix it several times, but it would never turn completely off.'

'So?'

'So, this morning, the tenant in the apartment below complained about water dripping through his ceiling. I came up here, knocked on the door, and when there was no answer, I opened it with my passkey. I came into the bathroom and found . . .' His voice choked.

A detective came into the bathroom. 'No liquor bottles in the cabinets, just wine.'

The *Kommandant* nodded. 'Right.' He pointed to the liquor bottle on the side of the tub. 'Have that tested for fingerprints.'

'Yes, sir.'

The *Kommandant* turned to Karl Goetz. 'Do you know where Herr Verbrugge is?'

'No. I always see him in the morning, when he leaves for work, but –' He made a helpless gesture.

'You did not see him this morning?'

'No.'

'Do you know if Herr Verbrugge was planning to take a trip somewhere?'

'No, sir. I do not.'

The *Kommandant* turned to the detective. 'Talk to the other tenants. Find out if Frau Verbrugge seemed

30

depressed lately, or if she and her husband quarrelled, and if she was a heavy drinker. Get all the information you can.' He looked at Karl Goetz. 'We will check on her husband. If you think of anything that might be helpful –'

Karl Goetz said, tentatively, 'I do not know whether this is helpful, but one of the tenants told me that an ambulance was parked in front of the building last night and he asked if anyone was sick. By the time I went outside to see what was happening, the ambulance was gone. Does that help?'

The *Kommandant* said, 'It will be looked into.'

'What – what about her – her body?' Karl Goetz asked, nervously.

'The medical examiner is on his way. Empty the tub and throw a towel over her.'

FOUR

'I'm afraid I have some bad news . . . murdered last night . . . we found his body under a bridge . . .'

For Diane Stevens, time had stopped. She wandered aimlessly through the large apartment filled with memories, and thought: Its comfort has gone . . . its warmth has gone . . . without Richard, it is only a collection of cold bricks. It will never come alive again.

Diane sank onto the couch and closed her eyes, thinking, Richard, darling, the day we were married, you asked what I would like as a gift. I told you I didn't want anything. But I do now. Come back to me. It doesn't matter if I can't see you. Just hold me in your arms. I'll know you're here. I need to feel your touch once more. I want to feel you stroking my breast . . . I want to imagine that I can hear your voice saying that I make the best paella in the world . . . I want to hear your voice asking me to stop pulling the bed covers off you . . . I want to hear you telling me that you love me. She tried to stop the sudden flow of tears, but it was impossible.

From the time Diane was told of Richard's murder, she spent the next several days locked away in their darkened apartment, refusing to answer the telephone or the door. She was like a wounded animal, hiding. She wanted to be alone with her pain. Richard, there were so many times I wanted to say 'I love you,' so that you would say 'I love you, too!' But I didn't want to sound needy. I was a fool. Now I'm needy, she thought.

Finally, when the constant ringing of the telephone and the incessant sound of the doorbell would not stop, Diane opened the door.

Carolyn Ter, one of Diane's closest friends, stood there. She looked at Diane and said, 'You look like hell.' Her voice softened. 'Everyone's been trying to reach you, honey. We've all been worried sick.'

'I'm sorry, Carolyn, but I just can't –'

Carolyn took Diane in her arms. 'I know. But there are a lot of friends who want to see you.'

Diane shook her head. 'No. It's im . . .'

'Diane, Richard's life is over, but yours isn't. Don't shut out the people who love you. I'll start making calls.'

Friends of Diane and Richard began telephoning and coming to the apartment, and Diane found herself listening to an endless litany of clichés:

'Think of it this way, Diane. Richard is at peace . . .'

'God called him, darling . . .'

'I know Richard is in heaven, shining down on you . . .'

'He's passed over to a better place . . .'

'He's joined the angels . . .'

Diane wanted to scream.

The stream of visitors seemed endless. Paul Deacon, the owner of the art gallery that displayed Diane's work, came to the apartment. He put his arms around Diane and said, 'I've been trying to reach you, but –'

'I know.'

'I'm so sad about Richard. He was a rare gentleman. But Diane, you can't shut yourself away like this. People are waiting to see more of your beautiful work.'

'I can't. It's not important any more, Paul. Nothing is. I'm through.'

She could not be persuaded.

The following day, when the doorbell rang, Diane reluctantly went to the door. She looked through the peephole and there seemed to be a small crowd outside. Puzzled, Diane opened the door. There were a dozen young boys in the hallway.

One of them was holding a little bouquet of flowers. 'Good morning, Mrs Stevens.' He handed the bouquet to Diane.

'Thank you.' She suddenly remembered who they were. They were members of the softball team that Richard had coached.

Diane had received countless baskets of flowers, cards of condolence, and E-mails, but this was the most touching gift of all.

'Come in,' Diane said.

The boys trooped into the room. 'We just wanted to tell you how bad we feel.'

'Your husband was a great guy.'

'He was really cool.'

'And he was an awesome coach.'

It was all Diane could do to hold back her tears. 'Thank you. He thought you were great, too. He was very proud of all of you.' She took a deep breath. 'Would you like some soft drinks or –?'

Tim Holm, the ten-year-old who had caught the fly ball, spoke up. 'No, thanks, Mrs Stevens. We just wanted to tell you that we'll miss him, too. We all chipped in for the flowers. They cost twelve dollars. Anyway, we just wanted you to know how sorry we are.'

Diane looked at them and said, quietly. 'Thank you, boys. I know how much Richard would appreciate your coming here.'

She watched as they mumbled their goodbyes, and left.

As Diane observed their departure, she remembered the first time she had watched Richard coach the boys. He had talked to them as though he were their age, in language they understood, and they loved him for it. That was the day I started falling in love with him, she thought.

Outside, Diane could hear the rumble of thunder and the first drops of rain beginning to roll down against the windows, like God's tears. *Rain.* It had been on a holiday weekend . . .

'Do you like picnics?' Richard asked.

'I adore them.'

He smiled. 'I knew it. I'll plan a little picnic for us. I'll pick you up tomorrow, at noon.'

It was a beautiful, sunny day. Richard had arranged for a picnic in the middle of Central Park. There was silverware and linens and when Diane saw what was in the picnic basket she laughed. Roast beef . . . a ham . . . cheeses . . . two large pâtés . . . an assortment of drinks and half-a-dozen desserts.

'There's enough for a small army! Who's going to join us?' And an unbidden thought popped into her mind. *A minister?* She blushed.

Richard was watching her. 'Are you all right?'

All right? I've never been so happy, Diane thought, as she said, 'Yes, Richard.'

He nodded. 'Good. We won't wait for the army. Let's start.'

While they ate, there was so much to talk about, and every word seemed to bring them closer. There was a strong sexual tension building up between them and they could both feel it. Then, in the middle of this perfect afternoon, it suddenly began to rain. In a matter of minutes, they were soaked.

Richard said ruefully, 'I'm sorry about this. I should have known better – the paper said no rain. I'm afraid it's spoiled our picnic, and –'

Diane moved close to him and said softly, 'Has it?'

And she was in his arms and her lips were pressed against his and she could feel the heat racing through her body. When she finally pulled back, she said, 'We have to get out of these wet clothes.'

He laughed. 'You're right. We don't want to catch –'

Diane said, 'Your place or mine?'

And Richard suddenly became very still. 'Diane, are you sure? I'm asking because . . . this isn't just a one-night stand.'

Diane said quietly, 'I know.'

Half an hour later they were in Diane's apartment, undressing, and their arms were around each other, and their hands were exploring tantalising places, and finally, when they could stand it no longer, they got into bed.

Richard was gentle and tender and passionate and frenzied and it was magical, and his tongue found her and moved slowly, and it felt as though warm waves were gently lapping at a velvet beach, and then he was deep inside her, filling her.

They spent the rest of the afternoon, and most of the night, talking and making love, and they opened their hearts to each other, and it was wonderful beyond words.

In the morning, while Diane was making their breakfast, Richard asked, 'Will you marry me, Diane?'

And she turned to him and said softly, 'Oh, yes.'

The wedding took place one month later. The ceremony was warm and wonderful, with friends and family congratulating the newlyweds, and Diane looked over at Richard's beaming face and thought of the fortune teller's ridiculous prediction, and smiled.

They had planned to leave for a honeymoon in France the week after the wedding, but Richard had called her from work. 'A new project has just come up and I can't get away. Is it all right if we do it in a few months? Sorry, baby.'

She had said, 'Of course it's all right, darling.'

'Do you want to come out and have lunch with me today?'

'I'd love that.'

'You like French food. I know a great French restaurant. I'll pick you up in half an hour.'

Thirty minutes later, Richard was outside, waiting for Diane. 'Hi, honey. I have to see one of our clients off at the airport. He's leaving for Europe. We'll say goodbye and then go on to lunch.'

She hugged him. 'Fine.'

When they arrived at Kennedy Airport, Richard said, 'He has a private plane. We'll meet him on the Tarmac.'

A guard passed them through to a restricted area where there was a Challenger waiting. Richard looked around. 'He's not here yet. Let's wait in the plane.'

'All right.'

They walked up the steps and entered the luxurious aircraft. The engines were running.

The stewardess walked in from the cockpit. 'Good morning.'

'Good morning,' Richard said.

Diane smiled. 'Good morning.'

They watched the flight attendant close the cabin door.

Diane looked at Richard. 'How late do you think your client is going to be?'

'He shouldn't be very long.'

The roar of the jets started getting louder. The plane began to taxi.

Diane looked out of the window and her face paled. 'Richard, we're moving.'

Richard looked at Diane in surprise. 'Are you sure?'

'Look out of the window.' She was panicking. 'Tell – tell the pilot –'

'What do you want me to tell him?'

'To stop!'

'I can't. He's already started.'

There was a moment of silence and Diane looked at Richard, her eyes wide. 'Where are we going?'

'Oh, didn't I tell you? We're going to Paris. You said you liked French food.'

She gasped. Then her expression changed. 'Richard, I can't go to Paris now! I have no clothes. I have no make-up. I have no –'

Richard said, 'I heard they have stores in Paris.'

She looked at him for a moment, then flung her arms around him. 'Oh, you fool, you. I love you.'

He grinned. 'You wanted a honeymoon. You've got it.'

FIVE

At Orly, a limousine was waiting to take them to the Hotel Plaza Athénée.

When they arrived, the manager said, 'Your suite is ready for you, Mr and Mrs Stevens.'

'Thank you.'

They were booked into Suite 310. The manager opened the door and Diane and Richard walked inside. Diane stopped, in shock. Half a dozen of her paintings were hanging on the walls. She turned to look at Richard. 'I – how did that –?'

Richard said innocently, 'I have no idea. I guess they have good taste here, too.'

Diane gave him a long, passionate kiss.

Paris was a wonderland. Their first stop was at Givenchy, to buy outfits for both of them, then over to Louis Vuitton, to choose luggage for all their new clothes.

They took a leisurely walk down the Champs-Elysées to the Place de la Concorde, and saw La Madeleine and the Palais Bourbon. They strolled along La Place Vendome, and spent a day at the Musée du Louvre. They wandered through the sculpture garden of the Musée Rodin, and had romantic dinners at Auberge de Trois Bonheurs, Au Petit Chez Soi, and D'Chez Eux.

The only thing that seemed strange to Diane were the telephone calls Richard received at peculiar hours.

'Who was that?' Diane asked once, at three a.m., as Richard finished a phone conversation.

'Just routine business.'

In the middle of the night? Diane wondered.

'Diane! Diane!'

She was shaken out of her reverie. Carolyn Ter was standing over her. 'Are you all right?'

'I'm – I'm fine.'

Carolyn put her arms around Diane. 'You just need time. It's only been a few days.' She hesitated. 'By the way, have you made arrangements for the funeral?'

Funeral. The saddest word in the English language. It carried the sound of death, an echo of despair.

'I – I haven't – been able to –'

'Let me help you with it. I'll pick out a casket and –'

'No!' The word came out harsher than Diane had intended.

44

Carolyn was looking at her, puzzled.

When Diane spoke again, her voice was shaky. 'Don't you see? This is – this is the last thing I can ever do for Richard. I want to make his funeral special. He'll want all his friends there, to say goodbye.' Tears were running down her cheeks.

'Diane –'

'I have to pick out Richard's casket to make sure he – he sleeps comfortably.'

There was nothing more Carolyn could say.

That afternoon, Detective Earl Greenburg was in his office when the call came.

'Diane Stevens is on the phone for you.'

'Oh, no, Greenburg remembered the slap in the face the last time he had seen her. What now? She probably has some new beef, he thought as he picked up the phone. 'Detective Greenburg.'

'This is Diane Stevens. I'm calling for two reasons. The first is to apologise. I behaved very badly, and I'm truly sorry.'

He was taken aback. 'You don't have to apologise, Mrs Stevens. I understand what you were going through.'

He waited. There was a silence.

'You said you had two reasons for calling.'

'Yes. My husband's –' Her voice broke. 'My husband's body is being held somewhere by the police. How do I get Richard back? I'm arranging for his – his funeral at the Dalton Mortuary.'

The despair in her voice made him wince. 'Mrs Stevens, I'm afraid that some red tape is involved. First, the coroner's office has to file a report on the autopsy, and then it's necessary to notify the various –' He was thoughtful for a moment, then made his decision. 'Look – you have enough on your mind. I'll make the arrangements for you. Everything will be set within two days.'

'Oh. I – I thank you. Thank you very –' Her voice choked up and the connection was broken.

Earl Greenburg sat there a long time, thinking about Diane Stevens and the anguish she was going through. Then he went to work cutting red tape.

The Dalton Mortuary was located on the east side of Madison Avenue. It was an impressive two-storey building with the façade of a Southern mansion. Inside, the décor was tasteful and understated, with soft lighting and whispers of pale curtains and drapes.

Diane said to the receptionist, 'I have an appointment with Mr Jones. Diane Stevens.'

'Thank you.'

The receptionist spoke into a phone and moments later the manager, a grey-haired, pleasant-faced man, came out to greet Diane.

'I'm Ron Jones. We spoke on the phone. I know how difficult everything is at a time like this, Mrs Stevens, and our job is to take the burden off you. Just tell me what you want and we will see that your wishes are carried out.'

Diane said uncertainly, 'I – I'm not even sure what to ask.'

Ron Jones nodded. 'Let me explain. Our services include a casket, a memorial service for your friends, a cemetery plot, and the burial.' He hesitated. 'From what I read of your husband's death in the newspapers, Mrs Stevens, you'll probably want a closed casket for the memorial service, so –'

'No!'

Jones looked at her in surprise. 'But –'

'I want it open. I want Richard to – to be able to see all his friends, before he . . .' Her voice trailed off.

Jones was studying her sympathetically. 'I see. Then if I may make a suggestion, we have a cosmetician who does excellent work where –' he said tactfully '– it's needed. Will that be all right?'

Richard would hate it, but – she thought, but she said, 'Yes.'

'There's just one thing more. We'll need the clothes you want your husband to be buried in.'

She looked at him, in shock. 'The –' Diane could feel the cold hands of a stranger violating Richard's naked body, and she shivered.

'Mrs Stevens?'

I should dress Richard myself. But I couldn't bear to see him the way he is. I want to remember – her thoughts were interrupted.

'Mrs Stevens?'

Diane swallowed. 'I hadn't thought about –' Her

voice was strangled. 'I'm sorry.' She was unable to go on.

He watched her stumble outside and hail a taxi.

When Diane returned home, she walked into Richard's closet. There were two racks filled with his suits. Each outfit held a treasured memory. There was the tan suit Richard had been wearing the night they had met at the art gallery. She remembered, 'I like your curves. They have the delicacy of a Rosetti or a Manet.' Could she let go of that suit? No.

Her fingers touched the next one. It was the light grey sport jacket Richard had worn to the picnic, when they had been caught in the rain. The memories flooded back: 'Your place or mine?'

How could she not keep it?

The pin-striped suit was next. 'You like French food . . . I know a great French restaurant . . .' She could almost hear his voice.

The navy blazer . . . the suede jacket . . . Diane wrapped the arms of a blue suit around herself and hugged it. *I could never let any of these go,* she thought. Each of them was a cherished remembrance. 'I can't.' Finally, sobbing, she grabbed a suit at random and fled.

The following afternoon, there was a message on Diane's voice mail:

Mrs Stevens, this is Detective Greenburg. I wanted to let you know that everything here has been cleared. I've talked to the Dalton Mortuary. You're free to go ahead with whatever plans you want to make . . . There was a slight pause. *I wish you well . . . Goodbye.*

Diane called Ron Jones at the Mortuary. 'I understand that my husband's body has arrived with you.'

'Yes, Mrs Stevens. I already have someone taking care of the cosmetics, and we've received the clothes you sent. Thank you.'

'I thought – would this coming Friday be all right for the funeral?'

'Friday will be fine. By then we will have taken care of all the necessary details. I would suggest 11 a.m.'

In three days, Richard and I will be parted for ever. Or until I join him.

On Thursday morning, Diane was busily preparing the final details of the funeral, verifying the long list of invitees and the pallbearers, when the telephone call came.

'Mrs Stevens?'

'Yes.'

'This is Ron Jones. I just wanted to let you know that we have followed your new instructions, just as your secretary ordered.'

Diane said, puzzled. 'My secretary –?'

'Yes, over the phone.'

'I don't have a –'

'Frankly, I was a little surprised, but, of course, it was your decision. We cremated your husband's body one hour ago.'

SIX

Paris, France

Kelly Harris had exploded into the world of fashion like a roman candle. She was in her mid-twenties, an African-American with skin the colour of melted honey and a face that was a photographer's dream. She had soft, brown, intelligent eyes, sensual full lips, lovely long legs, and a figure filled with erotic promise. Her dark hair was cut short in deliberate dishabille, with a few strands sprawling across her forehead. Earlier that year, the readers of *Elle* and *Mademoiselle* magazines had voted Kelly the Most Beautiful Model in the World.

As she finished dressing, Kelly looked around the penthouse, feeling, as always, a sense of wonder. The apartment was spectacular. It was on the exclusive Rue St-Louis-en-l'Ile, in the Fourth Arrondissement of Paris. The apartment had a double-door entry that opened into an elegant hall with high ceilings and soft yellow wall panels, and the living room was furnished with an eclectic mixture of French and Regency furniture. From the terrace, across the Seine, was a view of Notre Dame.

Kelly was looking forward to the coming weekend. Her husband was going to take her out for one of his surprise treats.

'I want you to get all dressed up, honey. You're going to love where we're going,' he had said.

Kelly smiled to herself. Mark was the most wonderful man in the world. Kelly glanced at her wristwatch and sighed. I had better get moving, she thought, the show starts in half an hour.

A few moments later, she left the apartment, heading down the hallway towards the lift. As she did so, the door of a neighbouring apartment opened and Madame Josette Lapointe came out into the corridor. A small, butterball of a woman, she always had a friendly word for Kelly.

'Good afternoon, Madame Harris.'

Kelly smiled. 'Good afternoon, Madame Lapointe.'

'You're looking beautiful, as always.'

'Thank you.' Kelly pressed the button for the lift.

A dozen feet away, a burly man in work clothes was adjusting a wall fixture. He glanced at the two women, then quickly turned his head.

'How is the modelling going?' Madame Lapointe asked.

'Very well, thank you.'

'I must come and see you in one of your fashion shows soon.'

'I'll be happy to arrange it any time.'

The lift arrived, and Kelly and Madame Lapointe stepped inside. The man in work clothes pulled out a small walkie-talkie, spoke hurriedly into it, and rapidly walked away.

As the lift door started to close, Kelly heard the telephone ring in her apartment. She hesitated. She was in a hurry, but it could be Mark calling.

'You go ahead,' she said to Madame Lapointe.

Kelly stepped out of the elevator, fumbled for her key, found it, and ran back into her apartment. She raced to the ringing telephone and picked it up. 'Mark?'

A strange voice said, 'Nanette?'

Kelly was disappointed. *'Il n'y a personne qui repond a ce nom ici.'*

'Pardonnez moi.'

A wrong number. Kelly put the phone down. As she did, there was a tremendous crash that shook the whole building. A moment later, there was a babble of voices and loud screams. Horrified, Kelly rushed into the hall to see what had happened. The sounds were coming from below. Kelly ran down the stairs and when she reached the lobby, she heard the clamour of voices in the basement.

Apprehensively, she went down the stairs to the basement and stood in shock as she saw the crushed lift car and the horribly mangled body of Madame Lapointe inside it. Kelly felt faint. That poor woman.

A minute ago she was alive and now . . . And I could have been in there with her. If not for that telephone call . . . she thought.

A crowd had gathered around the lift, and sirens could be heard in the distance. I should stay, Kelly thought guiltily, but I can't, I have to leave. She looked at the body and whispered, 'I'm so sorry, Madame Lapointe.'

When Kelly arrived at the fashion salon and walked in through the stage door, Pierre, the nervous fashion co-ordinator, was waiting.

He pounced on her. 'Kelly! Kelly! You're late! The show has already started and –'

'I'm sorry, Pierre. There – there was a bad accident.'

He looked at her in alarm. 'Are you hurt?'

'No.' Kelly closed her eyes for a moment. The idea of going to work after what she had witnessed was nauseating, but she had no choice. She was the star of the show.

'Hurry!' Pierre said. '*Vite!*'

Kelly started toward her dressing room.

The year's most prestigious fashion show was being held at 31 Rue Cambon, Chanel's original salon. The paparazzi were in the front rows. Every seat was occupied, and the back of the room was crowded with standees, eager to get the first glimpse of the coming season's new designs. The room had been decorated for the event with flowers and draped fabrics, but no one was paying any attention to the décor. The real attractions were on the long runway – a river of moving colours, beauty and style. In the background, music was playing, with a slow, sexy beat, accentuating the movements on stage.

As the lovely models glided back and forth, they were accompanied by a voice on a loudspeaker, giving a running commentary on the outfits.

An Asian brunette started down the runway: '. . . a satin wool jacket with edge top-stitching and georgette trousers and a white blouse . . .'

A slim blonde undulated the catwalk: '. . . is wearing a black cashmere turtleneck with white cotton cargo pants . . .'

A redhead appeared: '. . . a black leather jacket and black shantung trousers with a white knitted shirt . . .'

A French model: '. . . a pink, three-button, angora jacket, a pink cable-stitch rollneck and black cuffed trousers . . .'

A Swedish model: '. . . a navy satin wool suit and a lilac Charmeuse blouse . . .'

And then the moment everyone had been waiting for. The Swedish model had walked off, and the catwalk was deserted. The voice on the loudspeaker said, 'And now that the swimming season is here, we are pleased to display our new line of beachwear.'

There was a crescendo of anticipation, and then Kelly Harris appeared at the peak of it. She was wearing a white bikini, a bra that barely covered her firm, young breasts, and a figure-hugging bottom. As she floated sensuously down the runway, the effect was mesmerising. There was a wave of applause. Kelly gave a faint smile of acknowledgement, circled the runway and disappeared.

Backstage, two men were waiting for her.

'Mrs Harris, if I could have a moment –?'

'I'm sorry,' Kelly said apologetically. 'I have to make a quick change.' She started to walk away.

'Wait! Mrs Harris! We are with the *Police Judiciaire*. I am Chief Inspector Dune and this is Inspector Steunou. We need to talk.'

Kelly stopped. 'The police? Talk about what?'

'You are Mrs Mark Harris, yes?'

'Yes.' She was filled with sudden apprehension.

'Then I am sorry to inform you that – that your husband died last night.'

Kelly's mouth was dry. 'My husband –? How –?'

'Apparently, he committed suicide.'

There was a roar in Kelly's ears. She could barely make out what the Chief Inspector was saying. '. . . Tour Eiffel . . . midnight . . . note . . . very regrettable . . . deepest sympathy.'

The words were not real. They were pieces of sound with no meaning.

'Madame –'

'This weekend, I want you to get all dressed up, honey. You're going to love where we're going,' had been his last words.

'There is some – some mistake,' Kelly said. 'Mark wouldn't –'

'I am sorry.' The Chief Inspector was watching Kelly closely. 'Are you all right, Madame?'

'Yes.' Except that my life has just ended, she thought.

Pierre bustled over to Kelly, carrying a beautiful striped bikini. '*Cherie*, you must change quickly. There is no time to waste.' He thrust the bikini into her arms. '*Vite! Vite!*'

Kelly slowly let it drop to the floor. 'Pierre?'

He was looking at her in surprise. 'Yes?'

'You wear it.'

Kelly was taken back to her apartment in a limousine. The salon manager had wanted to send someone to be with her, but Kelly had refused. She wanted to be alone. Now, as she walked in through the entrance, Kelly saw the superintendent, Philippe Cendre, and a man in overalls, surrounded by a group of tenants.

One of the tenants said, 'Poor Madame Lapointe. What a terrible accident.'

The man in overalls held up two jagged ends of a heavy cable. 'It was no accident, Madame. Someone cut the lift's safety brakes.'

SEVEN

At four o'clock in the morning, Kelly was seated in a chair, staring out of the window in a daze, hearing a babble of voices. 'Police Judiciaire . . . we need to talk . . . Tour Eiffel . . . suicide note . . . Mark is dead . . . Mark is dead . . . Mark is dead.' The words became a dirge pulsing through Kelly's brain.

In her mind, Mark's body was tumbling down, down, down . . . She put her arms out to catch him just before he smashed against the pavement.

Did you die because of me? Was it something I did? Something I didn't do? Something I said? Something I didn't say? I was asleep when you left, darling, and I didn't have a chance to say goodbye, to kiss you and tell you how much I love you. I need you. I can't stand it without you, Kelly thought. Help me, Mark. Help me – the way you always helped me . . . She slumped back, remembering how it had been before Mark, in the awful early days . . .

Kelly had been born in Philadelphia, the illegitimate daughter of Ethel Hackworth, a black maid who worked for one of the town's most prominent white families. Her father was a judge. Ethel was seventeen and beautiful, and Ross, the handsome, blond, twenty-year-old son of the Turner family, had been attracted to her. He had seduced her, and, a month later, Ethel learned she was pregnant.

When she told Ross, he said, 'That's – that's wonderful.' And he rushed into his father's study to tell him the bad news.

Judge Turner called Ethel into his study the next morning and said, 'I won't have a whore working in this house. You're fired.'

With no money, no education and few skills, Ethel had taken a job as a cleaning lady in an industrial building, working long hours to support her newborn daughter. In five years, Ethel had saved enough money to buy a rundown clapboard house which she turned into a boarding house for men. The house consisted of a living room, a dining room, four small bedrooms, two bathrooms, a kitchen and a narrow little utility room which Kelly slept in.

From that time on, there was a series of men who were constantly arriving and leaving.

'These are your uncles,' Ethel told her. 'Don't bother them.'

Kelly was pleased that she had such a large family until she became old enough to realise that they were all strangers.

When Kelly was eight years old, she was asleep one night in her small, darkened bedroom when she was awakened by a gutteral whisper. 'Shhh! Don't make a sound.'

Kelly felt her nightgown being lifted and, before she could protest, one of her 'uncles' was on top of her and his hand was over her mouth. Kelly could feel him forcibly spreading her legs. She tried to struggle, but he held her down. She felt him tearing inside her body and she was filled with excruciating pain. He was merciless, forcing himself inside her, going deeper and deeper, rubbing her skin raw. Kelly could feel her warm blood gushing out. She was silently screaming, afraid she would faint. She was trapped in the terrifying blackness of her room.

Finally, after what seemed like an eternity, she felt him shudder and then withdraw.

He whispered, 'I'm leaving. But if you ever tell your mother about this, I'll come back and kill her.' And he was gone.

The next week was almost unbearable. She was in misery all the time, but she treated her lacerated body as best she could, until finally the pain subsided. She wanted to tell her mother what had happened, but she did not dare.

The incident had lasted only a few minutes, but those

few minutes altered Kelly's life. She changed from a young girl who had dreamed of having a husband and children, to someone who felt that she was tarnished and disgraced. She resolved that she would never let a man touch her again.

Something else had changed in Kelly. From that night on, she was afraid of the dark.

EIGHT

When Kelly turned ten, Ethel put her to work, helping around the boarding house. Kelly rose at five every morning, to clean the toilets, scrub the kitchen floor, and help prepare breakfast for the boarders. After school, she did the laundry, mopped the floor, dusted, and assisted with dinner. Her life became a dreadful, tedious routine.

She was eager to help her mother, hoping for a word of praise. It never came. Her mother was too pre-occupied with the boarders to pay any attention to her daughter.

When Kelly was very young, a kind boarder had read her the story of *Alice in Wonderland* and Kelly was fasci-nated by the way Alice escaped down a magic rabbit hole. That's what I need, Kelly thought, a way to escape. I can't spend the rest of my days scrubbing toilets and mopping floors and cleaning up after messy strangers.

And one day, Kelly found her magic rabbit hole. It was her imagination, which would take her anywhere she wanted to go. She re-wrote her life . . .

She had a father, and her mother and father were the same colour. They never got angry and yelled at her. They all lived in a beautiful home. Her mother and father loved her. Her mother and father loved her. Her mother and father loved her . . .

When Kelly was fourteen, her mother married one of the boarders, a bartender named Dan Berke, a surly, middle-aged man who was negative about everything. Kelly could do nothing to please him.

'The dinner is lousy . . .'

'That dress is the wrong colour for you . . .'

'The shade in the bedroom is still broken. I told you to fix it . . .'

'You haven't finished cleaning the bathrooms . . .'

Kelly's stepfather had a drinking problem. The wall between Kelly's bedroom and her mother and stepfather's bedroom was thin, and night after night, Kelly could hear the sounds of blows and screams. In the morning, Ethel would appear wearing heavy make-up that failed to cover bruises and black eyes.

Kelly was devastated. We should get out of here, she thought. My mother and I love each other.

One night, when Kelly was half asleep, she heard loud voices from the next room. 'Why didn't you get rid of the kid before she was born?'

'I tried to, Dan. It didn't work.'

Kelly felt as though she had been kicked in the gut. Her mother had never wanted her. No one did.

Kelly found another escape from the unending dreariness of her life: the world of books. She became an insatiable reader, and spent as much of her spare time as she could at the public library.

At the end of the week, there was never any money left for Kelly, and she got a job as a babysitter, envying the happy families she would never have.

At seventeen, Kelly was developing into the beauty her mother had once been. The boys at school began asking her for dates. She was repelled. She turned them all down.

On Saturday, when there was no school and Kelly's chores were finished, she would hurry to the public library and spend the afternoon reading.

Mrs Lisa Marie Houston, the librarian, was an intelligent, sympathetic woman with a quiet, friendly manner, whose clothes were as unpretentious as her personality. Seeing Kelly in the library so often, Mrs Houston became curious.

One day she said, 'It's nice to see a young person enjoying reading so much. You spend a lot of time here.'

It was the opening gambit of a friendship. As the weeks went by, Kelly poured out her fears and hopes and dreams to the librarian.

'What would you like to do with your life, Kelly?'

'Be a teacher.'

'I think you'd make a wonderful teacher. That's the most rewarding profession in the world.'

Kelly started to speak, then stopped. She was remembering a breakfast conversation with her mother and stepfather a week earlier. Kelly had said, 'I need to go to college. I want to be a teacher.'

'A teacher?' Berke had laughed. 'That's a dumbass idea. Teachers make zip. Do you hear me? Zip. You can make more sweeping floors. Anyway, your old lady and I don't have money to send you to college.'

'But I've been offered a scholarship and –'

'So what? You'll spend four years wasting your time. Forget it. With your looks, you could probably peddle your ass.'

Kelly had left the table.

Now she said to Mrs Houston, 'There's a problem. They won't let me go to college.' Her voice was choked. 'I'll spend the rest of my life doing what I'm doing!'

'Of course you won't.' Mrs Houston's tone was firm. 'How old are you?'

'In three months, I'll be eighteen.'

'You'll soon be old enough to make your own decisions. You're a beautiful young woman, Kelly. Do you know that?'

'No. Not really.' How can I tell her that I feel like a freak? I don't feel beautiful, she thought. 'I hate my life, Mrs Houston. I don't want to be like – I want to get away from this town. I want something different and I'll never have it.' She was trying hard to control her emotions. 'I'll never have a chance to do something, to be somebody.'

'Kelly –'

'I never should have read all those books.' Her voice was bitter.

'Why?'

'Because they're filled with lies. All those beautiful people and glamorous places and magic . . .' Kelly shook her head. 'There is no magic.'

Mrs Houston studied her for a moment. It was obvious that Kelly's sense of self-worth had been badly damaged. 'Kelly, there *is* magic, but you have to be the magician. You have to make the magic happen.'

'Really?' Kelly's tone was cynical. 'How do I do that?'

'First, you have to know what your dreams are. Yours are to have an exciting life, filled with interesting people and glamorous places. The next time you come in here, I'll show you how to make your dreams come true.'

Liar, Kelly thought.

The week after Kelly graduated, she returned to the library. Mrs Houston said, 'Kelly, do you remember what I said about making your own magic?'

Kelly said, sceptically, 'Yes.'

Mrs Houston reached behind her desk and pulled

out a handful of magazines: *Cosmogirl*, *Seventeen*, *Glamour*, *Mademoiselle*, *Essence*, *Allure* ... She handed them to Kelly.

Kelly looked at them. 'What am I supposed to do with these?'

'Have you ever thought of becoming a model?'

'No.'

'Look at these magazines. Then tell me if they give you any ideas that might bring magic into your life.'

She means well, Kelly thought, but she doesn't understand. 'Thank you, Mrs Houston, I will.'

Kelly took the magazines back to the boarding house and shoved them into a corner and forgot about them. She spent the evening doing her chores.

As Kelly started to get into bed that night, exhausted, she remembered the magazines Mrs Houston had given her. She picked up a few out of curiosity, and started to skim through them. It was another world. The models were beautifully dressed, with handsome, elegant men at their sides, in London and Paris and exotic places all over the world. Kelly felt a sudden sense of yearning. She hastily put on a dressing gown and walked down the hall to the bathroom.

She studied herself in the mirror. She supposed that perhaps she was attractive. Everyone always told her she was. Even if it's true, Kelly thought, I have no experience. She thought about her future life in Philadelphia, and looked in the mirror again. Everyone has to start somewhere. You have to be the magician, make your own magic, she told herself.

Early the next morning, Kelly went to the library to see Mrs Houston.

Mrs Houston looked up, surprised to see Kelly in the library so early. 'Good morning, Kelly. Have you had a chance to look at the magazines?'

'Yes.' Kelly took a deep breath. 'I would like to try being a model. The problem is that I have no idea where to start.'

Mrs Houston smiled. 'I do. I looked in the New York telephone directory. You said you wanted to leave this town.' Mrs Houston took a typed sheet of paper from her handbag and handed it to Kelly. 'This is a list of the top dozen modelling agencies in Manhattan, with their addresses and telephone numbers.' She squeezed Kelly's hand. 'Start at the top.'

Kelly was stunned. 'I – I don't know how to thank –'

'I'll tell you how. Let me see your photograph in these magazines one day.'

At dinner that evening, Kelly said, 'I've decided that I'm going to be a model.'

Her stepfather grunted. 'That's your stupidest idea yet. What the hell's the matter with you? All models are whores.'

Kelly's mother sighed. 'Kelly, don't make my mistake. I had false dreams, too. They'll kill you. You're black and poor. You're not going anywhere.'

The words sounded to Kelly like the lid of a coffin closing.

At five o'clock the following morning, Kelly packed a suitcase and headed for the bus station. In her handbag were two hundred dollars that she had earned babysitting.

The bus ride to Manhattan took two hours, and Kelly spent that time fantasising about her future. She was going to become a professional model. 'Kelly Hackworth' did not sound professional. I know what I'll do, she thought, I'll just use my first name. She said it in her mind over and over. 'And this is our top model, Kelly.'

She checked into a cheap hotel and, at nine o'clock, Kelly walked in through the front door of the modelling agency at the top of her list. Kelly had no make-up on and was wearing a dress wrinkled from the journey.

There was no one at the reception desk in the lobby. She approached a man sitting in an office, busily writing at a desk.

'Excuse me,' Kelly said.

The man grunted something without looking up.

Kelly hesitated. 'I wondered if you needed a model.'

'No,' the man muttered, 'we're not hiring.'

Kelly sighed. 'Thank you, anyway.' She turned to leave.

The man glanced up and his expression changed. 'Wait! Wait a minute. Come back here.' He had jumped to his feet. 'My God. Where did you come from?'

Kelly looked at him, puzzled. 'Philadelphia.'

'I mean – never mind. Have you ever modelled before?'

'No.'

'It doesn't matter. You'll learn it here, on the job.'

Kelly's throat was suddenly dry. 'Does that mean I'm – I'm going to be a model?'

He grinned. 'I'll say. We have clients who will go crazy when they see you.'

She could hardly believe it. This was the biggest model agency in the business and they –

'My name is Bill Lerner. I run this agency. What's your name?'

This was the moment Kelly had been dreaming of. This was the first time she was going to use her new, one-word, professional name.

Lerner was staring at her. 'Don't you know your own name?'

Kelly drew herself up to her full height and said confidently, 'Of course I do. Kelly.'

NINE

The sound of the plane buzzing low overhead brought a smile to Lois Reynolds' lips. Gary. He was late. Lois had offered to go to the airport to meet him, but he had said, 'Don't bother, sis. I'll take a taxi.'

'But Gary, I'll be glad to –'

'It will be better if you stay home and wait for me there.'

'Whatever you say, bro.'

Her brother had always been the most important person in Lois's life. Her growing-up years, in Kelowna, had been a nightmare. From the time Lois was a young girl, she felt that the world was against her: shamed by images in glamour magazines, of fashion models and female film stars – and just because she was a little plump. Where was it written that buxom girls could not be just as beautiful as sickly-looking, skinny girls? Lois Reynolds would constantly study her reflection in the mirror. She had long blonde hair, blue eyes, delicate pale features, and what Lois considered a pleasantly full-figured body. Men can go around with their beer bellies hanging over their pants and no one says a word, she would think but let a woman put on a few pounds and she's an object of scorn. What male moron had the right to decide that the ideal woman's figure should be 36–26–36? she thought.

For as long as Lois could remember, her schoolmates had mocked her behind her back – 'fat ass', 'tubby', 'porky'. The words hurt deeply. But Gary had always been there to defend her.

By the time Lois had been graduated from the University of Toronto, she had had enough of the teasing. If Mr Wonderful is looking for a real woman, I'm here, she would say to herself.

And one day, unexpectedly, Mr Wonderful appeared. His name was Henry Lawson. They met at a church social, and Lois was immediately attracted to him. He was a tall, thin, blond, with a face that seemed always ready to smile and a disposition that matched it. His father was the minister of the church. Lois spent most of her time at the social with Henry, and while they were talking, she learned that he owned a successful plant nursery and was a nature lover.

'If you're not busy tomorrow night,' he said, 'I'd like to take you to dinner.'

There was no hesitation on Lois's part. 'Yes, thank you.'

Henry Lawson took her to the Sassafraz, one of the finest restaurants in Toronto. The menu was tantalising, but Lois ordered a light dish because she did not want Henry to think she was a gourmand.

Henry noticed that she was eating only a salad and he said, 'That's not enough for you.'

'I'm trying to lose weight,' Lois lied.

He put his hand over hers. 'I don't want you to lose weight, Lois. I like you just the way you are.'

She felt a sudden thrill. He was the first man who had ever said that to her.

'I'm going to order you a steak, some potatoes, and a Caesar salad,' Henry said.

It was so wonderful, finally, to find a man who understood her appetite and approved of it.

Over the next few weeks they met as often as they could. Then, less than a month after their first date, Henry said, 'I love you, Lois. I want you to be my wife.'

Words Lois had always thought she would never hear. She put her arms around him and said, 'I love you, too, Henry. I want to be your wife.'

The wedding took place at the church where they had met, five days later. Gary and a few friends were there, and it was a beautiful ceremony, officiated by Henry's father. Lois had never been so happy.

'Where are you two going to honeymoon?' Reverend Lawson asked.

'Lake Louise,' Henry said. 'It's very romantic.'

'That sounds perfect.'

Henry put his arms around Lois. 'I expect every day to be a honeymoon for the rest of our lives.'

Lois was ecstatic.

Immediately after the wedding, they left for Lake Louise. It was a spectacular oasis in Banff National Park, in the heart of the Canadian Rockies.

They arrived in the late afternoon, with the sun sparkling over the lake.

Henry took Lois in his arms. 'Are you hungry?'

She looked into his eyes and smiled. 'No.'

'Neither am I. Why don't we get undressed?'

'Oh, yes, darling.'

Two minutes later, they were in bed and Henry was making exquisite love to her. It was wonderful. Exhausting. Exhilarating.

'Oh, darling, I love you so much.'

'I love you too, Lois,' Henry said. Then he stood up. 'Now we must fight carnal sin.'

Lois looked at him, confused. 'What?'

'Get on your knees.'

She laughed. 'Aren't you tired, darling?'

'Get on your knees.'

She smiled. 'All right.'

She got on her knees and watched, puzzled, as Henry took a large belt from his trousers. He walked up to her and, before she realised what was happening, he smashed the belt hard against her naked buttocks.

Lois screamed and started to get up. 'What are you –?'

He shoved her down. 'I told you, darling. We must fight carnal sin.' He raised the belt and struck her again.

'Stop it! Stop it!'

'Stay there.' His voice was filled with fervour.

Lois fought to get up, but Henry held her down with one strong hand and slammed the belt against her again.

Lois felt as though her backside had been flayed. 'Henry! My God! Stop it!'

Finally, Henry stood up and took a deep, quivery breath. 'It's all right now.'

It was difficult for Lois to move. She could feel the open cuts oozing. She painfully managed to get to her feet. She couldn't speak. She could only stare in horror at her husband.

'Sex is sinful. We must fight temptation.'

She shook her head, still speechless, still not believing what had just happened.

'Think of Adam and Eve, the beginning of the downfall of mankind.' He went on.

Lois began to weep, huge gulping sobs.

'It's all right now.' He took Lois in his arms. 'It's all right. I love you.'

Lois said uncertainly, 'I love you too, but –'

'Don't worry. We have conquered it.'

Which means that will be the last time that happens, Lois thought. It probably has something to do with his being a minister's son. Thank God it's over.

Henry held her close. 'I love you so much. Let's go out to dinner.'

In the restaurant, Lois was barely able to sit down. The pain was terrible, but she was too embarrassed to ask for a cushion.

'I'll order,' Henry said. He ordered a salad for himself and an enormous meal for Lois. 'You have to keep your strength up, my dearest.'

During the meal, Lois thought about what had just happened. Henry was the most wonderful man she had ever known. She had been taken aback by his – what was it, she wondered – fetish? Anyway, that was over. She could look forward to spending the rest of her life taking care of this man, and being taken care of.

When they had finished their entrées, Henry ordered an extra dessert for Lois and said, 'I like a lot of woman.'

She smiled. 'I'm glad I please you.'

When dinner was over, Henry said, 'Shall we go back to our room?'

'Fine.'

When they returned to their room, they undressed and, as Henry took Lois in his arms, her pain seemed to disappear. His lovemaking was sweet and gentle and was even more enjoyable than before.

Lois hugged her husband and said, 'That was wonderful.'

'Yes,' he nodded. 'Now we must atone for carnal sin. Get on your knees.'

In the middle of the night, while Henry was asleep, Lois quietly packed a suitcase and fled. She took a plane to Vancouver and called Gary. They met for lunch, and she told him what had happened.

'I'm filing for divorce,' Lois said, 'but I have to move out of town.'

Gary thought for a moment. 'I have a friend who owns an insurance agency, sis. It's in Denver and that's 1500 miles away.'

'That would be perfect.'

Gary said, 'I'll talk to him.'

Two weeks later, Lois was working at the insurance agency.

Gary had kept in constant touch with Lois. She bought a small, charming bungalow with a view of the Rockies in the distance, and from time to time her brother would visit her. They had some great weekends together – skiing, or fishing, or simply sitting on the sofa, talking. 'I'm so proud of you, sis,' he'd always tell her, and Lois was proud of Gary's accomplishments, as well. He had earned his Ph.D. in science, was working for an international corporation, and had taken up flying as a hobby.

As Lois was thinking about Gary, there was a knock at the front door. She looked out of the window to see who was calling, and recognised him. Tom Huebner. He was a tall, rugged-looking charter pilot, a friend of Gary's.

Lois opened the door and Huebner walked in.

'Hi, Tom.'

'Lois.'

'Gary isn't here yet. I think I heard his plane a little while ago. He should be here any minute. Would you like to wait or –?'

Tom was staring at her. 'You haven't been watching the news?'

Lois shook her head. 'No. What's going on? I hope we're not going to get into another war and –'

'Lois, I'm afraid I have some bad news. Really bad news.' His voice was tight. 'It's about Gary.'

She stiffened. 'What about him?'

'He was killed on his way here to see you.' He watched the light go out of her eyes. 'I'm so sorry. I know how much you loved each other.'

Lois tried to speak, but she was hyperventilating. 'How – how – how –?'

Tom Huebner took her hand and gently led her to the couch.

Lois sat down and took deep breaths. 'What – what happened?'

'Gary's plane hit the side of a mountain a few miles outside of Denver.'

Lois felt faint. 'Tom, I'd like to be alone.'

He studied her, worried. 'Are you sure, Lois? I could stay and –'

'Thank you, but please go.'

Tom Huebner stood there, irresolutely, then nodded. 'You have my number. Call if you need me.'

Lois did not hear him leave. She sat there in a state of shock. It was as if someone had told her *she* had died. Her mind started flashing back to their childhood. Gary had always been her protector, fighting boys who teased her and, as they got older, escorting her to baseball games, the movies and parties. The last time they had been together was a week ago, and she saw the scene in her mind, unspooling like a blurred film through her tears.

The two of them were seated at the dining-room table. 'You're not eating, Gary.'

'It's delicious, sis. I'm just not very hungry.'

She watched him for a moment. 'Anything you want to talk about?'

'You always know, don't you?'

'It's something to do with your work?'

'Yes.' He pushed his plate away. 'I think my life is in danger.'

Lois looked at him, startled. '*What?*'

'Sis, only half a dozen people in the world know about what's happening. Monday, I'm flying back here to spend the night. On Tuesday morning, I'm heading for Washington.'

Lois was puzzled. 'Why Washington?'

'To tell them about Prima.'

And then Gary explained.

* * *

81

Now, Gary was dead. 'I think my life is in danger,' he had said. Her brother had not been killed in an accident. He had been murdered.

Lois looked at her watch. It was too late to do anything now, but in the morning she was going to make the phone call that would avenge her brother's murder. She was going to finish what Gary had planned to do. Lois felt suddenly drained. It was an effort to get up from the couch. She had had no dinner, but the idea of food nauseated her.

Lois headed for the bedroom and fell onto the bed, too tired to undress. She lay there, dazed, until she finally fell asleep.

Lois dreamed that she and Gary were on a speeding train, and that all the passengers in the carriage were smoking. It was getting hot, and the smoke made her cough. Her coughing woke her up, and she opened her eyes. She looked around in shock. Her bedroom was on fire, the blaze racing up the curtains, the room filled with smoke. Lois stumbled out of bed, choking. Trying to hold her breath, she staggered into the living room. The entire room was engulfed in flames and thick with smoke. She took half a dozen steps towards the door, felt her legs give way and fell to the floor.

The last thing Lois Reynolds remembered was the flames hungrily licking their way towards her.

TEN

To Kelly, everything was happening at a dizzying pace. She quickly learned about the most important aspects of modelling, the agency had given her training courses in image projection, poise and carriage. Much of modelling was attitude, and to Kelly that meant acting, because she felt neither beautiful nor desirable.

The phrase 'overnight sensation' could have been invented for Kelly. She projected not only an exciting, provocative image, but an air of untouchability that was a challenge to men. Within two years, Kelly had risen to the top tier of models. She was advertising products in a dozen countries. Much of Kelly's time was spent in Paris, where some of her agency's most important clients were located.

Once, after a fashion extravaganza in New York, before heading back to Paris, Kelly went to see her mother. She looked older and more careworn. I've got to get her out of here, Kelly thought, I'll buy a nice apartment for her, and take care of her.

Her mother seemed pleased to see her. 'I'm glad you're doing so well, Kelly. Thanks for your monthly cheques.'

'You're welcome. Mother, there's something I want to talk to you about. I have a plan all worked out. I want you to leave –'

'Well, look who's come to pay us a visit – her highness.' Her stepfather had just walked in. 'What are you doing here? Shouldn't you be strutting around in them fancy clothes?'

I'll have to do this another time, Kelly thought.

Kelly had one more stop to make. She went to the public library where she had spent so many wonderful hours, and as she walked through the door holding half a dozen magazines, her mind was dancing with memories.

Mrs Houston was not at her desk. Kelly walked inside and saw her standing in one of the side aisles, looking radiant in a sleek, tailored dress, busily filling a shelf with books.

As Mrs Houston heard the door open, she said, 'I'll be with you in a moment.' She turned. 'Kelly!' It was almost a scream. 'Oh, Kelly.'

They ran to each other and embraced.

Mrs Houston pulled back and looked at Kelly. 'I can't believe it's you. What are you doing in town?'

'I came to see my mother, but I wanted to see you, too.'

'I'm so proud of you. You have no idea.'

'Mrs Houston, do you remember when I asked how I could thank you? You said I could let you see my picture in a fashion magazine. Here.' And Kelly put the pile of magazines in Mrs Houston's arms. There were copies of *Elle*, *Cosmopolitan*, *Vanity Fair* and *Vogue*. She was on the cover of each one.

'They're beautiful.' Mrs Houston was beaming. 'I want to show you something.' She went behind her desk and pulled out copies of the same magazines.

It took a moment before Kelly could speak. 'What can I ever really do to thank you? You changed my life.'

'No, Kelly. You changed your life. All I did was give you a little push. And Kelly –'

'Yes?'

'Thanks to you I've become a fashion plate too!'

Since Kelly valued her privacy, her fame was sometimes troublesome. The constant barrage of photographers annoyed her, and she had what amounted to a phobia of being approached by people she did not know. Kelly enjoyed being alone, and thinking about Mark, bringing the past to life. She remembered the first time . . .

She was having lunch at *Restaurant Le Cinq* at the George V hotel, when a badly dressed man passing by stopped to stare at her. He had the pallid, unhealthy complexion of someone who spent all his time indoors. He was carrying a copy of *Elle*, opened to a page of photographs of Kelly.

'Excuse me,' the stranger said.

Kelly looked up, annoyed. 'Yes?'

'I saw your – I read this article about you and it says that you were born in Philadelphia.' His voice grew enthusiastic. 'I was born there too, and when I saw your pictures, I felt like I knew you and –'

Kelly said coldly, 'You don't, and I don't like strange men bothering me.'

'Oh, I'm sorry.' He swallowed. 'I didn't mean to – I'm not strange. I mean – my name is Mark Harris and I work for Kingsley International. When I saw you here, I – I thought maybe you didn't like having lunch alone and that you and I could –'

Kelly gave him a scathing look. 'You thought wrong. Now I'd like you to leave.'

He was stammering. 'I – I didn't mean to intrude. It's just that I –' He saw the look on her face. 'I'm going.'

Kelly watched him walk out of the door carrying the magazine with him. Good riddance, she thought.

Kelly had signed to do a week of layouts for several fashion magazines. The day after her encounter with Mark Harris, she was in the models' dressing room, getting dressed, when three dozen roses arrived for her. The card read, *Please forgive me for bothering you. Mark Harris.*

Kelly ripped up the card. 'Send the flowers to the Children's Hospital.'

The next morning the wardrobe mistress came into the dressing room again, with a package. 'Some man left this for you, Kelly.'

In it was a single orchid. The card read, *I hope I'm forgiven. Mark Harris.*

Kelly tore up the card. 'Keep the flower.'

After that, Mark Harris's gifts came almost daily: a small basket of fruit, a mood ring, a toy Santa Claus. Kelly threw them all away. The next gift that arrived was different: it was an adorable French poodle puppy with a red ribbon around its neck with a card attached: *This is 'Angel'. I hope you'll love her as much as I do. Mark Harris.*

Kelly dialled Information and got the number of the Kingsley International Group. When their operator answered, Kelly asked, 'Do you have a Mark Harris working there?'

'*Oui, Mademoiselle.*'

'Could I speak with him, please?'

'One moment.'

A minute later Kelly heard his familiar voice. 'Hello?'

'Mr Harris?'

'Yes.'

'This is Kelly. I've decided to take you up on your invitation to lunch.'

There was a stunned silence, then 'Really? That's – that's wonderful.'

Kelly could hear the excitement in his voice.

'Meet me at Laurent today, at one?'

'That will be great. Thank you so much. I –'

'I'll make the reservation. Goodbye.'

Mark Harris was standing, waiting at a table at Laurent, when Kelly strode in, carrying the puppy.

Mark's face lit up. 'You – you came. I wasn't sure that – and you brought Angel.'

'Yes.' Kelly planted the dog in Mark's arms. 'She can join you for lunch,' Kelly said, icily, and turned to leave.

Mark said, 'I don't understand. I thought –'

'Well, I'm going to explain it for you for the last time,' Kelly snapped. 'I want you to stop annoying me. Do you understand that?'

Mark Harris's face turned a bright red. 'Yes. Yes, of course. I'm sorry. I didn't – I didn't mean to – I just thought – I don't know what to . . . I'd like to explain. Would you sit down just for a moment?'

Kelly started to say 'no', then sat, a look of contempt on her face. 'Yes?'

Mark Harris took a deep breath. 'I'm really so sorry. I didn't mean to annoy you. I sent you those things to apologise for intruding. All I wanted was a chance to – when I saw your picture, I felt as though I had known you all my life. And then when I saw you in person and you were even more –' He was stammering, mortified. 'I – I should have known that someone like you could never be interested in someone like . . . I –

I acted like a stupid schoolboy. I'm so embarrassed. It's just that I – I didn't know how to tell you how I felt, and . . .' His voice trailed off. There was a naked vulnerability about him. 'I'm just not good at . . . at explaining my feelings. I've been alone all my life. No one ever . . . when I was six years old, my parents got a divorce, and there was a custody battle. Neither one of them wanted me.'

Kelly was watching him, silent. His words were resonating in her mind, bringing back long-buried memories: 'Why didn't you get rid of the kid before she was born?'

He went on. 'I grew up in half a dozen different foster homes, where nobody cared . . .'

'These are your uncles. Don't bother them.' Kelly could hear her mother's voice.

'It seems I couldn't do anything right . . .' Mark continued, as did the voices in Kelly's head: 'The dinner is lousy . . . That dress is the wrong colour for you . . . You haven't finished cleaning the bathrooms . . .'

'They wanted me to quit school to work at a garage, but I – I wanted to be a scientist. They said I was too dumb . . .'

Kelly was becoming more and more engrossed in what he was saying, as she remembered her own past: 'All models are whores . . .'

'I dreamed of going to college, but they said with the kind of work I would be doing, I – I didn't need an education. When I got a scholarship to MIT, my foster parents said I would probably flunk out . . .'

Listening to this stranger was like hearing a replay of her own life: 'College? You'll waste four years of your life . . .' Kelly sat there, deeply touched, feeling the same painful emotions as the stranger seated across from her.

'When I finished at MIT, I came here to work for a branch of Kingsley International Group. But I've been so lonely.' There was a long pause. 'Somewhere, a long time ago, I read that the greatest thing in life is to find someone to love, who loves you . . . and I believed it.'

Kelly sat there, quiet.

Mark Harris said, awkwardly, 'But I never found that person and I was ready to give up. And then the other day I saw you . . .' He could not go on.

He stood up, holding Angel in his arms. 'I'm so ashamed about all this. I promise never to bother you again. Goodbye.'

Kelly watched him start to walk away. 'Where are you going with my dog?' she called.

Mark Harris turned, confused. 'I'm sorry?'

'Angel is mine. You gave her to me, didn't you?'

Mark stood there, nonplussed. 'Yes, but you said –'

'I'll make a deal with you, Mr Harris. I'll keep Angel, but you can have visiting rights.'

It took him a moment, and then his smile lit up the room. 'You mean I can – you'll let me –?'

Kelly said, 'Why don't we discuss it at dinner tonight?'

She had no idea that she had just set herself up as a target for assassination.

ELEVEN

Paris, France

At Reuilly Police Headquarters on Rue Hénard in the 12th Arrondissement, an interrogation was taking place. The Superintendent of the Eiffel Tower was being questioned by Detectives André Belmondo and Pierre Marais.

Monday, May 6

10 a.m.

Subject: René Pascal

BELMONDO: Monsieur Pascal, we have reason to believe that Mark Harris, the man who supposedly fell from the observation deck of the Eiffel Tower, was murdered.

PASCAL: Murdered? But – I was told it was an accident and –

MARAIS: He could not possibly have fallen over that parapet by accident. It is much too high.

BELMONDO: And we have established that the victim was not suicidal. In fact, he had made elaborate plans with his wife for the weekend. She's Kelly – the model.

PASCAL: I'm sorry, gentlemen, but I don't see what that – why was I brought here?

MARAIS: To help us clarify a few matters. What time did the restaurant close that night?

PASCAL: At ten o'clock. Because of the storm, the Jules Verne was empty, so I decided to –

MARAIS: What time were the lifts shut down?

PASCAL: They usually run until midnight, but on that night, since there were no sightseers or diners, I closed them down at ten p.m.

BELMONDO: Including the lift which goes to the observation deck?

PASCAL: Yes. All of them.

MARAIS: Is it possible for someone to get to the observation deck without using the lift?

PASCAL: No. On that night everything was closed off. I don't understand what this is all about. If –

BELMONDO: I will tell you what it is all about. Monsieur Harris was thrown from the observation deck. We know it was the observation deck because when we examined the parapet, the top had been scraped, and traces of cement embedded in the soles of Harris's shoes matched that of the scraped cement on the parapet. If the floor was locked off, and the lifts were not working, how did he get up there at midnight?

PASCAL: I don't know. Without the lift, it would be – it would be impossible.

MARAIS: But a lift was used to take Monsieur Harris up to the observation tower, and to take up his assassin – or assassins – and bring them down again.

BELMONDO: Could a stranger run the lifts?

PASCAL: No. The operators never leave them when they are on duty, and at night the lifts are locked down with a special key.

MARIAS: How many keys are there?

PASCAL: Three. I have one, and the other two are kept here.

BELMONDO: You are certain that the last lift was shut down at ten o'clock?

PASCAL: Yes.

MARAIS: Who was running it?

PASCAL: Toth. Gérard Toth.

MARAIS: I would like to speak with him.

PASCAL: So would I.

MARAIS: I beg your pardon?

PASCAL: Toth has not shown up for work since that night. I called his apartment. There was no answer. I got hold of his landlord. Toth has moved out.

MARAIS: And left no forwarding address?

PASCAL: That's right. He's vanished into thin air.

'*Vanished into thin air?* Are we talking about The Great Houdini, or a damned lift operator?'

The speaker was Secretary General Claude Renaud, in charge of Interpol Headquarters. Renaud was a short, dynamic man in his fifties, who had worked his way up the police hierarchy over a period of twenty years.

Renaud was chairing a meeting in the main conference room at the seven-storey Interpol Headquarters. The international police organisation is the clearing house of information for 126 police forces in seventy-eight countries. The building is located in St-Cloud, six miles west of Paris, is manned by former detectives from the *Sûreté Nationale*, and the *Préfecture de Paris*.

There were twelve men seated at the large conference table. They had been questioning Detective Belmondo for the past hour.

Secretary General Renaud said sourly, 'So you and Detective Marais were unable to get any information about how a man was murdered in an area it would be impossible for him to be in, in the first place, and impossible for his assassins to get to or escape from? Is that what you're telling me?'

'Marais and I talked to everyone who –'

'Never mind. You may go.'

'Yes, sir.'

They watched the chastened detective walk out of the room. One of the men said, 'Well, he was no help.'

Secretary General Renaud sighed. 'On the contrary. Everything he said confirmed what we already suspected.'

They were all looking at him in surprise.

'Gentlemen, we have a riddle wrapped in a mystery,

inside an enigma. In the fifteen years I have been in this office, we have investigated serial killers, international gangs, mayhem, patricide, and every other crime imaginable.' He paused. 'But in all those years, I have never come across anything like this. I am sending a NOTICE to the New York office.'

Manhattan, New York

Chief of Manhattan Detectives, Frank Bigley, was reading the file Secretary General Renaud had sent, when Earl Greenburg and Robert Praegitzer entered his office.

'You wanted to see us, Chief?'

'Yes. Sit down.'

They each took a chair.

Chief Bigley held up a piece of paper. 'This is a NOTICE that Interpol sent this morning.' He started reading. 'Six years ago, a Japanese scientist named Akira Iso committed suicide, hanging himself in his hotel room in Tokyo. Mr Iso was in perfect health, had just received a promotion and was reported to be in high spirits.'

'Japan? What does that have to do with –?'

'Let me go on. Three years ago, Madeleine Smith, a thirty-two-year-old Swiss scientist, turned on the gas in her Zurich apartment and committed suicide. She was pregnant and about to marry the father of her baby. Friends said they'd never seen her happier.' He looked up at the two detectives. 'In the past three days: a Berliner named Sonja Verbrugge drowned herself in her bathtub. The same night, Mark Harris, an American, did a swan dive off the observation deck of the Eiffel Tower. A day later, a Canadian named Gary Reynolds crashed his Cessna into a mountain outside Denver.'

Greenburg and Praegitzer were listening, more and more puzzled.

'And yesterday, you two found the body of Richard Stevens on the bank of the East River.'

Earl Greenburg was looking at him, perplexed. 'What do all these cases have to do with us?'

Chief Bigley said quietly, 'They're all the same case.'

Greenburg was staring at him. '*What?* Let me see if I have this right. A Japanese six years ago, a Swiss three years ago, and in the past few days a German, a Canadian, and two Americans.' He was silent for a moment. 'What connects these cases?'

Chief Bigley handed Greenburg the NOTICE from Interpol. As Greenburg read it, his eyes widened. He looked up, and said slowly, 'Interpol believes that the think-tank, Kingsley International Group, is behind these murders? That's ridiculous.'

Praegitzer said, 'Chief, we're talking about the biggest think-tank in the world.'

'All those people were murdered, and each one had a connection with KIG. The company is owned and run by Tanner Kingsley. He's the President and CEO of Kingsley International Group, Chairman of the Presidential Science Committee, head of the National Advanced Planning Institute, and on the Defence Policy

Board at the Pentagon. I think you and Greenburg had better have a talk with Mr Kingsley.'

Earl Greenburg swallowed, 'Right.'

'And Earl . . .'

'Yes?'

'Walk softly and carry a small stick.'

Five minutes later, Earl Greenburg was talking to Tanner Kingsley's secretary. When he had finished, he turned to Praegitzer. 'We have an appointment Tuesday at ten a.m. Right now Mr Kingsley is appearing at a Congressional Committee hearing, in Washington.'

Washington, DC

At the hearing before the Senate Select Committee on the Environment, in Washington, DC, a panel of six Senate Committee members and three dozen spectators and reporters listened attentively to the testimony of Tanner Kingsley.

Tanner Kingsley was in his forties, tall and handsome, with steely blue eyes that blazed with intelligence. He had a Roman nose, a strong chin and a profile that could have graced a coin.

The Committee head, Senior Senator Pauline Mary van Luven, was an imposing figure with an almost aggressive self-confidence. She looked at Tanner and said, crisply, 'You may begin now, Mr Kingsley.'

Tanner nodded. 'Thank you, Senator.' He turned to the other members of the Committee, and when he spoke, his voice was impassioned. 'While some of our politicians in the government are still quibbling about the consequences of global warming and the green-house effect, the hole in the ozone layer is rapidly grow-ing. Because of that, half the world is suffering droughts, and the other half floods. In the Ross Sea, an iceberg the size of Jamaica has just collapsed because of global warming. The ozone hole over the South Pole has reached the record size of ten million square miles.' He paused for effect, and repeated slowly, 'Ten million square miles.

'We're witnessing a record number of hurricanes, cyclones, typhoons and storms that are ravaging parts of Europe. Due to the radical changes in the weather, millions of people in countries around the world are facing starvation and extinction. But those are just words: starvation and extinction. Stop thinking of them as words. Think of their meaning – men, women and children, hungry and homeless and facing death.

'This past summer, more than 20,000 people died in a heat wave in Europe.' Tanner's voice rose. 'And what have we done about it? Our government has refused to ratify the Kyoto Protocol, the global environmental summit. The message is that we don't give a damn what happens to the rest of the world. We'll just go ahead and do what suits us. Are we so dense, so self-absorbed that we can't see what we're doing to –?'

Senator van Luven interrupted. 'Mr Kingsley, this is

not a debate. I will ask you to adopt a more moderate tone.'

Tanner took a deep breath, and nodded. In a less impassioned tone, he continued. 'As all of us are aware, the greenhouse effect is caused by the burning of fossil fuels and other related factors completely under our control, and yet these emissions have reached their highest point in half a million years. They're polluting the air that our children and grandchildren breathe. The pollution can be stopped. And why isn't it? Because it would cost big business money.' His voice rose again. 'Money! How much is a breath of fresh air worth compared to the life of a human being? A gallon of gas? Two gallons of gas?' His voice became even more fervent. 'As far as we know, this earth is the only place that's habitable for us, yet we're poisoning the land and the oceans and the air we breathe as fast as we can. If we don't stop –'

Senator van Luven interrupted again. 'Mr Kingsley –'

'I apologise, Senator. I'm angry. I can't watch the destruction of our universe without protesting.'

Kingsley spoke for another thirty minutes. When he was finished, Senator van Luven said, 'Mr Kingsley, I would like to see you in my office, please. This hearing is adjourned.'

Senator van Luven's office had originally been furnished in typical, sterile, bureaucratic fashion: a desk, a table, six chairs, and rows of filing cabinets, but the Senator had added her own feminine touches, with colourful fabrics, paintings and photographs.

When Tanner entered, there were two people in the office besides Senator van Luven.

'These are my assistants, Corinne Murphy and Karolee Trost.'

Corinne Murphy, an attractive young redhead, and Karolee Trost, a petite blonde, both in their twenties, took seats next to the Senator. They were obviously fascinated by Tanner.

'Sit down, Mr Kingsley,' Senator van Luven said.

Tanner took a seat. The Senator studied him for a moment. 'Frankly, I don't understand you.'

'Oh really? I'm surprised, Senator. I thought I made myself perfectly clear. I feel –'

'I know how you feel. But your company has contracts for many projects with our government, and yet you're challenging the government on the environment issue. Isn't that bad for business?'

Tanner said, coldly, 'This isn't about business, Senator van Luven. This is about humanity. We're seeing the beginning of a disastrous global destabilisation. I'm trying to get the Senate to allocate funds to correct it.'

Senator van Luven said, sceptically, 'Some of those funds could go to your company, couldn't they?'

'I don't give a damn who gets the money. I just want to see action taken before it's too late.'

Corinne Murphy said warmly, 'That's admirable. You're a very unusual man.'

Tanner turned to her. 'Miss Murphy, if you mean by that, that the majority of people seem to believe that money is more important than morals, I regret to say you're probably right.'

Karolee Trost spoke up. 'I think what you're trying to do is wonderful.'

Senator van Luven gave each of her assistants a disapproving look, then turned to Tanner. 'I can't promise anything, but I will talk with my colleagues and get their point of view on the environmental issue. I will get back to you.'

'Thank you, Senator. I would be most appreciative.' He hesitated. 'Perhaps sometime when you're in Manhattan, I can take you around KIG and show you our operation. I think you might find it interesting.'

Senator van Luven nodded indifferently. 'I'll let you know.'

The meeting was over.

TWELVE

Paris, France
From the moment people heard of Mark's death, Kelly Harris had been flooded with phone calls and flowers and E-mails. The first to call was Sam Meadows, a colleague and close friend of Mark's.

'Kelly! My God. I can't believe it! I – I don't know what to say, I'm just devastated. Every time I turn around, I expect to see Mark there. Kelly – is there anything I can do for you?'

'No, thank you, Sam.'

'Let's stay in touch. I want to be of help in any way I can . . .'

After that came a dozen calls from Mark's friends, and from models Kelly worked with.

Bill Lerner, the head of the model agency, telephoned. He offered his condolences and then said, 'Kelly, I realise this is not the appropriate time, but

I think that getting back to work might be good for you right now. Our phone has been ringing off the hook. When do you think you'll be ready to go to work?'

'When Mark comes back to me.'

Kelly dropped the telephone.

Now the phone was ringing again. Finally, Kelly picked it up. 'Yes?'

'Mrs Harris?'

Was she still Mrs Harris? There was no Mr Harris any more, but she would always, always be Mark's wife.

She said firmly, 'This is Mrs Mark Harris.'

'This is Tanner Kingsley's office.'

The man Mark works – worked for, Kelly thought. 'Yes?'

'Mr Kingsley would appreciate it if you could come and see him in Manhattan. He would like to have a meeting with you at the company headquarters. Are you free?'

Kelly was free. She had told the agency to cancel all her bookings. But she was surprised. Why does Tanner Kingsley want to see me? She wondered. 'Yes.'

'Will it be convenient for you to leave Paris on Friday?'

Nothing would ever be convenient again. 'Friday. All right.'

'Good. There will be a United Airlines ticket waiting for you at Charles de Gaulle Airport.' He gave her the flight number. 'A car will meet you in New York.'

Mark had spoken to her about Tanner Kingsley. Mark had met with him and thought he was a genius and a wonderful man to work for. Perhaps we could share some memories of Mark: the thought cheered Kelly up.

Angel came running in and jumped onto her lap. Kelly hugged her. 'What am I going to do with you while I'm away? Mama would take you with her, but I'm only going to be gone a few days.'

Suddenly, Kelly knew who would take care of the puppy.

She walked down the stairs to the building superintendent's office. Workmen were installing a new lift, and Kelly winced every time she passed them.

The superintendent of the building, Philippe Cendre, was a tall, attractive man with a warm personality, and his wife and daughter had always gone out of their way to be helpful. When they had heard the news about Mark, they had been devastated. Mark's funeral had been held at the Père Lachaise cemetery, and Kelly had invited the Cendre family to attend.

Kelly approached Philippe's apartment door and knocked. When Philippe opened the door, Kelly said, 'I have a favour to ask of you.'

'Come in. Anything you wish, Madame Harris.'

'I have to go to New York for three or four days. I wonder if you would mind taking care of Angel while I'm gone.'

'Mind? Ana Maria and I would love it.'

'Thank you. I would appreciate it.'

'And I promise to do everything I can to spoil her.'

Kelly smiled. 'Too late. I've already spoiled her.'

'When do you plan to leave?'

'Friday.'

'Very well. I will see to everything. Did I tell you that my daughter has been accepted at La Sorbonne?'

'No. That's wonderful. You must be very proud.'

'I am. She starts in two weeks. We're all very excited. It's a dream come true.'

On Friday morning, Kelly took Angel down to Philippe Cendre's apartment.

Kelly handed the superintendent some paper bags. 'Here's Angel's favourite food and some toys for her to play –'

Philippe stepped back and behind him Kelly saw a pile of dog toys on the floor.

Kelly laughed. 'Angel, you're in good hands.' She gave the puppy a final hug. 'Goodbye, Angel. Thank you so much, Philippe.'

As Kelly was leaving, Nicole Paradis, the switchboard operator at the apartment building, was standing at the door to say goodbye. An ebullient grey-haired woman, she was so tiny that when she was seated behind the desk at her switchboard, only the top of her head was visible.

She smiled at Kelly and said, 'We will miss you, Madame. Please hurry back to us.'

Kelly took her hand. 'Thank you. I'll be back soon, Nicole.' And minutes later, she was on her way to the airport.

The Charles de Gaulle Airport was crowded beyond belief, as always. It was a surrealistic maze of ticket counters, shops, restaurants, stairways, and giant escalators crawling up and down like prehistoric monsters.

When Kelly arrived, the airport manager escorted her to a private lounge. Forty-five minutes later, her flight was announced. As Kelly started towards the boarding gate, a woman standing nearby watched her go through. The moment Kelly was out of sight, the woman picked up her cell phone and made a call.

Kelly sat in her airplane seat, thinking constantly about Mark, oblivious to the fact that most of the men and women in the cabin were covertly staring at her.

What was Mark doing on the observation deck of the Eiffel Tower, at midnight? Who was he going to meet? And why? she wondered. And the worst question of all – Why would Mark commit suicide? We were so happy together. We loved each other so much. I don't believe he killed himself. Not Mark . . . not Mark . . . not Mark.

Kelly closed her eyes and let her thoughts drift back . . .

It was their first date. She had dressed for the evening in a prim black skirt and a high-necked white blouse, so that Mark would not get the idea that she was trying to tempt him in any way. This was just going to be a casual, congenial evening. Kelly found that she was nervous. Because of the unspeakable thing that had happened to her when she was a child, Kelly had not been out with any men except for business reasons or obligatory charity events.

Mark isn't really a date, Kelly kept telling herself. He and I are just going to be friends. He can be my escort around town, and there won't be any romantic complications. Even as she was thinking it, the door-bell rang.

Kelly took a hopeful breath and opened the door. Mark stood there, smiling, holding a box and a paper bag. He was wearing an ill-fitting grey suit, a green shirt, a bright red tie and brown shoes. Kelly almost laughed aloud. The fact that Mark had no sense of style was somehow endearing. She had known too many men whose egos were involved in how elegant they thought they looked.

'Come in,' Kelly said.

'I hope I'm not late.'

'No, not at all.' He was twenty-five minutes early.

Mark handed Kelly the box. 'This is for you.'

It was a five-pound box of chocolates. Over the years Kelly had been offered diamonds and furs and pent-houses, but never chocolates. Exactly what every model needs, she thought, amused.

Kelly smiled. 'Thank you.'

Mark held out the bag. 'And these are treats for Angel.'

As if on cue, Angel came bouncing into the room and ran up to Mark, her tail wagging.

Mark picked Angel up and petted her. 'She remembers me.'

'I really want to thank you for her,' Kelly said. 'She's a wonderful companion. I've never had one before.'

Mark looked at Kelly and his eyes said it all.

The evening went unexpectedly well. Mark was a charming companion and Kelly was touched by how obviously thrilled he was to be with her. He was intelligent and easy to talk to, and the time went by more quickly than Kelly had anticipated.

At the end of the evening, Mark said, 'I hope we can do this again.'

'Yes. I would like that.'

'What's your favourite thing to do, Kelly?'

'I enjoy soccer games. Do you like soccer?'

A blank look came over Mark's face. 'Oh – er – yes. I – I love it.'

He's such a poor liar, Kelly thought. A mischievous idea came into her head. 'There's a championship game on Saturday night. Would you like to go?'

Mark swallowed and said, weakly, 'Sure. Great.'

When they arrived back at Kelly's apartment building, Kelly found herself tensing. This was always the moment for:

'How about a good-night kiss . . . ? Why don't I

come in for a bit, and we'll have a nightcap . . . ? You don't want to spend the night alone . . .

As they reached Kelly's door, Mark looked at her and said, 'Do you know what I first noticed about you, Kelly?'

Kelly held her breath. Here it comes, she thought: You have a great ass . . . I love your boobs . . . I'd like to have your long legs wrapped around my neck . . .

'No,' Kelly said icily. 'What did you first notice?'

'The pain in your eyes.'

Before she could reply, Mark said. 'Good-night.'

And Kelly watched him leave.

THIRTEEN

When Mark arrived the following Saturday night, he brought another box of chocolates and a large paper bag. 'The candy is for you. The treats are for Angel.'

Kelly took the bags. 'I thank you, and Angel thanks you.'

She watched Mark petting Angel, and asked, innocently, 'Are you looking forward to the game?'

Mark nodded and said, enthusiastically, 'Oh, yes.'

Kelly smiled. 'Good. So am I.' She knew that Mark had never even seen a soccer game.

The Paris St-Germain stadium was packed to capacity, with sixty-seven thousand eager fans waiting for the championship game between Lyons and Marseilles to begin.

As Kelly and Mark were ushered to their seats directly

above midfield, Kelly said, 'I'm impressed. These seats are hard to get.'

Mark smiled and said, 'When you love soccer as much as I do, nothing is impossible.'

Kelly bit her lip to keep from laughing. She could not wait for the game to begin.

At 2 o'clock, both teams entered the stadium, standing at attention while the band played the *Marseillaise*, the French national anthem. As the line-ups for Lyons and Marseilles faced the stands for introductions, a player stepped forward, wearing the Lyons logo in the team colours of blue and white.

Kelly decided to relent and let Mark know what was happening. She leaned towards him. 'That's their goalie,' Kelly explained. 'He's –'

'I know,' Mark said. 'Grégory Coupet. He's the best goalie in the league. He won a championship against Bordeaux last April. He won a UEFA Cup and a Champions League the year before that. He's thirty-one years old, six feet tall, and weighs 180 pounds.'

Kelly looked at Mark in astonishment.

The announcer continued. 'Playing forward, Sidney Gouvou . . .'

'Number fourteen,' Mark enthused. 'He's incredible. Last week, against Auxerre, he scored a goal in the last minute of the game.'

Kelly listened in amazement as Mark knowledgeably discussed all the other players.

The game began and the crowd went wild.

'Look. He's starting with a bicycle kick,' Mark crowed.

It was a frenzied, exciting game, and goalies for both teams fought hard to keep their opponents from scoring. It was difficult for Kelly to concentrate. She kept looking at Mark, amazed by his expertise. *How could I have been so wrong?* she thought.

In the middle of play, Mark exclaimed, 'Gouvou's going for a flick kick! He made it!'

A few minutes later, Mark said, 'Watch! Carrière's going to be fined for handling the ball.'

And he was right.

When Lyons won, Mark was euphoric. 'What a great team!'

As they were leaving the stadium, Kelly asked, 'Mark – how long have you been interested in soccer?'

He looked at Kelly sheepishly and said, 'About three days. I've been researching it on my computer. Since you were so interested, I thought I should learn about it.'

Kelly was incredibly touched. It was unbelievable that Mark had spent so much time and effort, just because she enjoyed the game.

They had made a date for the following day, after Kelly finished a modelling assignment.

'I can pick you up at your dressing room, and –'

'No!' She did not want him to meet the other models.

Mark was looking at her, puzzled.

'I mean – there's a rule that men aren't allowed in the dressing rooms.'

'Oh.'

Kelly was really thinking, I don't want you to fall in love with –

'Ladies and gentlemen, please fasten your seat belts and return your seat backs and trays to their upright and locked positions. We're approaching Kennedy Airport and we'll be landing in just a few minutes.'

Kelly was jolted back to the present. She was in New York to meet Tanner Kingsley, the man for whom Mark had worked.

Someone had informed the media. When the plane landed, they were waiting for Kelly. She was surrounded by reporters with television cameras and microphones.

'Kelly, would you look this way?'

'Can you tell us what you think happened to your husband?'

'Is there going to be a police investigation?'

'Were you and your husband planning a divorce?'

'Are you moving back here to the States?'

'How did you feel when you heard what happened?'

The most insensitive question of all.

Kelly saw a pleasant-faced, alert-looking man standing in the background. He smiled and waved to Kelly and she motioned for him to come over to her.

Ben Roberts was one of the most popular and respected talk-show hosts on network television. He had interviewed Kelly before, and they had become friends. She watched as Ben made his way through the crowd of reporters. They all knew him.

'Hey, Ben! Is Kelly going to be on your show?'

'Do you think she'll talk about what happened?'

'Can I get a picture of you and Kelly?'

By this time, Ben had reached Kelly's side. The tide of reporters was pushing against them. Ben called out, 'Let's give her a break, boys and girls. You can talk to her later.'

Reluctantly, the reporters began to give way.

Ben took Kelly's hand and said, 'I can't tell you how sorry I am. I liked Mark so much.'

'That was mutual, Ben.'

As Kelly and Ben made their way towards the exit, he asked, 'Off the record, what *are* you doing in New York?'

'I'm here to see Tanner Kingsley.'

Ben nodded. 'He's a powerful man. I'm sure you'll be well taken care of.'

'Kelly, if there is anything I can do for you, you can always reach me at the network.' He looked around. 'Are you being picked up? If not, I'll –'

At that moment, a uniformed chauffeur came up to Kelly. 'Mrs Harris? I'm Colin. The car is right outside, Mr Kingsley has checked you into a suite at the Metropolitan Hotel. If you'll give me your tickets, I'll attend to your luggage.'

Kelly turned to Ben. 'Will you call me?'

'Of course.'

Ten minutes later, Kelly was on her way to the hotel. As they weaved through traffic, Colin said, 'Mr Kingsley's secretary will telephone you and set up an appointment. The car will be at your disposal when-ever you need it.'

'Thank you.'

What am I doing here? Kelly wondered.

She was about to get the answer.

FOURTEEN

Manhattan, New York

Tanner Kingsley was reading the headline of the afternoon newspaper: *Hailstorm Batters Iran*. The rest of
the story went on to call it a 'freakish event'. The idea
of a hailstorm happening in summer, in a hot climate,
was bizarre. Tanner buzzed for his secretary. When she
came in, he said, 'Kathy, clip this article and send it to
Senator van Luven, with a note: "A global warming
update. Sincerely . . ."'

'Right away, Mr Kingsley.'

Tanner Kingsley glanced at his watch. The two
detectives were due at KIG in half an hour. He looked
around his extravagant office. He had created all of
this. KIG. He thought about the power behind those
three simple initials, and how surprised people would
be if they knew the astonishing story of KIG's humble

beginnings, a mere seven years ago. The memories of the past raced through his mind . . .

He remembered the day he had designed the new KIG logo. 'Pretty fancy for a nothing company,' someone had said, and Tanner had single-handedly turned that nothing company into a world powerhouse. When Tanner thought about the beginnings, he felt as though he had performed a miracle.

Tanner Kingsley had been born five years after his brother Andrew, and that had totally shaped the direction of his life. Their parents divorced and their mother had remarried and moved away. Their father was a scientist, and the boys had followed in his footsteps, and had grown up to be science prodigies. Their father had died of a heart attack aged forty.

The fact that Tanner was five years younger than his brother was a constant frustration. When Tanner won the top award in his science class, he was told, 'Andrew was number one in his class five years ago. It must run in the family . . .'

When Tanner won an oratorical contest, the professor said, 'Congratulations, Tanner. You're the second Kingsley to get this award.'

On joining the tennis team: 'I hope you're as good as your brother Andrew . . .'

When Tanner was graduated: 'Your valedictorian speech was inspiring. It reminded me so much of Andrew's . . .'

He had grown up in the shadow of his brother, and

118

it was galling to know that he was considered second best only because Andrew had got there first.

There were similarities between the two brothers: they were both handsome, intelligent and talented, but as they grew older, major differences became apparent. While Andrew was altruistic and self-effacing, Tanner was an extrovert, gregarious and ambitious. Andrew was shy around women, while Tanner's looks and charm drew them to him like a magnet.

The most important difference between the brothers was their goals in life. While Andrew was deeply concerned with organising charity events and assisting others, Tanner's ambition was to become rich and powerful.

Andrew was graduated from college *summa cum laude*, and immediately accepted an offer to work at a think-tank. There he learned what a significant contribution an organisation like that could make, and five years later, Andrew decided to start his own think-tank, on a modest scale.

When Andrew told Tanner about the idea, Tanner was excited. 'That's brilliant! Think-tanks get government contracts worth millions, not to mention corporations that hire –'

Andrew interrupted. 'That's not my idea, Tanner. I want to use it to help people.'

Tanner was staring at him. 'Help people?'

'Yes. There are dozens of Third World countries that have no access to modern methods of agriculture and manufacturing. There's a saying that if you give a man a fish, he can have a meal. If you teach him to fish, he can eat for the rest of his life.'

You could cut down an oak tree with that old saw, Tanner thought. 'Andrew, countries like that can't afford to pay us –'

'That doesn't matter. We'll send experts to Third World countries to teach them modern techniques that will change their lives. I'm making you a partner. We'll call our think-tank "Kingsley Group". What do you say?'

Tanner was thoughtful for a moment. He nodded. 'As a matter of fact, it's not a bad idea. We can start with the kind of countries you're talking about, then go after the big money – the government contracts and –'

'Tanner, let's just concentrate on making the world a better place.'

Tanner smiled. It was going to be a compromise. They would start the way Andrew wanted to, and then they would gradually build up the company to its real potential.

'Well?'

Tanner held out his hand. 'Here's to our future, partner.'

Six months later, the two brothers were standing in the rain, outside a small redbrick building with an unimpressive little sign that read 'Kingsley Group'.

'How does it look?' Andrew asked, proudly.

'Beautiful.' Tanner managed to keep the irony out of his voice.

'That sign is going to bring happiness to so many people around the world, Tanner. I've already started hiring some experts to go to Third World countries.'

Tanner started to object and stopped. His brother could not be rushed. He had a stubborn streak. But the time is coming, the time is coming, Tanner thought as he looked up at the little sign again. Some day it will read, 'KIG, Kingsley International Group'.

John Higholt, a college friend of Andrew's, had invested 100,000 dollars to help get the think-tank started, and Andrew had raised the rest of the money.

Half a dozen people were hired and sent to Mombasa, Somalia and Sudan, to teach the local populations how to better their lives. But no money was coming in.

It made no sense to Tanner. 'Andrew, we could get contracts from some of the big companies and –'

'That's not what we do, Tanner.'

What in the hell do we do? Tanner wondered. 'The Chrysler Corporation is looking for –'

Andrew smiled and said, 'Let's do our real job.'

It took all of Tanner's willpower to control himself.

Andrew and Tanner each had their own laboratory at the think-tank. They were both immersed in their own projects. Andrew frequently worked far into the night.

One morning, when Tanner arrived at the plant, Andrew was still there. He saw Tanner come in, and Andrew jumped to his feet. 'I'm excited about this new nanotechnology experiment. I'm developing a method of . . .'

Tanner's mind drifted to something more important: the hot little redhead he had met the night before. She had joined him at the bar, had a drink, taken him to her apartment, and given him a wonderful time. When she had held his –

'. . . and I think it's really going to make a difference. How does that sound, Tanner?'

Caught by surprise, Tanner said, 'Oh. Yes, Andrew. Great.'

Andrew smiled. 'I knew you would see its possibilities.'

Tanner was more interested in his own secret experiment. If mine works, he thought, I'll own the world.

One evening, shortly after his graduation, Tanner was at a cocktail party, when a pleasant, feminine voice behind him said, 'I've heard a lot about you, Mr Kingsley.'

Tanner turned around in anticipation and then tried to conceal his disappointment. The speaker was an unremarkable-looking young woman. All that kept her from being plain was a pair of intense brown eyes and a bright, slightly cynical smile. The *sine qua non* for Tanner was the physical beauty of a woman, and it was clear that this woman didn't make the cut.

Even as he said, 'Nothing too bad, I hope,' he was thinking up an excuse to get rid of her.

'I'm Pauline Cooper. My friends call me Paula. You

dated my sister Ginny in college. She was mad about you.'

Ginny, Ginny . . . Short? Tall? Dark? Blonde? Tanner stood there, smiling, trying to remember. There had been so many.

'Ginny wanted to marry you.'

That was no help. So did a lot of others. 'Your sister was very nice. We just didn't seem to be –'

She gave Tanner a sardonic look. 'Save it. You don't even remember her.'

He was embarrassed. 'Well, I –'

'It's all right. I just attended her wedding.'

Tanner was relieved. 'Ah. So, Ginny is married.'

'Yes, she is.' There was a pause. 'But I'm not. Would you like to have dinner tomorrow night?'

Tanner took a closer look at her. Even though she was not up to his standards, she appeared to have a nice body and seemed pleasant enough. And this was certainly an easy lay. Tanner thought of his dates in baseball terms. He would throw a woman one pitch. That was it. If she didn't hit a home run, she was out.

She was watching him. 'I'll pay.'

Tanner laughed. 'I can handle it – if you're not a world-class gourmand.'

'Try me.'

He looked into her eyes and said softly, 'I will.'

The following evening, they dined at a trendy restaurant uptown. Paula was dressed in a white, low-cut silk

123

blouse, a black skirt, and high-heeled shoes. As Tanner watched her stride into the restaurant, it seemed to him that she was a lot better looking than he had remembered. In fact, she had the bearing of a princess from some exotic country.

Tanner stood up. 'Good evening.'

She took his hand. 'Good evening.' There was a self-assured air about her that was almost regal.

When they were seated, she said, 'Let's start over, shall we? I have no sister.'

Tanner looked at her, confused. 'But you told me –?'

She smiled. 'I just wanted to test your reaction, Tanner. I've heard a lot about you from some of my friends, and I became interested.'

Was she talking about sex? He wondered whom she had spoken to. It could have been so many –

'Don't jump to conclusions. I'm not talking about your swordsmanship. I'm talking about your mind.'

It was as though she had been reading his thoughts. 'So, you're – er – interested in minds?'

'Among other things,' she said, invitingly.

This is going to be an easy home run, Tanner thought as he reached over and took her hand. 'You're really something.' He stroked her arm. 'You're very special. We're going to have a good time together tonight.'

She smiled. 'Are you feeling horny, darling?'

Tanner was taken aback by her bluntness. She was an eager little thing. Tanner nodded. 'Always, Princess.'

She smiled. 'Fine. Get out your little black book and

we'll try to find someone who's available for you tonight.'

Tanner froze. He was used to making sport of women, but none of them had ever mocked him before. Tanner stared at her. 'What are you saying?'

'That we're going to have to improve your line, love. Do you have any idea how trite it is?'

Tanner felt his face getting red. 'What makes you think it's a line?'

She looked him in the eye. 'It was probably invented by Methuselah. When you talk to me, I want you to say things that you've never said to any woman before.'

Tanner looked at her, trying to conceal his fury.

Who does she think she's dealing with – some high-school kid? he fumed to himself. She is too damned insolent for her own good. Strike one. The bitch is out.

FIFTEEN

The world headquarters of the Kingsley International Group was located in lower Manhattan, two blocks from the East River. The compound occupied five acres of land and consisted of four large concrete buildings, along with two small staff houses, fenced in and guarded electronically.

At ten o'clock in the morning, Detectives Earl Greenburg and Robert Praegitzer entered the lobby of the main building. It was spacious and modern, furnished with sofas and tables, and half a dozen chairs.

Detective Greenburg glanced at the assortment of magazines on a nearby table: *Virtual Reality*, *Nuclear and Radiological Terrorism*, *Robotics World* . . . He held up a copy of *Genetic Engineering News*, and turned to Praegitzer. 'Don't you get tired of reading these in your dentist's office?'

Praegitzer grinned. 'Yeah.'

The two detectives approached the receptionist and identified themselves. 'We have an appointment with Mr Tanner Kingsley.'

'He's expecting you. I'll have someone escort you to his office.' She gave them each a KIG badge. 'Please, turn these in when you leave.'

'No problem.'

The receptionist pressed a buzzer and, a moment later, an attractive young woman appeared.

'These gentlemen have an appointment with Mr Tanner Kingsley.'

'Yes. I'm Retra Tyler, one of Mr Kingsley's assistants. Follow me, please.'

The two detectives walked down a long, sterile corridor with tightly closed office doors on each side. At the end of the corridor was Tanner's office.

In Tanner's waiting room, Kathy Ordonez, Tanner's bright, young secretary, was seated behind a desk.

'Good morning, gentlemen. You can go right in.'

She got up and opened the door to Tanner's private office. As the detectives stepped inside, they stopped to stare, in awe.

The huge office was crammed with arcane electronic equipment, and the soundproofed walls were lined with wafer-thin television sets displaying live scenes from cities around the world. Some of the views were of busy conference rooms, offices and laboratories, while others showed hotel suites where meetings were taking place. Each set had its own audio system and, even though the volume was barely audible, it was eerie to hear snippets of sentences spoken simultaneously in a dozen different languages.

Captions appeared at the bottom of each screen identifying the cities: Milan . . . Johannesburg . . . Zurich . . . Madrid . . . Athens . . . At the far wall was an eight-tier bookshelf filled with leather-bound volumes.

Tanner Kingsley was seated behind a mahogany desk that contained a console with half a dozen different coloured buttons. He was elegantly dressed in a tailored grey suit with a light-blue shirt and a blue checked tie.

Tanner rose as the two detectives walked in. 'Good morning, gentlemen.'

Earl Greenburg said, 'Good morning. We're –'

'Yes, I know who you are. Detectives Earl Greenburg and Robert Praegitzer.' They shook hands. 'Sit down, please.'

The detectives took seats.

Praegitzer was staring at the swiftly-changing, world-wide pictures on the profusion of television sets. He shook his head in admiration. 'Talk about today's state of the art! This is –'

Tanner raised a hand. 'We're not talking here about today's state of the art, Detective. This technology won't be on the market for another two or three years. With these, we're able to watch teleconferences in a dozen different countries simultaneously. The information that pours in from our offices around the world is automatically categorised and recorded by these computers.'

Praegitzer asked, 'Mr Kingsley, forgive a simplistic question. What does a think-tank do, exactly?'

'Bottom line? We're problem solvers. We figure out solutions to problems that may lie ahead. Some think-tanks concentrate in only one area – the military or economics or politics. We deal in national security, communications, microbiology, environmental issues . . . KIG functions as an independent analyst and critic of long-range global consequences for various govern-ments.'

'Interesting,' said Praegitzer.

'Eighty-five per cent of our research staff hold advanced degrees and more than sixty-five per cent have Ph.D.s.'

'That's impressive.'

'My brother Andrew founded Kingsley International Group to assist Third World countries, so we're also heavily involved in start-up projects around the world.'

There was a sudden rumble of thunder and a flash of lightning from one of the television sets. They all turned to look.

Detective Greenburg said, 'Didn't I read something about a weather experiment you were doing?'

Tanner grimaced. 'Yes, it's known around here as Kingsley's folly. It's one of the few major failures KIG has ever had. It was the one project that I most hoped would work. Instead, we're closing it down.'

Praegitzer asked, 'Is it possible to control the weather?'

Tanner shook his head. 'Only to a limited degree. A

lot of people have tried. As long ago as 1900, Nikola Tesla was doing experiments with weather. He discovered that ionisation of the atmosphere could be altered by radio waves. In 1958, our Defence Department experimented with dropping copper needles into the ionosphere. Ten years later, there was Project Popeye, where the government attempted to extend the monsoon season in Laos, to increase the amount of mud in the Ho Chi Minh Trail. They used a silver iodide nuclei agent, and generators shot banks of silver iodide into the clouds, to become seeds for raindrops.'

'Did it work?'

'Yes, but on a confined local basis. There are several reasons why no one will ever be able to control the weather. One problem is that El Niño creates warm temperatures in the Pacific Ocean that disrupt the world's ecological system, while La Niña creates cold weather temperatures in the Pacific, and the two of them combined completely negate any realistic weather control planning. The southern hemisphere is about eighty per cent ocean, while the northern hemisphere is sixty per cent ocean, causing another imbalance. In addition to that, the jet stream determines the path of storms, and there is no way to control that.'

Greenburg nodded, then hesitated. 'Do you know why we're here, Mr Kingsley?'

Tanner studied Greenburg for a moment. 'I trust that that is a rhetorical question. Otherwise, I would find it offensive. Kingsley International Group is a think-tank.

Four of my employees have died or disappeared mysteriously within a period of twenty-four hours. We have already started our own investigation. We have offices in major cities around the world, with 1,800 employees, and it is obviously difficult for me to keep in contact with all of them. But what I have learned so far is that two of the employees who were murdered were apparently involved in illegal activities. It cost them their lives – but I assure you, it is not going to cost Kingsley International Group its reputation. I expect our people to resolve this very quickly.'

Greenburg spoke up. 'Mr Kingsley, there's something else. We understand that six years ago, a Japanese scientist named Akira Iso committed suicide in Tokyo. Three years ago a Swiss scientist named Madeleine Smith committed suicide in –'

Tanner interrupted. 'Zurich. Neither of them committed suicide. They were murdered.'

The two detectives looked at him in surprise. Praegitzer asked, 'How do you know that?'

There was a hardened tone in Tanner's voice. 'They were killed because of me.'

'When you say –'

'Akira Iso was a brilliant scientist. He worked for a Japanese electronics conglomerate called Tokyo First Industrial Group. I met Iso at an international industry convention in Tokyo. We got along well. I felt that KIG could offer him a better atmosphere than the company he was with. I made him an offer to work here, and he accepted. In fact, he was very excited about it.' Tanner was fighting to keep his voice steady. 'We agreed to keep it confidential until he was legally able to leave his job, but he obviously mentioned it to someone, because there was an item about it in a newspaper column, and . . .' Tanner stopped again for a long moment, then went on. 'The day after the item appeared, Iso was found dead in a hotel room.'

Robert Praegitzer asked, 'Mr Kingsley, couldn't there have been other reasons that might explain his death?'

Tanner shook his head. 'No. I didn't believe he committed suicide. I hired investigators and sent them and some of my own people to Japan, to try to learn what had happened. They couldn't find any evidence of foul play, and I thought that perhaps I was wrong, that possibly there was some tragedy in Iso's life that I knew nothing about.'

'Then why are you so sure now that he was murdered?' Greenburg wanted to know.

'As you mentioned, a scientist named Madeleine Smith supposedly committed suicide in Zurich, three years ago. What you don't know is that Madeleine Smith also wanted to leave the people she worked for and come to our company.'

Greenburg frowned. 'What makes you think the two deaths are connected?'

Tanner's face was stone. 'Because the company she worked for is a branch of the same Tokyo First Industrial Group.'

There was a stunned silence.

Praegitzer said, 'There's something I don't understand.

Why would they murder an employee just because she wants to quit? If –'

'Madeleine Smith wasn't just an employee. Neither was Iso. They were brilliant physicists who were about to solve problems that would have made the company a fortune larger than you can imagine. That's why they didn't want to lose either of them to us.'

'Did the Swiss police investigate Smith's death?'

'Yes. So did we. But again, we could prove nothing. As a matter of fact, we're still working on all the deaths that occurred, and I expect that we will solve them. KIG has far-reaching connections all over the world. If I get any useful information, I will be happy to share it with you. I hope you will reciprocate.'

Greenburg said, 'That's fair enough.'

A gold-plated phone on Tanner's desk rang. 'Excuse me.' He walked over to the desk and picked up the phone. 'Hello . . . Yes . . . The investigation's coming along very satisfactorily. As a matter of fact, two detectives are in my office at this moment, and they have agreed to co-operate with us.' He glanced over at Praegitzer and Greenburg. 'Right . . . I'll let you know when we have any further news.' He replaced the receiver.

Greenburg asked, 'Mr Kingsley, are you working on anything sensitive here?'

'You mean, are we working on something sensitive enough to have half a dozen people murdered? Detective Greenburg, there are more than a hundred think-tanks around the world, some of them working on exactly the same problems we are. We're not building atomic bombs here. The answer to your question is "no".'

The door opened and Andrew Kingsley walked into the office carrying a stack of papers. Andrew Kingsley bore little resemblance to his brother. His features seemed to be blurred. He had thinning grey hair, a lined face, and he walked in a slightly stooped posture. Whereas Tanner Kingsley was brimming with vitality and intelligence, Andrew Kingsley appeared to be slow-witted and apathetic. He spoke haltingly and seemed to have trouble putting sentences together.

'Here are those – you know – those notes you asked for, Tanner. I'm sorry I didn't finish – finish them earlier.'

'That's perfectly all right, Andrew.' Tanner turned to the two detectives. 'This is my brother, Andrew. Detectives Greenburg and Praegitzer.'

Andrew looked at them uncertainly and blinked.

'Andrew, do you want to tell them about your Nobel Prize?'

Andrew looked at Tanner and said, vaguely, 'Yes, the Noble Prize . . . the Nobel Prize . . .'

They watched as he turned and shuffled out of the room.

Tanner sighed. 'As I mentioned, Andrew was the founder of this company, a truly brilliant man. He was awarded the Nobel Prize for one of his discoveries seven years ago. Unfortunately, he became involved in an experiment that went wrong and it – it changed him.' His tone was bitter.

'He must have been a remarkable man.'

'You have no idea.'

Earl Greenburg rose and held out his hand. 'Well, we won't take up any more of your time, Mr Kingsley. We'll keep in touch.'

'Gentlemen –' Tanner's voice was steel. 'Let's get these crimes solved – fast.'

SIXTEEN

All the morning newspapers were filled with the same story. A drought in Germany had caused at least a hundred deaths and had wiped out millions of dollars worth of crops.

Tanner buzzed for Kathy. 'Send this article to Senator van Luven, with a note: "Another global warming update. Sincerely . . .'''

Tanner could not stop thinking about the evening he had spent with Paula. And the more he thought about how insolent she had been and how she had ridiculed him, the more incensed he became. He remembered her exact words: 'We're going to have to improve your line, love. Do you have any idea how trite it is?' It was as though he needed to exorcise her. He decided he would see her once more, to give her the comeuppance she deserved, and then forget about her.

Tanner waited three days and telephoned.

'Princess?'

'Who is this?'

He was ready to slam down the phone. How many goddamn men called her 'Princess'? he wondered, but he managed to keep his voice calm. 'This is Tanner Kingsley.'

'Oh, yes. How are you?' Her tone was completely indifferent.

I've made a mistake, Tanner thought. I should never have called her.

'I thought we could have dinner again some time, but you're probably busy, so let's forget –'

'What about this evening?'

Tanner was caught off guard again. He could not wait to teach the bitch a lesson.

Four hours later, Tanner was seated across a table from Paula Cooper at a small French restaurant east of Lexington Avenue. He was surprised by how pleased he was to see her again. He had forgotten how vital and alive she was.

'I've missed you, Princess,' Tanner said.

She smiled. 'Oh, I've missed you, too. You're really something. You're very special.'

They were his words coming back to him, mocking him. Damn her.

It looked as though the evening was going to be a replay of their last meeting. On Tanner's other romantic evenings, he had always been the one to control the conversation. With Paula, he had the unsettling feeling that she was always one step ahead of him. She had a quick comeback for everything he had to say. She was witty and swift and took no nonsense from him.

The women Tanner usually dated were beautiful and willing, but for the first time in his life, Tanner felt that perhaps something had been missing. They had been too easy. They were all agreeable, but they were *too* agreeable. There was no challenge. Paula, on the other hand . . .

'Tell me about you,' Tanner said.

She shrugged. 'My father was rich and powerful and I grew up as a spoiled brat – maids and butlers – waiters to serve us by the swimming pool, Radcliffe and a finishing school – the whole bit. Then my father lost it all and died. I've been working as an executive assistant to a politician ever since then.'

'Are you enjoying it?'

'No. He's boring.' Her eyes met his. 'I'm looking for something more interesting.'

The next day, Tanner called Paula again. 'Princess?'

'I was hoping you would call, Tanner.' Her voice was warm.

Tanner felt a small *frisson* of pleasure. 'Were you?'

'Yes. Where are you taking me to dinner tonight?'

He laughed. 'Anywhere you would like to go.'

'I'd like to go to Maxim's, in Paris, but I'll settle for going anywhere if I can be with you.'

She had thrown him off guard again, but for some reason, her words warmed him.

They had dinner at La Côte Basque on 55th Street, and throughout the meal, Tanner kept looking at her and wondering why he was so attracted to her. It was not her looks; it was her mind and personality that were dazzling. Her whole essence blazed with intelligence and self-confidence. She was the most independent woman he had ever known.

Their conversations ranged over myriad subjects and Tanner found her to be remarkably knowledgeable.

'What do you want to do with your life, Princess?'

She studied Tanner for a moment before answering. 'I want power – the power to make things happen.'

Tanner smiled. 'Then we're a lot alike.'

'How many women have you said that to, Tanner?'

He found himself getting angry. 'Will you stop doing that? When I say you're different from any woman I've ever –'

'Ever what?'

Tanner said, exasperated. 'You frustrate me.'

'Poor darling. If you're frustrated, why don't you go take a shower –?'

The anger started again. He had had enough. He rose. 'Never mind. There's no use trying to –'

'– at my place?'

Tanner could hardly believe what he was hearing. 'Your place?'

'Yes, I have a little *pied-à-terre* on Park Avenue,' she said. 'Would you like to take me home?'

They skipped dessert.

The little *pied-à-terre* was a sumptuous apartment, beautifully furnished. Tanner looked around, amazed at how luxurious it was, and how elegant. The apartment suited her. A collection of eclectic paintings, a refectory table, a large chandelier, an Italian settee and a set of six Chippendale chairs. That was all that Tanner had time to take in before she said, 'Come see my bedroom.'

The bedroom was done in white, with all white furniture, and a large mirrored ceiling over the bed.

Tanner looked around and said, 'I'm impressed. This is the most –'

'Shh.' Paula began to undress him. 'We can talk later.'

When she had finished, she started slowly taking off her own clothes. She had a body that was erotic perfection. Her arms were around Tanner and she was pressed against him, and she put her lips to his ear and whispered, 'That's enough foreplay.'

They were in bed and she was ready for him, and when he was inside her, she squeezed her hips and thighs tightly together and then relaxed them, and squeezed again and repeated it, getting Tanner more and more excited. She kept shifting her body slightly, so that each sensation was different for him. She gave him voluptuous gifts he had never imagined, stimulating him to an ecstatic pitch of excitement.

Later, they talked into the night.

They were together every evening after that. Paula was constantly surprising Tanner with her humour and charm, and gradually, in his eyes, she became beautiful.

One morning, Andrew said to Tanner, 'I've never seen you smile so much. Is it a woman?'

Tanner nodded. 'Yes.'

'Is it serious? Are you going to marry her?'

'I've been thinking about it.'

Andrew regarded Tanner for a moment. 'Maybe you should tell her.'

Tanner squeezed Andrew's arm. 'Maybe I will.'

The following night, Tanner and Paula were alone in her apartment.

Tanner began, 'Princess, you once asked me to say to you something I had never said to a woman before.'

'Yes, darling?'

'Here it is. I want you to marry me.'

There was a moment's hesitation, and she grinned and flew into his arms. 'Oh, Tanner!'

He looked into her eyes. 'Is that a yes?'

'I want to marry you, darling, but – I'm afraid we have a problem.'

'What problem?'

'I told you. I want to do something important. I want

enough power to make things happen – to change things. And the root of that is money. How can we have a future together if you don't have a future?'

Tanner took her hand. 'There's no problem. I own half of an important business, Princess. One day I'm going to make enough money to give you everything you want.'

She shook her head. 'No. Your brother Andrew tells you what to do. I know all about you two. He won't let the company grow, and I need more than you can give me now.'

'You're wrong.' Tanner reflected for a moment. 'I want you to meet Andrew.'

The three of them had lunch the following day. Paula was charming and it was obvious that Andrew liked her immediately. Andrew had been worried about some of the women his brother had been taking out. This one was different. She was personable and intelligent and witty. Andrew looked over at his brother, and his nod meant 'good choice'.

Paula said, 'I think that what KIG is doing is wonderful, Andrew, helping so many people around the world. Tanner's told me all about it.'

'I'm grateful that we can do it. And we're going to do even more.'

'You mean the company's going to expand?'

'Not in that sense. I mean that we're going to send more people to more countries where they can be helpful.'

143

Tanner said quickly, 'Then we'll start to get contracts for assignments here and –'

Andrew smiled. 'Tanner is so impatient. There's no hurry. Let's do what we were meant to do first, Tanner. Help others.'

Tanner looked over at Paula. Her expression was noncommittal.

The next day, Tanner called her, 'Hi, Princess. What time should I pick you up?'

There was a moment of silence. 'Darling, I'm so sorry. I can't keep our date tonight.'

Tanner was caught by surprise. 'Is anything wrong?'

'No. A friend of mine is in town and I have to see him.'

Him? Tanner felt a pang of jealousy. 'I understand. Then tomorrow night, we'll –'

'No, I can't tomorrow. Why don't we make it Monday?'

She was going to spend the weekend with whoever it was. Tanner hung up, worried and frustrated.

On Monday night, Paula apologised. 'I'm sorry about the weekend, darling. It's just that an old friend came to town to see me.'

Into Tanner's mind flashed a picture of Paula's beautiful apartment. There was no way she could afford that on her salary. 'Who is he?'

'I'm sorry. I can't tell you his name. He's – he's too well known and he doesn't like publicity.'

'Are you in love with him?'

She took Tanner's hand and said, softly, 'Tanner, I'm in love with you. And only you.'

'Is he in love with you?'

She hesitated. 'Yes.'

Tanner immediately thought: I have to find a way to give her everything she wants. I can't lose her.

The next morning, at 4.58 a.m., Andrew Kingsley was awakened by the sound of his ringing telephone.

'I have a call for you, from Sweden. Hold on, please.'

A moment later, a voice with a slight Swedish accent said: 'Congratulations, Mr Kingsley. The Nobel Committee has chosen you to receive the Nobel Prize for Science for this year, for your innovative work in nanotechnology . . .'

The Nobel Prize! When the conversation was over, Andrew hurriedly dressed and went straight to his office. The minute Tanner arrived, Andrew rushed to tell his brother the news.

Tanner threw his arms around him. 'The Nobel! That's wonderful, Andrew! Wonderful!'

And it was. Because now all of Tanner's problems were about to be solved.

Five minutes later, Tanner was talking to Paula. 'Do you see what this means, darling? Now that KIG has a Nobel Prize, we can get all the business we can handle. I'm talking about big government contracts and huge corporations. I'll be able to give you the world.'

'That's fabulous, darling.'

145

'Will you marry me?'

'Tanner, I want to marry you more than anything in the world.'

When Tanner replaced the receiver, he was euphoric. He hurried into his brother's office. 'Andrew, I'm getting married!'

Andrew looked up and said, warmly, 'That's great news. When is the wedding?'

'We'll set it up soon. The whole staff will be invited.'

When Tanner went into his office the following morning, Andrew was waiting for him. He was wearing a boutonnière.

'What's that for?'

Andrew grinned. 'I'm getting ready for your wedding. I'm so happy for you.'

'Thank you, Andrew.'

The news spread quickly. Since the wedding had not been officially announced, no one said anything to Tanner, but there were knowing looks and smiles.

Later, Tanner went into his brother's office. 'Andrew, with the Nobel, everybody will be coming to us. And with the prize money –'

Andrew interrupted. 'With the prize money, we can afford to hire more people to send to Eritrea and Uganda.'

Tanner said slowly, 'But you're going to use this award to build up the business, aren't you?'

Andrew shook his head. 'We're doing just what we set out to do, Tanner.'

Tanner looked at his brother for a long moment. 'It's your company, Andrew.'

Tanner telephoned Paula as soon as he had made his decision. 'Princess, I have to go to Washington on business. You may not hear from me for a day or two.'

She said, teasingly, 'No blondes, brunettes or redheads.'

'No chance. You're the only woman in the world I'm in love with.'

'And I'm in love with you.'

The following morning, Tanner Kingsley was at the Pentagon, meeting with the Army Chief of Staff, General Alan Barton.

'I thought your proposal was very interesting,' General Barton said. 'We are currently discussing whom we are going to use for the test.'

'Your test involves micro-nanotechnology, and my brother just got a Nobel Prize for his work in that field.'

'We are well aware of that.'

'He is so excited about this that he would like to do it *pro bono*.'

'We're flattered, Mr Kingsley. We don't have many Nobel laureates offering their services.' He looked up to make sure the door was closed. 'This is top secret. If it works, it's going to be one of the most important components of our armament. Molecular nanotechnology can give us control of the physical world at the level of individual atoms. Until now, efforts to make chips even smaller than they are have been blocked by the electron interference called "cross talk", when electrons are uncontrolled. If this experiment is successful, it will give us significant new defence and attack weapons.'

Tanner said, 'There's no danger to this experiment, is there? I don't want anything to happen to my brother.'

'You need not worry. We will send over all the equipment you need, including the safe suits and two of our scientists to work with your brother.'

'Then we have a go-ahead?'

'You have a go-ahead.'

On his way back to New York, Tanner thought, Now all I have to do is convince Andrew.

SEVENTEEN

Andrew was in his office looking at a colourful booklet that the Nobel Committee had sent him, along with a note: *We're looking forward to your arrival.* There were pictures of the huge Stockholm concert hall, with the audience applauding a Nobel Laureate as he walked across the stage to receive his award from King Carl XVI Gustav of Sweden. And soon I'll be up there, Andrew thought.

The door opened and Tanner walked in. 'We have to talk.'

Andrew set the booklet aside. 'Yes, Tanner?'

Tanner took a deep breath. 'I've just committed KIG to assist the Army in an experiment they're conducting.'

'You *what*?'

'The test involves cryogenics. They need your help.'

Andrew shook his head. 'No. I can't get involved in that, Tanner. This isn't the sort of thing we're doing here.'

'This isn't about money, Andrew. This is about the defence of the United States of America. It's very important to the Army. You'd be doing this for your country. *Pro bono*. They need you.'

Tanner spent another hour persuading him. Finally, Andrew gave in. 'All right. But this is the last time we get off the track, Tanner. Agreed?'

Tanner smiled. 'Agreed. I can't tell you how proud I am of you.'

Tanner called Paula. Her voice mail came on. 'I'm back, darling. We have a very important experiment coming up. I'll call you when it's over. I love you.'

Two Army technicians arrived to brief Andrew on the progress they had made so far. Andrew had been reluctant at first, but as they discussed the project, Andrew became more and more excited. If the problems could be solved, it would be a major breakthrough.

An hour later, Andrew watched as an Army truck drove through the gates of KIG, escorted by two Army staff cars, carrying armed soldiers. He went out to meet the Colonel in charge of the cadre.

'Here it is, Mr Kingsley. What do we do with it?'

'I'll handle it from here,' Andrew said. 'Just unload it and we'll take over.'

'Yes, sir.' The Colonel turned to two soldiers standing at the rear of the truck. 'Let's unload it. And be careful. I mean *very* careful.'

The men reached inside the truck and gingerly

brought out a small, heavy-duty metallic carrying case.

Within minutes, two staff assistants were carrying the case into a laboratory, under Andrew's supervision.

'On that table,' he said, 'very gently.' He watched as they set it down. 'Fine.'

'One of us could have carried it. It's very light,' one of the assistants commented.

'You wouldn't believe how heavy it is,' Andrew told them.

The two assistants looked at him, puzzled. 'What?'

Andrew shook his head. 'Never mind.'

Two expert chemists, Perry Stanford and Harvey Walker, had been selected to work on the project with Andrew.

The two men had already donned the heavy protective suits that were required for the experiment.

'I'll get suited up,' Andrew said. 'Be right back.'

He walked down the corridor to a closed door and opened it. Inside were racks holding full chemical gear resembling space suits, along with gas masks, goggles, special shoes and heavy gloves.

Andrew walked into the room to put on his suit, and Tanner was there to wish him luck.

When Andrew returned to the laboratory, Stanford and Walker were waiting. The three men meticulously sealed the room so that it was airtight, then carefully secured the door. They could all feel the excitement in the air.

'All set?'

Stanford nodded. 'Ready.'

Walker confirmed, 'Ready.'

'Masks.'

They donned their protective gas masks.

'Let's begin,' Andrew said. He cautiously lifted the lid from the metallic box. Inside were six small vials fitted snugly into protective cushions. 'Be careful,' he warned. 'These genies are 222 degrees below zero.' His voice was muffled by the gas mask.

Stanford and Walker watched as Andrew gently lifted the first vial and opened it. It began hissing, and steam rising from the vial turned into a freezing cloud that seemed to saturate the room.

'All right,' Andrew said. 'Now, the first thing we have to do – the first thing –' His eyes widened. He was choking, his face turning chalky white. He tried to speak, but no words came out.

Stanford and Walker watched in horror as Andrew's body tumbled to the floor. Walker hastily capped the vial and closed the case. Stanford hurried to the wall and pressed a button to activate a giant fan that swept the frigid gas vapour out of the lab.

When the air was clear, the two scientists opened the door and hurriedly carried Andrew outside. Tanner, walking down the hallway, saw what was happening, and a panicky look came over his face.

He ran over to the two men and looked down at his brother. 'What the hell is going on?'

Stanford said, 'There's been an accident and –'

'What kind of accident?' Tanner was screaming like

a madman. 'What have you done to my brother?' People were starting to gather around. 'Call 911. Never mind. We haven't time for that. We'll get him to the hospital in one of our cars.'

Twenty minutes later, Andrew was lying on a bed in a room of the emergency ward at St Vincent's Hospital in Manhattan. There was a pulsating oxygen mask on his face and an intravenous drip in his arm. Two doctors were hovering over him.

Tanner was frantically pacing up and down. 'You've got to take care of whatever is wrong,' he yelled. 'Now!'

One of the doctors said, 'Mr Kingsley, I must ask you to leave the room.'

'No,' Tanner shouted. 'I'm staying right here with my brother.' He walked over to the bed where Andrew was lying, unconscious, and took his hand and squeezed it. 'Come on, bro. Wake up. We need you.'

There was no response.

Tears filled Tanner's eyes. 'You're going to be fine. Don't worry. We're going to fly in the best doctors in the world. You're going to get well.' He turned to the doctors. 'I want a private suite and twenty-four-hour private nurses, and I want an extra bed put in his room. I'm staying with him.'

'Mr Kingsley, we'd like to finish our examination.'

Tanner said defiantly, 'I'll be waiting in the hall.'

Andrew was rushed downstairs for a number of MRI and CAT scans, as well as extensive blood work. A more sophisticated test, a PET scan, was scheduled. Afterwards, he was moved to a suite where three doctors tended to him.

Tanner was in the hallway, sitting in a chair, waiting. When one of the doctors finally came out of Andrew's room, Tanner leaped to his feet. 'He's going to be all right, isn't he?'

The doctor hesitated. 'We're transferring him immediately to the Walter Reed Army Medical Center, in Washington, for further diagnosis, but frankly, Mr Kingsley, we don't have much hope.'

'What the hell are you talking about?' Tanner was yelling. 'Of course he's going to get well. He was in that lab only for a few minutes.'

The doctor was about to reprimand him, but he looked up and saw that Tanner's eyes were filled with tears.

Tanner rode to Washington in the ambulance plane with his unconscious brother. He kept reassuring him during the entire flight. 'The doctors say you're going to be fine . . . They're going to give you something to make you well . . . All you need is a little rest.' Tanner put his arms around his brother. 'You've got to get well in time for us to go to Sweden to pick up your Nobel Prize.'

For the next three days, Tanner slept on a cot in Andrew's room and stayed by his brother's side as much as the doctors would allow it. Tanner was in the waiting room at Walter Reed when one of the attending doctors approached him.

'How is he doing?' Tanner asked. 'Is he –?' He saw the expression on the doctor's face. 'What is it?'

'I'm afraid it's very bad. Your brother is lucky to be alive. Whatever that experimental gas was, it was extremely toxic.'

'We can bring in doctors from –'

'It's no use. I'm afraid the toxins have already affected your brother's brain cells.'

Tanner winced. 'But isn't there a cure for – for what he has?'

The doctor said, caustically, 'Mr Kingsley, the Army doesn't even have a name for it yet, and you want to know if there's a cure? No. I'm sorry. I'm afraid he's – he's never going to be himself again.'

Tanner stood there, his fists clenched, his face white.

'Your brother's awake now. You can go in and see him, but only for a few minutes.'

When Tanner walked into Andrew's hospital room, Andrew's eyes were open. He stared at his visitor, a blank expression on his face.

The phone rang and Tanner moved to answer it. It was General Barton. 'I'm terribly sorry about what happened to –'

'You bastard! You told me that my brother wouldn't be in any danger.'

'I don't know what went wrong, but I assure you –'

Tanner slammed down the receiver. He heard his brother's voice, and turned.

'Where – where am I?' Andrew mumbled.

'You're at Walter Reed Hospital, in Washington.'

'Why? Who's sick?'

'You are, Andrew.'

'What happened?'

'Something went wrong with the experiment.'

'I don't remember –'

'It's all right. Don't worry. You'll be taken care of. I'll see to it.'

Tanner watched Andrew's eyes close. He took one last look at his brother lying in bed, and left the room.

Paula sent flowers to the hospital. Tanner planned to call her, but his secretary said, 'Oh, she phoned. She had to go out of town. She'll call you as soon as she returns.'

A week later, Andrew and Tanner were back in New York. Word about what had happened to Andrew had raced through KIG. Without him in charge, would the think-tank continue to exist? When the news of the accident became public, it was sure to damage the reputation of the company.

That doesn't matter, Tanner thought. I'm going to make this the biggest think-tank in the world. Now I can give Princess more than she ever dreamed of. In a few years –

Tanner's secretary buzzed. 'There's a limousine driver here to see you, Mr Kingsley.'

Tanner was puzzled. 'Send him in.'

A uniformed chauffeur walked in, holding an envelope. 'Tanner Kingsley?'

'Yes.'

'I was asked to deliver this to you personally.'

He handed Tanner the envelope and left.

Tanner looked at the envelope and grinned. He recognised Paula's handwriting. She had planned some kind of surprise for him. Eagerly, he opened the envelope. The note read:

It isn't going to work, my dearest. Right now, I need more than you can give me, so I'm marrying someone who is able to do that. I love you and always will. I know you will find this hard to believe, but what I am doing is for the good of both of us.

Tanner's face had gone pale. He stared at the note for a long time and then he dropped it nervelessly into the wastebasket.

His triumph had come one day too late.

EIGHTEEN

Tanner was sitting quietly at his desk when his secretary buzzed. 'There's a committee here to see you, Mr Kingsley.'

'A committee?'

'Yes, sir.'

'Send them in.'

Supervisors from several KIG departments walked into Tanner's office. 'We'd like to talk to you, Mr Kingsley.'

'Sit down.'

They took seats.

'What's the problem?'

One of the foremen said, 'Well, we're kind of worried. After what's happened to your brother . . . Is KIG going to stay in business?'

Tanner shook his head. 'I don't know. At this point I'm still in shock. I can't believe what's happened to

Andrew.' He was thoughtful for a moment. 'I'll tell you what I'll do. I can't predict our chances, but I'm going to make every effort to see if we can stay afloat. That's a promise. I'll keep you informed.'

There were murmurs of thank yous, and Tanner watched the men depart.

The day that Andrew got out of the hospital, Tanner set him up in a little staff house on the KIG site, where he could be taken care of, and gave him an office next to his. The employees were stunned to see what had happened to Andrew. He had changed from a brilliant, alert scientist to a zombie. Most of the day Andrew sat in his chair, looking out of the window, half asleep, but he seemed happy to be back at KIG, even though he had little idea of what was going on. All the employees were touched by how well Tanner treated his brother, and how solicitous and caring he was of him.

The atmosphere at KIG changed almost overnight. When Andrew was running it, it had been casual. Now suddenly it had become more formal and was being run as a business instead of a philanthropy. Tanner sent out agents to sign up clients for the company. Business began to flourish at an extraordinary pace.

Word about Paula's goodbye note had spread quickly through KIG. The employees had been prepared for the marriage and they wondered how Tanner had taken this blow. There was a great deal of speculation among the staff about what he would do after being jilted.

Two days after Tanner had received the letter, an item had appeared in the newspapers announcing that Tanner's bride-to-be had married Edmond Barclay, a billionaire media tycoon. The only changes in Tanner Kingsley seemed to be an increased moodiness and a work ethic that was even stronger than it had been before. Every morning he spent two hours in the red brick building, working on a project that was shrouded in secrecy.

One evening, Tanner was invited to speak at MENSA, the high IQ society. Since many of the employees at KIG were members, he agreed to accept.

When Tanner came into headquarters the following morning, he was accompanied by one of the most beautiful women his staff had ever seen. She was Latin-looking, with dark eyes, an olive complexion and a sensational figure.

Tanner introduced her to the staff. 'This is Sebastiana Cortez. She spoke at MENSA last night. She was brilliant.'

Tanner's whole attitude suddenly seemed lighter. Tanner took Sebastiana into his office, and they did not reappear for more than an hour. After they came out, they had lunch in Tanner's private dining room.

One of the employees looked up Sebastiana Cortez on the Internet. She was a former Miss Argentina, and her home was in Cincinnati, where she was married to a prominent businessman.

When Sebastiana and Tanner went back into his office after lunch, Tanner's voice could be heard in the reception room through the intercom, that had accidentally been left open.

'Don't worry, darling. We'll find a way to make it work.'

The secretaries started gathering around the intercom, eagerly listening to the conversation.

'We have to be very careful. My husband is a jealous man.'

'There's no problem. I'll make arrangements for us to keep in touch.'

It did not take a genius to figure out what was happening. It was all that the secretaries could do to keep from giggling.

'I'm sorry you have to go home just now.'

'I am, too. I wish I could stay, but – it can't be helped.'

When Tanner and Sebastiana left the office, they were the picture of decorum. The staff took delight in the idea that Tanner had no clue they were aware of what was going on.

The day after Sebastiana departed, Tanner arranged for a gold-plated phone to be installed in his office with a digital scrambler. His secretary and assistants had orders never to answer it.

From that time on, Tanner spoke on the gold phone

almost every day, and at the end of each month, he went away for a long weekend, and came back looking refreshed. He never told his staff where he had been, but they knew.

Two of Tanner's aides were talking, and one of them said to the other, 'Does the word "rendezvous" ring a bell?'

Tanner's love life had started again, and the change in him was remarkable. Everybody was happy.

NINETEEN

The words kept echoing through Diane Stevens' brain: 'This is Ron Jones. I just wanted to let you know that we have followed your new instructions, just as your secretary ordered . . . We cremated your husband's body one hour ago.'

How could the mortuary have made such a mistake? Lost in her grief, could she have called and asked them to cremate Richard? Never. And she had no secretary. None of it made any sense. Someone at the mortuary had misunderstood, confused Richard's name with a similar name of another body.

They had delivered an urn with Richard's ashes in it. Diane stood, staring at it. Was Richard really in there . . . ? Was his laughter in there . . . ? The arms that had held her close . . . the warm lips that had pressed against hers . . . the mind that had been so bright and funny . . . the voice that had said, 'I love you' . . . were all his dreams and passions and a thousand more things in that little urn?

Diane's thoughts were interrupted by the ringing of the telephone.

'Mrs Stevens?'

'Yes?'

'This is Tanner Kingsley's office. Mr Kingsley would appreciate it if he could make an appointment for you to come and meet with him.'

That had been two days ago, and now Diane was walking through the entrance of KIG and approaching the reception desk.

The receptionist said, 'May I help you?'

'My name is Diane Stevens. I have an appointment to see Tanner Kingsley.'

'Oh, Mrs Stevens! We're all so sorry about Mr Stevens. What a terrible thing to happen. Terrible.'

Diane swallowed. 'Yes.'

Tanner was talking to Retra Tyler. 'I have two meetings coming up. Let's do a complete scan on both of them.'

'Yes, sir.'

He watched his assistant leave.

The intercom buzzed. 'Mrs Stevens is here to see you, Mr Kingsley.'

Tanner pressed one of the buttons on the electronic panel on his desk and Diane Stevens appeared on one of the television screens on the wall. Her blonde hair was tied back in a knot and she was wearing a white and navy pin-striped skirt, and a white blouse. She looked pale.

'Send her in, please.'

He watched Diane walk through the door and rose to greet her. 'Thank you for coming, Mrs Stevens.'

Diane nodded. 'Good morning.'

'Please, sit down.'

Diane took a chair opposite his desk.

'Needless to say, all of us were shocked by your husband's brutal murder. You can be sure that whoever is responsible will be brought to justice as quickly as possible.'

Ashes . . .

'If you don't mind, I would like to ask you a few questions.'

'Yes?'

'Did your husband often discuss his work with you?'

Diane shook her head. 'Not really. It was a separate part of our lives together because it was so technical.'

In the surveillance room down the hall, Retra Tyler had turned on a voice recognition machine, a voice stress analyser and a television recorder, and was taping the scene taking place in Tanner's office.

'I know how difficult it must be for you to discuss this,' Tanner said, 'but how much do you know about your husband's connection with drugs?'

Diane was staring at him, too dumbfounded to speak. Finally, she found her voice. 'What – what are you asking? Richard would never have had anything to do with drugs.'

'Mrs Stevens, the police found a threatening note from the Mafia in his pocket, and –'

The idea of Richard being involved with drugs was unthinkable. Could Richard have had a secret life that she knew nothing about? *No, no, no.*

Diane's heart began to pound, and she felt the blood rushing to her face. They killed him to punish *me*, she thought. 'Mr Kingsley, Richard didn't –'

Tanner's tone was sympathetic, but at the same time determined. 'I'm so sorry to put you through this, but I fully intend to get to the bottom of what happened to your husband.'

I'm the bottom, Diane thought, miserably. I'm the one you're looking for. Richard died because I testified against Altieri. She was beginning to hyperventilate.

Tanner Kingsley was watching her. He said, 'I won't keep you, Mrs Stevens. I can see how upset you are. We'll talk again later. Perhaps there's something you'll remember. If you think of anything that might be helpful, I would appreciate it if you would call me.' Tanner reached into a drawer and pulled out an embossed business card. 'This has my private cell phone number on it. You can reach me day or night.'

Diane took the card. All that was on it was Tanner's name and a number.

Diane rose, her legs trembling.

'I apologise for having to put you through this. In the meantime, if there is anything that I can do for you – anything you need, I am at your service.'

Diane was barely able to speak. 'Thank you. I – thank you.' She turned and walked out of the office, numb.

As Diane reached the reception room, she heard the woman behind the desk saying, 'If I were a superstitious person, I would think someone had put a curse on KIG. And now *your* husband, Mrs Harris. We were all so shocked to hear about the dreadful thing that happened to him. To die like that is just awful.'

The words sounded ominously familiar to Diane. What had happened to the woman's husband? Diane turned to see whom the receptionist was addressing. It was a stunning-looking, young, African-American woman, dressed in black trousers and a silk turtleneck sweater. On her finger was a large emerald ring and a diamond wedding ring. Diane had a sudden feeling that it was important that she speak to her.

As Diane started to approach her, Tanner's secretary came in. 'Mr Kingsley will see you now.' And Diane watched Kelly Harris disappear into Tanner's office.

Tanner rose to greet Kelly. 'Thank you for coming, Mrs Harris. Did you have a satisfactory flight?'

'Yes, thank you.'

'Would you like anything? Coffee or –?'

Kelly shook her head.

'I know what a difficult time this must be for you, Mrs Harris, but I need to ask you a few questions.'

In the surveillance room, Retra Tyler was watching Kelly on the television set and recording the scene.

'Did you and your husband have a close relationship?' Tanner asked.

'Very close.'

'Would you say that he was honest with you?'

Kelly looked at him, puzzled. 'We had no secrets. Mark was the most honest, open human being I've ever known. He –' Kelly found it difficult to go on.

'Did he often discuss his work with you?'

'No. What Mark did was very – complicated. We didn't talk much about it.'

'Did you and Mark have many Russian friends?'

Kelly looked at him, confused. 'Mr Kingsley, I don't know what these questions –'

'Did your husband tell you he had a big deal coming up and that he was going to make a lot of money?'

Kelly was getting upset. 'No. If that were so, Mark would have told me.'

'Did Mark ever discuss Olga?'

Kelly was filled with a sudden foreboding. 'Mr Kingsley, exactly what is this all about?'

'The Paris police found a note in your husband's

pocket. It mentioned a reward for some information, and was signed, "Love, Olga".'

Kelly sat there, stunned. 'I – I don't know what . . .'

'But you did say he discussed everything with you?'

'Yes, but –'

'From what we have been able to learn, your husband was apparently involved with this woman and –'

'No!' Kelly was on her feet. 'This isn't my Mark we're talking about. I told you, we had no secrets between us.'

'Except whatever secret it was that caused your husband's death.'

Kelly felt suddenly faint. 'You'll – you'll have to excuse me, Mr Kingsley. I'm not feeling well.'

He was instantly apologetic. 'I understand. I want to help you in any way I can.' Tanner handed her his embossed business card. 'You can reach me through this number at any time, Mrs Harris.'

Kelly nodded, unable to speak, and blindly walked out of the office.

Kelly's mind was churning as she left the building. Who was Olga? And why had Mark been involved with Russians? Why would he –?

'Excuse me. Mrs Harris?'

Kelly turned. 'Yes?'

An attractive blonde woman was standing outside the building. 'My name is Diane Stevens. I'd like to talk to you. There's a coffee shop across the way and we –'

'Sorry. I – I can't talk now.' Kelly started to move on.

'It's about your husband.'

Kelly stopped abruptly and turned. 'Mark? What about him?'

'Can we talk where it's more private?'

In Tanner's office, his secretary's voice came over the intercom. 'Mr Higholt is here.'

'Send him in.'

A moment later, Tanner was greeting him. 'Good afternoon, John.'

'Good? It's a *hell* of an afternoon, Tanner. It seems that everyone in our company is being murdered. What the devil is going on?'

'That's what we're trying to find out. I don't believe the sudden deaths of three of our employees are a co-incidence. Someone is out to damage the reputation of this company, but they're going to be found and stopped. The police have agreed to co-operate with us, and I have men tracing the final movements of the employees who were killed. I would like you to listen to two interviews that I've just recorded. These are the widows of Richard Stevens and Mark Harris. Are you ready?'

'Go ahead.'

'This is Diane Stevens.' Tanner pressed a button and his interview with Diane Stevens appeared on the screen. At the right-hand corner of the screen was a graph, tracing lines up and down as Diane spoke.

How much do you know about your husband's connection with drugs?

What – what are you asking? Richard would never have had anything to do with drugs.

The graphic images remained steady.

Tanner pressed the fast-forward button. 'This is Mrs Mark Harris, whose husband was pushed or fell from the top of the Eiffel Tower.'

A picture of Kelly flashed on the television screen.

Did Mark ever discuss Olga?

Mr Kingsley, exactly what is this all about?

The Paris police found a note in your husband's pocket. It mentioned a reward for some information, and was signed, 'Love, Olga'.

I – I don't know what . . .

From what we have been able to learn, your husband was apparently involved with this woman and –

No! This isn't my Mark we're talking about. I told you, we had no secrets between us.

The lines on the graph remained even. Kelly's image disappeared.

'What was that line on the screen?' John Higholt asked.

'That's a voice stress analyser, a CVSA. It registers micro-tremors in the human voice. If the subject is lying, the modulations of the audio frequencies increase. It's state of the art. It doesn't require wires, like a polygraph. I'm convinced that both women told the truth. They must be protected.'

John Higholt frowned. 'What do you mean? Protected from what?'

'I think they're in danger, that subconsciously, they have more information than they realise. They were both close to their husbands. I'm convinced that at some point, something revealing might have been said that slipped by them at the time, but is dormant in their memories. The chances are that as they start to think about it, they're going to remember what it was. The moment they do, their lives could be at risk, because whoever killed their husbands could be planning to kill them. I intend to see that no harm comes to them.'

'You're going to have them followed?'

'That was yesterday, John. Today it's electronic equipment. I've put the Stevens' apartment under surveillance – cameras, telephones, microphones – everything. We're using every bit of technology at our disposal to guard them. The moment anyone tries to attack her, we'll know.'

John Higholt was thoughtful for a moment. 'What about Kelly Harris?'

'She's in a hotel. Unfortunately we couldn't get into her suite to prepare it. But I have men staking out the lobby, and if it looks as if there might be trouble, they'll handle it.' Tanner hesitated. 'I want KIG to put up a five-million-dollar reward leading to the arrest of –'

'Wait a minute, Tanner,' John Higholt objected. 'That's not necessary. We'll get this solved and –'

'Very well. If KIG won't do it, I'll personally offer a five-million-dollar reward. My name is identified with this company.' His voice hardened. 'I want whoever is behind this, caught.'

TWENTY

In the coffee shop across the street from KIG head-quarters, Diane Stevens and Kelly Harris were seated at a corner booth. Kelly was waiting for Diane to speak.

Diane was not sure how to begin. She wondered if she should simply ask: What was the dreadful thing that happened to your husband, Mrs Harris? Had he been murdered, like Richard?

Kelly said, impatiently, 'Well? You said you wanted to talk to me about my husband. How well did you know Mark?'

'I didn't know him, but –'

Kelly was furious. 'You said you –'

'I said I wanted to talk about him.'

Kelly rose. 'I don't have time for this, lady.' She started to walk away.

'Wait! I think we might both have the same prob-lem, and we may be able to help each other.'

Kelly stopped. 'What are you talking about?'

'Please, sit down.'

Reluctantly, Kelly returned to her seat in the booth. 'Go ahead.'

'I wanted to ask you if –'

A waiter approached the table with a menu. 'What would you ladies like?'

To be out of here, Kelly thought as she said, 'Nothing.'

Diane said, 'Two coffees please.'

Kelly looked at Diane and said defiantly, 'Make mine tea.'

'Yes, ma'am.' The waiter left.

Diane said, 'I think that you and I –'

She was interrupted as a young girl came up to the table and said to Kelly, 'Can I have your autograph?'

Kelly looked at her. 'Do you know who I am?'

'No, but my mother says you're important.'

Kelly said, 'I'm not.'

'Oh.'

They both watched the little girl leave, and Diane looked at Kelly, puzzled. 'Should I know who you are?'

'No.' Then Kelly added pointedly, 'And I don't like busybodies prying into my life. What is this all about, Mrs Stevens?'

'Diane, please. I heard that something terrible had happened to your husband and –'

'Yes, he was killed.'

'My husband was killed, too. And they both worked for KIG.'

Kelly said impatiently, 'Is that it? Well, so do

thousands of other people. If two of them caught colds, would you call it an epidemic?'

Diane leaned forward. 'Look, this is important. First of all . . .'

Kelly cut her short, 'Sorry. I'm not in the mood to listen to this.' She picked up her handbag.

'I'm not in the mood to talk about it either,' Diane snapped, 'but it could be very –'

Diane's voice suddenly echoed through the coffee shop.

'There were four men in the room . . .'

Startled, Diane and Kelly turned toward the sound. Diane's voice was coming from a television set above the bar. She was in the courtroom, on the witness stand.

'. . . One of them was in a chair, tied up. Mr Altieri seemed to be questioning him while the two other men stood next to him. Mr Altieri pulled out a gun, yelled something, and shot the man in the back of the head.'

The anchorman appeared on the screen. 'That was Diane Stevens testifying in the murder trial of accused Mafia head Anthony Altieri. The jury has just brought in a verdict of not guilty.'

Diane sat there, stunned. *'Not guilty?'*

'The murder that took place almost two years ago charged Anthony Altieri with killing one of his

employees. In spite of Diane Steven's testimony, the jury believed other witnesses who contradicted her.'

Kelly was staring at the set, wide-eyed. A new witness appeared on the stand.

Jake Rubenstein asked, 'Dr Russell, do you have a practice in New York?'

No. I work only in Boston.'

'On the day in question, did you treat Mr Altieri for a heart problem?'

'Yes. About nine a.m. I kept him under observation for the whole day.'

'So he could not have been in New York on October 14?'

'No.'

Another witness appeared on the screen: 'Would you tell us your occupation, sir?'

'I'm the manager of the Boston Park Hotel.'

'Were you on duty on the October 14 in question?'

'Yes, I was.'

'Did anything unusual happen that day?'

'Yes. I received an urgent phone call from the penthouse suite to send a doctor up there immediately.'

'What happened next?'

'I called Dr Joseph Russell and he came right over. We went to the penthouse suite to check on the guest, Anthony Altieri.'

'What did you see when you got there?'

'Mr Altieri, lying on the floor. I thought he was going to die in our hotel.'

Diane had turned pale. 'They're lying,' she said hoarsely. 'Both of them.'

Anthony Altieri was being interviewed. He looked frail and sickly.

'Do you have any plans for the immediate future, Mr Altieri?'

'Now that justice has been done, I'm just going to take it easy for a while.' Altieri smiled thinly. *'Maybe clean up a few old debts.'*

Kelly was dumbstruck. She turned to Diane. 'You testified against *him*?'

'Yes. I saw him kill –'

Kelly's trembling hands spilled some tea and knocked over a salt shaker. 'I'm getting out of here.'

'What are you so nervous about?'

'What am I nervous about? You tried to have the head of the Mafia sent to prison and he's free, and he's going to clean up a few old debts, and you want to know what *I'm* nervous about? *You* should be nervous.' Kelly rose and threw some money on the table. 'I'll pick up the check. You'd better save your money for travelling expenses, Mrs Stevens.'

'Wait! We haven't talked about our husbands or –'

'Forget it.' Kelly headed for the door and Diane reluctantly pursued her.

'I think you're overreacting,' Diane argued.

'Do you?'

As they reached the door, Kelly said, 'I don't understand how you could be so stupid as to –'

An elderly man, entering on crutches, slipped and started to fall. For an instant, Kelly was in Paris and it was Mark who was falling, and she reached down to save him, and at the same time, Diane moved to catch him. At that moment, from across the street two loud shots rang out, the bullets smashing into the wall where the women had been standing. The explosions brought Kelly back to instant reality. She was in Manhattan and had just had tea with a crazy woman.

'My God!' Diane exclaimed. 'We –'

'This is no time to pray. Let's get the hell out of here!'

Kelly propelled Diane to the kerb where Colin was waiting. He pulled the car door open, and Kelly and Diane tumbled into the back seat.

'What was that noise?' Colin asked.

The two women sat there, huddled in the seat, too unnerved to speak.

Finally, Kelly said, 'It – er, must have been a car backfiring.' She turned to Diane, who was fighting to regain her composure. 'I hope I'm not overreacting,' she said sarcastically. 'I'll drop you off. Where do you live?'

Diane took a deep breath and gave Colin the address of her apartment building. The two women rode there in stony silence, shaken by what had just happened.

*   *   *

When the car pulled up in front of her building, Diane turned to Kelly. 'Will you come in? I'm a little jittery. I have a feeling something more might happen.'

Kelly said curtly, 'I have the same feeling – but it's not going to happen to me. Goodbye, Mrs Stevens.'

Diane looked at Kelly for a moment, started to say something, then shook her head and got out of the car.

Kelly watched as Diane walked into the foyer and started up the steps to her apartment on the first floor. Kelly gave a sigh of relief.

Colin said, 'Where would you like to go, Mrs Harris?'

'Back to the hotel, Colin, and –'

There was a loud scream from inside the apartment building. Kelly hesitated an instant, then opened the car door and raced inside. Diane had left the door to her apartment wide open. She was standing in the middle of the room, trembling.

'What happened?' asked Kelly.

'Someone – someone's broken in here. Richard's briefcase was on this table and it's gone. It was filled with his papers. They left his wedding ring in its place.'

Kelly looked around nervously. 'You'd better call the police.'

'Yes.' Diane remembered the card that Detective Greenburg had left on the hall table. She walked over to it and picked it up. A minute later, she was on the phone, saying, 'Detective Earl Greenburg, please.'

There was a brief delay.

'Greenburg here.'

'Detective Greenburg, this is Diane Stevens. Something

183

has happened here. I wonder if you could come by the apartment and . . . Thank you.'

Diane took a deep breath and turned to Kelly. 'He's coming. If you don't mind waiting until he –'

'I do mind. This is your problem. I don't want any part of it. And you might mention that someone just tried to kill you. I'm leaving for Paris. Goodbye, Mrs Stevens.'

Diane watched as Kelly walked outside and headed for the limousine.

'Where to?' Colin asked.

'Back to the hotel, please.'

Where she would be safe.

TWENTY-ONE

When Kelly returned to her hotel room, she was still unnerved by what had happened. The experience of coming so close to being killed had been terrifying. The last thing I need right now is some blonde airhead trying to get me murdered, she thought.

Kelly sank down onto a sofa to calm herself and closed her eyes. She tried to meditate and concentrate on a mantra, but it was no use. She was too shaken. There was an empty, lonely feeling deep inside her. She could not stop her thoughts: Mark, I miss you so much. People said that as time went by, I would feel better. It's not true, my darling. Every day makes it worse.

The sound of a food cart being wheeled down the corridor outside made Kelly realise that she had not eaten all day. She was not hungry, but she knew she had to keep up her strength.

She phoned Room Service. 'I'd like a shrimp salad and some hot tea, please.'

'Thank you. It should be there in twenty-five to thirty minutes, Mrs Harris.'

'Fine.' Kelly replaced the receiver. She sat there, replaying in her mind the meeting with Tanner Kingsley, and she felt as though she had been plunged into a chilling nightmare. What was going on?

Why had Mark never mentioned Olga? Was it a business relationship? An affair? Mark, darling, I want you to know that if you did have an affair, I forgive you because I love you. I will always love you. You taught me how to love. I was cold and you warmed me. You gave me my pride back, and made me feel like a woman.

She thought about Diane. That busybody put my life at risk. She's someone to stay away from. That won't be difficult. Tomorrow I'll be in Paris, with Angel.

Her reverie was interrupted by the sound of a knock at the door. 'Room Service.'

'Coming.' As Kelly started towards the door, she stopped, puzzled. She had ordered just a few minutes ago. It's too soon, she thought. 'Just a moment,' she called.

'Yes, ma'am.'

Kelly picked up the phone and dialled Room Service. 'My order is not here yet.'

'We're working on it, Mrs Harris. It should be there in fifteen or twenty minutes.'

Kelly replaced the receiver, her heart pounding. She dialled the main desk.

'There's – there's a man trying to get into my room.'

'I'll send a security officer right up, Mrs Harris.'

Two minutes later, she heard another knock. Kelly walked over to the door, warily.

'Who is it?'

'Security.'

Kelly looked at her watch. Too fast, she thought. 'I'll be right there.' She hurried over to the telephone and called the main desk again. 'I called down about security. Is –'

'He's on his way up, Mrs Harris. He should be up there in a minute or two.'

'What is his name?' Her voice was strangled with fear.

'Thomas.'

Kelly could hear low, low whispers in the hall. She pressed her ear against the door, until the voices faded. She stood there, filled with blind fear.

A minute later, there was a knock at the door.

'Who is it?'

'Security.'

'Bill?' Kelly asked. She held her breath.

'No, Mrs Harris. It's Thomas.'

Kelly quickly opened the door and let him in.

He regarded her for a moment, and said, 'What happened?'

'Some – some men tried to get in here.'

'Did you see them?'

'No. I – I heard them. Would you walk me out to a taxi?'

'Certainly, Mrs Harris.'

Kelly was trying to force herself to stay calm. Too much was happening too fast.

Thomas stayed close by Kelly's side as they got into the lift.

When they reached the lobby, Kelly glanced around, but she could see nothing suspicious. Kelly and the security guard walked outside and as they reached the taxi stand, Kelly said, 'Thank you very much. I appreciate it.'

'I'll make sure that everything is all right when you come back. Whoever tried to break into your room is gone for now.'

Kelly got into a taxi. As she glanced out of the rear window, she saw two men hurrying into a parked limousine.

'Where to?' the cab driver asked Kelly.

The limousine had pulled up behind the taxi. Ahead, at the corner, a policeman was directing traffic.

'Go straight ahead,' Kelly told him.

'OK.'

As they approached the green light, Kelly said urgently, 'I want you to slow down, and wait until the light changes to amber, then make a quick left turn.'

The driver glanced at her in the rear-view mirror. '*What?*'

'Don't go through the green light until it turns amber.' She saw the expression on the driver's face.

Kelly forced a smile. 'I'm trying to win a bet.'

'Oh.' Kelly could see him thinking, Crazy damn passengers.

As the light changed from green to amber, Kelly said, 'Now!'

The taxi made a fast left turn as the light turned red. Behind them, the oncoming traffic was stopped by the policeman. The men in the limousine turned to each other, frustrated.

When the taxi reached the next junction, Kelly said, 'Oh, I forgot something. I've got to get out here.'

The driver pulled over to the kerb and Kelly got out of the cab and handed him some money. 'Here.'

He watched Kelly hurry into the entrance to a medical building, thinking to himself, I hope she's seeing a psychiatrist.

At the corner, the moment the light turned green, the limousine made a left turn. The taxi was two blocks ahead, and they raced after it.

Five minutes later, Kelly was hailing another taxi.

In Diane Stevens' apartment, Detective Greenburg was saying, 'Mrs Stevens, did you get a look at the person who took a shot at you?'

Diane shook her head. 'No, it happened so fast . . .'

'Whoever it was, was serious. Ballistics dug the bullets out of the wall. They were .45 calibres, capable of piercing body armour. You were lucky. Do you have any idea who might have a reason to kill you?'

Diane remembered Altieri's words: 'I'm just going to

take it easy for a while, maybe clean up a few old debts.'

Greenburg was waiting for an answer.

Diane hesitated. Putting it into words made it seem too real. 'The only one I can think of who might believe he has a motive is Anthony Altieri.'

Greenburg studied her for a moment. 'I understand. We'll check on that. About the briefcase that is missing, do you have any idea what was in it?'

'I'm not sure. Richard took it to the laboratory with him every morning and brought it home every night. I saw some of the papers once and they were very technical.'

Greenburg picked up the wedding ring that was on the table. 'And you said that your husband never took off his wedding ring?'

'That's – that's right.'

'In the days before his death, did your husband act differently than usual, as though he might be under some kind of pressure, or be worried about something? Do you remember anything out of the ordinary that he said or did the last time you saw him?'

Diane remembered: It was early morning. They were in bed, naked. Richard gently stroked her thighs and said, 'I'm going to be working late tonight, but save an hour or two for me, when I get home, honey.'

She touched him where he liked being touched and said, 'Braggart.'

'Mrs Stevens –'

190

Diane was jolted back to reality. 'No. There was nothing unusual.'

'I'll see that you have protection,' Greenburg said. 'And if —'

The front doorbell rang.

'Were you expecting anyone?'

'No.'

Greenburg nodded. 'I'll get it.'

He walked over to the door and opened it. Kelly Harris stormed in and brushed by him.

Kelly marched up to Diane. 'We need to talk.'

Diane looked at her in surprise. 'I thought you were on your way to Paris?'

'I took a detour.'

Greenburg had joined them. 'This is Detective Earl Greenburg. Kelly Harris.'

Kelly turned to Greenburg. 'Someone just tried to break into my hotel room, Detective.'

'Did you report it to hotel security?'

'Yes. The men were gone by the time the guard arrived.'

'Do you have any idea who they were?'

'No.'

'When you say someone tried to break in, you mean they tried to force the door?'

'No, they — they just stood out in the hall. They pretended they were from Room Service.'

'Had you ordered Room Service?'

'Yes, but I —'

Diane interrupted, 'Then you're probably imagining

things because of what happened this morning, and –'

Kelly snapped at her. 'Listen, I told you, I don't want any part of this, or of you. I'm going to pack and fly back to Paris this afternoon. You tell your Mafia friends to leave me alone.'

They watched Kelly turn and leave.

'What was that all about?' Greenburg asked.

'Her husband was – was killed. He worked for the same company Richard worked for, Kingsley International Group.'

When Kelly returned to the lobby of her hotel, she walked over to the reception desk. 'I'm checking out,' she said. 'Would you please get me a reservation on the next plane to Paris?'

'Certainly, Mrs Harris. Any particular airline?'

'Just get me out of here.'

Kelly crossed the hotel lobby, stepped into the lift, and pressed the button for the fourth floor. As the lift door started to close, two men pushed it open and got in. Kelly studied them for an instant, then quickly backed out into the lobby. She waited until the lift door closed, then headed for the stairs and started to walk up. No use taking any chances, Kelly thought.

As she reached the fourth-floor landing, a huge man was blocking the way.

'Excuse me,' Kelly said. She started to move past him.

'Shh!' He was pointing a gun with a silencer at her.

Kelly turned pale. 'What are you –?'

'Shut up. I bet you got exactly the right number of holes, lady. Unless you want an extra one, be quiet. I mean – very quiet. You and I are going downstairs.'

The man was smiling, but as Kelly looked closer, she saw that a knife-like crease on his upper lip had pulled his mouth up into a fixed grin. He had the coldest eyes Kelly had ever seen.

'Let's go.'

Kelly was furious. No! I'm not going to die because of that bitch. 'Wait a minute. You have the wrong –'

She felt the gun smash so hard into her ribs that she wanted to scream.

'I told you to shut up! We'll walk down.'

He was holding Kelly's arm in a painful vice-like grip, the gun concealed in his hand behind her back.

Kelly was fighting hysteria. 'Please,' she said softly, 'I'm not the –' The pain as he stabbed the muzzle of the gun hard against her back was excruciating. He was squeezing her arm so hard that she could feel the blood draining out.

They started down the stairs. They reached the lobby. It was crowded, and as Kelly was debating whether to call for help, the man said, 'Don't even think about it.'

Then they were outside. There was a station wagon waiting at the kerb. Two cars ahead, a traffic policeman was writing a parking ticket. Kelly's captor led her to the back door of the station wagon. 'Get in,' he ordered.

Kelly glanced ahead at the policeman. 'All right,'

Kelly said, in a loud, angry voice, 'I'll get in, but I want to tell you something. What you want me to do to you will cost an extra hundred dollars. I think it's disgusting.'

The policeman had turned to watch.

The burly man was staring at Kelly. 'What the hell are you –?'

'If you won't pay it, then forget it, you cheap bastard.'

Kelly started rapidly walking towards the policeman. The man looked after her. His lips were smiling, but his eyes were deadly.

Kelly pointed to him. 'That pervert has been bothering me.'

She glanced back to see the policeman moving towards the thug. Kelly stepped into a waiting taxi.

As the man started to get into the station wagon, the policeman said, 'Just a minute, sir. It's against the law in this state to solicit prostitutes.'

'I wasn't –'

'Let me see some identification. What's your name?'

'Harry Flint.'

Flint watched as Kelly's taxi sped away.

That whore! I'll kill her. Slowly, he vowed.

TWENTY-TWO

Kelly alighted from the taxi in front of Diane's apartment building for the second time, stormed up to the front door and pressed the bell hard.

The door was opened by Detective Greenburg again. 'Can I –?'

Kelly saw Diane in the living room and moved past the detective.

'What's going on?' Diane asked. 'You said you –'

'You tell *me* what's going on. They tried to grab me again. Why are your Mafia buddies trying to kill me?'

'I – I have no idea. They wouldn't – maybe they saw us together and thought we were friends and –'

'Well we're *not* friends, Mrs Stevens. Get me out of this.'

'What are you talking about? How can I –?'

'The same way you got me into it. I want you to tell your buddy, Altieri, that you and I just met, and you don't know me. I'm not going to let someone murder me because of some stupid thing you did.'

Diane said, 'I can't –'

'Oh, yes, you can. You're going to talk to Altieri and you're going to talk to him *now*. I'm not leaving here until you do.'

Diane said, 'What you're asking is impossible. I'm sorry if I got you involved in this, but . . .' She was thoughtful for a long moment, then turned to Greenburg. 'Do you think if I talked to Altieri he might leave us both alone?'

Greenburg said, 'That's an interesting question. He might – especially if he thinks we're watching him. Would you like to talk to him personally?'

Diane said, 'No, I –'

Kelly interrupted, 'She means "yes".'

Anthony Altieri's home was a classic stone and frame colonial-style house, in Hunterdon County, New Jersey. The enormous house was at the end of a cul-de-sac, on fifteen acres of land, surrounded by a huge, high, iron fence. On the grounds were tall shady trees, ponds and a colourful garden.

A guard sat in a booth inside the front gate. As the car with Greenburg, Kelly and Diane drove up, the guard walked out to meet it.

He recognised Greenburg. 'Afternoon, Lieutenant.'

'Hello, Caesar. We want to see Mr Altieri.'

'Do you have a warrant?'

'It's not that kind of visit. This is a social call.'

The guard glanced at the two women. 'Wait here.' He walked inside the booth. A few minutes later he came out and opened the gate, 'You can go in.'

'Thanks,' said Greenburg and drove up to the front of the house.

As the three of them got out of the car, a second guard appeared. 'Follow me.'

He led them inside. The large living room was an eclectic combination of antiques and modern and French furniture. In spite of the fact that the day was warm, there was a roaring fire in the huge stone fireplace. The trio followed the guard through the living room into a large darkened bedroom. Anthony Altieri was in bed, attached to a respirator. He was pale and gaunt and seemed to have aged greatly since the short time he had appeared in court. A priest and a nurse were at his side.

Altieri looked at Diane, Kelly and Greenburg, and then turned back to Diane. When he spoke, his voice was hoarse and raspy. 'What the hell do you want?'

Diane said, 'Mr Altieri, I want you to leave Mrs Harris and me alone. Call off your men. It's enough that you killed my husband and –'

Altieri cut in. 'What are you talking about? I never even heard of your husband. I read about that bullshit note found on his body.' He sneered. '"He'll swim with the fishes." Somebody's seen *The Sopranos* too many times. I'll tell you something for free, lady. No Italian wrote that. I'm not after you. I don't give a damn whether you live or die. I'm not after anybody. I –' He winced in pain. 'I'm busy making my peace with God. I –' He began to choke.

The priest turned to Diane. 'I think it would be better if you left now.'

Detective Greenburg asked, 'What is it?'

The priest said, 'Cancer.'

Diane looked at the man in the bed and thought about what he had just said. He was telling the truth.

Diane was filled with a sudden, blinding panic.

On the drive back from Altieri's, Detective Greenburg looked worried. 'I have to tell you, I think Altieri meant what he said.'

Kelly reluctantly nodded. 'So do I. The man is dying.'

'Do you know of any reason why someone would try to kill the two of you?'

'No,' Diane said. 'If it isn't Altieri –' She shook her head. 'I have no idea.'

Kelly swallowed. 'Neither have I.'

Detective Greenburg escorted Diane and Kelly back into Diane's apartment. 'I'm going to get to work on this now,' he said, 'but you'll be safe here. In fifteen minutes there will be a police cruiser outside your apartment building for the next twenty-four hours, and we'll see what we can find out by then. If you need me, call.'

And he was gone.

Diane and Kelly stared at each other in an awkward silence.

'Would you like some tea?' Diane asked.

Kelly said, perversely, 'Coffee.'

Diane looked at her for a moment, irritated, and sighed. 'Right.'

Diane walked into the kitchen to start the coffee. Kelly wandered around the living room, looking at the paintings on the walls.

When Diane came out of the kitchen, Kelly was studying one of Diane's paintings. She looked at the signature, 'Stevens.' She turned to Diane. 'Did you paint this?'

Diane nodded. 'Yes.'

Kelly said, in a dismissive tone of voice, 'Pretty.'

Diane's lips tightened. 'Oh? Do you know a lot about art?'

'Not much, Mrs Stevens.'

'Who do you like? Grandma Moses, I suppose.'

'She's interesting.'

'And what other primitive painters touch your heart?'

Kelly turned to face Diane. 'To be honest, I prefer the curvilinear, non-representational form. There are exceptions, of course. For instance, in Titian's, *Venus of Robin*, the diagonal sweep of her form is breathtaking, and –'

From the kitchen, they could hear the coffee percolating.

Diane said curtly, 'The coffee is ready.'

They were seated across from each other in the dining room, taciturn, letting their coffee get cold.

Diane broke the silence. 'Can you think of any reason why someone would try to kill us?'

'No.' Kelly was silent for a moment. 'The only connection you and I have is that both our husbands worked at KIG. Maybe they were involved in some top-secret project. And whoever killed them thinks they might have told us about it.'

Diane paled. 'Yes . . .'

They looked at each other in dismay.

In his office, Tanner was watching the scene taking place in Diane's apartment, on one of the wall television sets. His chief security guard stood next to him.

The Stevens' apartment had been wired with state-of-the-art television and sound. Just as Tanner had told his partner, the house was filled with cutting-edge technology. There were concealed video systems in every room, with a web-based camera the size of a button resting among the books, bent fibre optical wires under the doors, and a wireless picture-frame camera. In the attic, a video server the size of a laptop computer had been installed to service six cameras. Attached to the server was a wireless modem that allowed the equipment to function through cellular technology.

As Tanner leaned forward, watching the screen intently, Diane said, 'We have to find out what our husbands were working on.'

'Right. But we're going to need help. How do we go about that?'

'We'll call Tanner Kingsley. He's the only one who can help us, and he's already trying to find out who's behind all this.'

'Let's do it.'

Diane said, 'You can spend the night here. We'll be safe. There's a police car stationed outside.' She walked over to the window and pulled the curtain back. There was no car.

She stared for a long moment and felt a sudden chill. 'That's strange,' Diane said. 'There was supposed to be a patrol car here. Let me make a phone call.'

Diane took Detective Greenburg's card from her handbag, went to the telephone and called the number. 'Detective Greenburg, please.' She listened for a moment. 'Are you sure? . . . I see. Then could I speak to Detective Praegitzer?' There was another moment of silence. 'Yes, thank you.' Diane slowly replaced the receiver.

'What is it?'

Diane said, 'Detectives Greenburg and Praegitzer have been transferred to another precinct.'

Kelly swallowed. 'That's a real coincidence, isn't it?'

Diane said, 'And I just remembered something.'

'What?'

'Detective Greenburg asked me if Richard had done or said anything out of his usual routine lately. There was one thing I forgot to mention. Richard was going to Washington, to see somebody. Sometimes I travel with him, but this time he insisted it would be better if he went alone.'

Kelly was watching her with a surprised expression. 'That's strange. Mark told me *he* had to go to Washington, and had to go alone too.'

'We have to find out why.'

Kelly walked over to the window and pulled back the curtains. 'There's still no car.' She turned to Diane. 'Let's get out of here.'

'Right,' Diane said. 'I know a little out-of-the-way hotel in Chinatown called The Mandarin. No one will ever think of looking for us there. We'll call Mr Kingsley from the room.'

Tanner turned to his chief security officer, Harry Flint, the thug with the perpetual half-smile. 'Kill them,' he said.

TWENTY-THREE

Harry Flint will take good care of the women, Tanner thought with satisfaction. Flint had never failed him.

It amused Tanner to think about how Flint had come into his life. Years ago, his brother Andrew, poster boy for the bleeding hearts of the world, had started a half-way house for newly released prisoners, to help them adjust to civilian life. Then he would find jobs for them.

Tanner had a more useful plan for these men, because he believed that there was no such thing as an ex-felon. Through his private sources, he would get inside information on the backgrounds of recently released prisoners, and if they had the qualifications that Tanner needed, they went from the half-way house to working for Tanner directly, doing what he called 'delicate private tasks'.

He had arranged for an ex-felon named Vince Carballo to come to work for KIG. Carballo was a huge man with a straggly beard and blue eyes that were like daggers. He had a long prison record. He had been on trial for murder. The evidence against him was overwhelming, but a member of the jury stubbornly held out for acquittal, and the case had ended up in a hung jury. Only a few people knew that the juror's little daughter had disappeared, and that a note had been left behind: *If you keep quiet about this, your daughter's fate will be determined by the jury's verdict.* Carballo was the kind of man that Tanner Kingsley admired.

Tanner had also heard about an ex-felon named Harry Flint. He had investigated Flint's life thoroughly, and decided he was perfect for his needs.

Harry Flint had been born in Detroit, into a middle-class family. His father was a bitter, failed salesman who spent his time sitting around the house complaining. He was a sadistic martinet, and at his son's slightest infraction, he enjoyed whipping him, using a ruler, a belt, or anything else that was handy, as though he could beat success into his son to make up for his own inadequacy.

The boy's mother worked as a manicurist at a barber shop. While Harry's father was tyrannical, his mother was devoted and doting, and as young Harry grew up, he was emotionally whipsawed between the two.

Doctors had told Harry's mother that she was too old to have a child, so she considered her pregnancy a miracle. After Harry was born, she lovingly fondled him and was constantly hugging him, patting him, and kissing him, until eventually Harry felt smothered by her love. As he got older, he loathed being touched.

When Harry Flint was fourteen years old, he trapped a rat in the basement and stomped on it. As he stared at the rat slowly, painfully dying, Harry Flint had an epiphany. He suddenly realised he had the awesome power to take life, to kill. It made him feel like God. He was omnipotent. He needed to have that feeling again, and he began to stalk small animals around the neighbourhood, and they became his prey. There was nothing personal or malicious about what Flint was doing. He was just using his God-given talent.

Angry neighbours whose pets were being tortured and killed complained to the authorities, and a trap was set. The police put a Scottish terrier on the front lawn of a house, on a lead to keep her from running away. They staked out the site and, one night, as the police watched, Harry Flint approached the animal. He pried the dog's jaws open, and started to put a lit firecracker in her mouth. The police pounced. When Harry Flint was frisked, he had a bloody rock and a five-inch fillet knife in his pocket.

He was sent to Challenger Memorial Youth Center for twelve months.

One week after Flint arrived, he attacked one of the other boys, maiming him badly. The psychiatrist who examined Flint diagnosed him as a paranoid schizophrenic.

'He's psychotic,' the doctor warned the guards in charge. 'Be careful. Keep him away from the others.'

When Harry Flint had served his time, he was fifteen years old and was released on probation. He returned to school. Several of his classmates looked upon Flint as a hero. They had become involved in petty crimes such as purse snatching, pick-pocketing and shoplifting, and Flint soon became their leader.

In an alley fight one night, a knife sliced a corner of Flint's lip, giving him a constant half-smile.

As the boys grew older, they turned to car-jacking, burglary and robbery. One of the robberies became violent and a shopkeeper was killed. Harry Flint was convicted of armed robbery and abetting a murder, and sentenced to ten years in prison. He was the most vicious prisoner the warden had ever seen.

There was something in Harry Flint's eyes that made other prisoners leave him alone. He constantly terrorised them, but no one dared report him.

One day, as a guard passed Harry Flint's cell, he stared inside, unbelievingly. Flint's cellmate was lying on the floor in a pool of blood. He had been beaten to death.

The guard looked at Flint, and there was a smile of satisfaction on his face. 'All right, you bastard. You won't get out of this one. We can start warming up the chair for you.'

Flint glared at him and slowly raised his left arm. A bloody butcher's knife was deeply embedded in it.

Flint said coldly, 'Self-defence.'

The prisoner in the cell across from Flint never told anyone that he had seen Flint savagely beat his cellmate to death, then pull out a knife from under his mattress, and slice the knife through his own arm.

The characteristic that Tanner most admired about Flint was that Flint enjoyed his work so much.

Tanner remembered the first time that Flint had proved to him how useful he could be. It was during an emergency trip to Tokyo . . .

'Tell the pilot to warm up the Challenger. We're going to Japan. There will be two of us.'

The news had come at a bad time, but it had to be taken care of immediately, and it was too sensitive to entrust to anyone else. Tanner had arranged for Akira Iso to meet him in Tokyo, and to take a room at the Okura Hotel.

While the plane was crossing the Pacific Ocean, Tanner was planning his strategy. By the time the plane landed, he had worked out a win-win situation.

The drive from Narita Airport took one hour, and Tanner was amazed by how Tokyo never seemed to change. In boom times and in depressions, the city always seemed to wear the same impassive face.

Akira Iso was waiting for him at the Fumiki Mashimo restaurant. Iso was in his fifties, a spare figure, grey hair and bright brown eyes. He stood up to greet Tanner.

'It is an honour to meet you, Mr Kingsley. Frankly, I was surprised to hear from you. I cannot imagine why you would come all this way to meet me.'

Tanner smiled. 'I'm the bearer of good news that I thought was too important to discuss on the telephone. I think I'm going to make you a very happy man, and a very rich one.'

Akira Iso was looking at him curiously. 'Yes?'

A white-jacketed waiter had come to the table.

'Before we talk business, why don't we order?'

'As you wish, Mr Kingsley. Are you familiar with Japanese dishes or shall I order for you?'

'Thank you. I can order. Do you like sushi?'

'Yes.'

Tanner turned to the waiter. 'I'll have *hamachi-temaki*, *kaibashira* and *ama-ebi*.'

Akira Iso smiled. 'That sounds good.' He looked at the waiter. 'I'll have the same.'

While they were eating, Tanner said, 'You work for a very fine company, the Tokyo First Industrial Group.'

'Thank you.'

'How long have you worked there?'

'Ten years.'

'That's a long time.' He looked Akira Iso in the eye and said, 'In fact, it might be time to make a change.'

'Why would I want to do that, Mr Kingsley?'

'Because I'm going to make you an offer you can't refuse. I don't know how much money you make, but I am willing to pay you twice as much to leave your job and come to work for KIG.'

'Mr Kingsley, that is not possible.'

'Why not? If it's because of a contract, I can arrange –'

Akira Iso put down his chopsticks. 'Mr Kingsley, in Japan, when we work for a company, it is like a family. And when we can no longer work, they take care of us.'

'But the money I'm offering you –'

'No. *Ai-shya-sei-shin.*'

'What?'

'It means that we put loyalty above money.' Akira Iso looked at him curiously. 'Why did you choose me?'

'Because I've heard very flattering things about you.'

'I'm afraid you have taken a long trip for nothing, Mr Kingsley. I would never leave Tokyo First Industrial Group.'

'It was worth a try.'

'There are no hard feelings?'

Tanner leaned back and laughed. 'Of course not. I wish all my employees were as loyal as you are.' He remembered something. 'By the way, I brought you and your family a little gift. An associate of mine will bring it to you. He'll be at your hotel in an hour. His name is Harry Flint.'

A maid found Akira Iso's body hanging from a hook in the wardrobe. The official verdict was suicide.

TWENTY-FOUR

The Mandarin Hotel was a seedy, two-storey building in the heart of Chinatown, three blocks from Mott Street.

As Kelly and Diane got out of the taxi, Diane saw a large billboard across the street, with a picture of Kelly in a beautiful evening gown, holding up a bottle of perfume. Diane looked at it in surprise. 'That's who you are.'

'You're wrong,' Kelly said. 'That's what I do, Mrs Stevens. It's not who I am.' She turned and walked into the lobby and an exasperated Diane followed.

A young Chinese man was seated behind the desk in the small hotel lobby, reading a copy of *The China Post*.

'We would like a room for the night,' Diane said.

The man glanced up at the two elegantly dressed

211

women and almost said aloud, *Here?* He rose. 'Certainly.' He took a closer look at their designer clothes. 'That will be a hundred dollars a night.'

Kelly looked at him, shocked. 'A hun –?'

Diane cut in quickly, 'That will be fine.'

'In advance.'

Diane opened her purse, took out some bills and gave them to the man. He handed her a key.

'Room Ten, straight down the hall, on the left. Do you have luggage?'

'It's coming later,' Diane told him.

'If you need anything, just ask for Ling.'

Kelly said, 'Ling?'

'Yes. She's your chambermaid.'

Kelly gave him a sceptical look. 'Right.'

The two women started down the dreary, dimly-lit hallway.

'You paid too much,' Kelly said.

'What's a safe roof over your head worth?'

'I'm not so sure this place is such a good idea,' Kelly said.

'It will have to do until we think of something better. Don't worry. Mr Kingsley will take care of us.'

When they reached number ten, Diane unlocked the door and they stepped inside. The small room looked and smelled as though it had been unoccupied for a long time. There were twin beds with rumpled bed covers and two worn chairs next to a scarred desk.

Kelly looked around. 'It may be small, but it sure is

ugly. I'll bet it's never been cleaned.' She touched a cushion and watched the dust rise. 'I wonder how long ago Ling passed away.'

'It's only for tonight,' Diane assured her. 'I'm going to phone Mr Kingsley now.'

Kelly watched as Diane went to the telephone and called the number on the card that Tanner Kingsley had given her.

The call was answered immediately. 'Tanner Kingsley.'

Diane sighed in relief. 'Mr Kingsley, this is Diane Stevens. I'm sorry to bother you, but Mrs Harris and I need your help. Someone is trying to kill us and we have no idea what's going on. We're on the run.'

'I'm very glad you called, Mrs Stevens. You can relax. We just found out what's behind all this. You won't have any more problems. I can assure you that from now on, both you and Mrs Harris will be perfectly safe.'

Diane closed her eyes for an instant. Thank God, she thought. 'Can you tell me who –?'

'I'll tell you all about it when I see you. Stay where you are. I'll have someone there to pick you up in thirty minutes.'

'That's –' The connection was broken. Diane replaced the receiver and turned to Kelly, grinning. 'Good news! Our problems are over.'

'What did he say?'

'He knows what's behind all this and he says from now on, we're safe.'

Kelly gave a deep sigh. 'Great. Now I can go back to Paris and start my life over again.'

'He's sending someone to pick us up in half an hour.'

Kelly looked around the dingy room. 'It will sure be hard to leave all this,' she said, sarcastically.

Diane turned to her and said wistfully, 'It's going to be strange.'

'What is?'

'Going back to a life without Richard. I can't imagine how I'll be able to –'

'Then don't.' Kelly snapped as she thought, Don't take me there, lady, or I'll fall apart. I can't even think about it. Mark was my whole life, my only reason for living . . .

Diane looked at Kelly's emotionless expression and thought, She's like a lifeless work of art – beautiful and cold.

Kelly turned and sat on one of the beds, her back to Diane. She closed her eyes against the pain inside her and slowly . . . slowly . . . slowly . . .

Kelly was walking along the Left Bank with Mark, chatting about everything and nothing, Kelly felt that she had never been so completely comfortable with anyone before.

She said to Mark, 'Tomorrow evening there's a gallery opening, if you're interested in –'

'Oh, I'm sorry, Kelly. Tomorrow night I'm busy.'

Kelly felt an unexpected stab of jealousy. 'Going on another date?' She tried to keep her tone light.

'No. No. I'm going alone. It's a banquet –' He saw the look on Kelly's face. 'I – I mean it's just a dinner for scientists. You'd be bored.'

'Would I?'

'I'm afraid so. There – there will be people using a lot of words you've probably never heard before and –'

'I think I've heard them all,' Kelly said, piqued. 'Why don't you try me?'

'Well, I don't really think –'

'I'm a big girl. Go ahead.'

He sighed. 'All right. "Anatripsology" . . . "malacostracology" . . . "aneroidograph" . . . "term ag –"'

'Oh.' Kelly said, taken aback. 'Those kind of words.'

'I knew you wouldn't be interested. I –'

'You were wrong. I am.' Because you're interested, Kelly thought.

The banquet was held at the Prince de Galles Hotel and turned out to be a major event. There were three hundred people in the ballroom, among them, some of the most important dignitaries in France. One of the guests at the front table where Kelly and Mark were seated was an attractive man with a warm, engaging personality.

'I'm Sam Meadows,' he said to Kelly. 'I've heard a lot about you.'

'I've heard a lot about *you*,' Kelly replied. 'Mark says you're his mentor and best friend.'

Sam Meadows smiled. 'I'm honoured to be his friend. Mark is a very special person. We've worked together for a long time. He's the most dedicated –'

Mark was listening, embarrassed. 'Would you like some wine?' he interrupted.

The master of ceremonies appeared on stage, and the speeches began. Mark had been right about the evening being uninteresting for Kelly. Technical scientific prizes were being awarded, and as far as Kelly was concerned, the speakers could all have been talking in Swahili. But Kelly watched the enthusiasm on Mark's face, and she was glad she was there.

When the dinner plates had been cleared, the president of the French Science Academy appeared on stage. He began by praising the scientific accomplishments that France had made in the past year, and it was not until the end of his speech, when he held up a gold statuette and called out Mark Harris's name that Kelly realised that Mark was the star of the evening. He had been too modest to tell her. That's why he tried to talk me out of coming, she thought, as she watched Mark get up and go on stage, while the audience warmly applauded him.

'He never said a word to me about this,' Kelly told Sam Meadows.

Meadows smiled. 'That's Mark.' He studied Kelly for a moment. 'You know he's madly in love with you. He wants to marry you.' He paused, and said pointedly, 'I hope he doesn't get hurt.'

And as Kelly listened, she felt a sudden rush of guilt: I can't marry Mark. He's a great friend, but I'm not in love with him. What have I been doing? I don't want to hurt him. It's better if I stop seeing him. How am I going to tell –?

'*Have you heard a word I've said?*'

Diane's angry voice shook Kelly out of her reverie. The beautiful ballroom disappeared and she was in a crummy hotel room with a woman she wished she had never met. 'What?'

Diane said urgently, 'Tanner Kingsley said someone's going to pick us up here in half an hour.'

'You told me that. So?'

'He didn't ask where we were.'

'He probably thinks we're still at your apartment.'

'No. I told him that you and I are on the run.'

There was a moment of silence. Kelly's lips pursed into a long, silent 'Oh'.

They turned to look at the clock on the bedside table.

The man at the reception desk glanced up as Flint entered the lobby of the Mandarin Hotel. 'Can I help you?' He saw Flint's smile and returned it.

'My wife and her friend just checked in here. My wife is a blonde. Her friend is a hot black chick. What room are they in?'

'Room Ten, but I'm afraid I can't let you go in. You'll have to teleph –'

Flint raised a .45 calibre Ruger pistol equipped with a silencer, and put a bullet in the man's forehead. Flint shoved the body behind the desk and started down the hall, the gun at his side. When he reached number ten, he stepped back, took two steps forward, shouldered the door open, and stepped into the room.

The room was empty, but through the closed bathroom door, Flint could hear the sound of a shower running. He walked over to the bathroom door and shoved it open. The shower was turned on full force, and the closed curtains were gently swaying. Flint fired four shots into the curtains, waited for a moment, then pulled them open.

There was no one there.

In a diner across the street, Diane and Kelly had watched Flint's station wagon arrive, and had seen him go into the hotel.

'My God,' Kelly said, 'that's the man who tried to kidnap me.'

They waited. When Flint came out a few minutes later, his lips were smiling, but his face was a mask of fury.

Kelly turned to Diane. 'There goes Godzilla. What's our next false move?'

'We have to get out of here.'

'And go where? They're going to be watching the airports, train stations, bus depots . . .'

Diane was thoughtful for a moment. 'I know a place where they can't touch us.'

'Let me guess. The space ship that brought you here.'

TWENTY-FIVE

The neon sign in front of the building read *Wilton Hotel for Women*.

In the lobby, Kelly and Diane were registering under false names. The woman behind the desk handed Kelly a key. 'Suite 424. Do you have luggage?'

'No, we –'

'It got lost,' Diane cut in. 'It will be here in the morning. By the way, our husbands are picking us up in a little while. Would you send them to our room and –'

The receptionist shook her head. 'I'm sorry. Men are not allowed upstairs.'

'Oh?' Diane gave Kelly a complacent smile.

'If you wish to meet them down here –'

'Never mind. They'll just have to suffer without us.'

*   *   *

Suite 424 was beautifully appointed, with a living room containing a sofa, chairs, tables and an armoire, and in the bedroom, two comfortable-looking double beds.

Diane looked around. 'This is pleasant, isn't it?'

Kelly said acidly, 'What are we doing – going for the Guinness Book of Records – a different hotel every half-hour?'

'Do you have a better plan?'

'This is no plan,' Kelly said scornfully. 'This is a game of cat and mice, and we're the mice.'

'It's extraordinary when you think about it, the men in the biggest think-tank in the world are out to murder us,' Diane said.

'Then don't think about it.'

'Easier said than done. There are enough eggheads at KIG to make an omelette the size of Kansas.'

'Well, we'll just have to out-think them.' Kelly frowned. 'We need some kind of weapon. Do you know how to use a gun?'

'No.'

'Damn. Neither do I.'

'It doesn't matter. We don't have one.'

'How about karate?'

'No, but I was on the debating team in college,' Diane said, drily. 'Maybe I can argue them out of killing us.'

'Right.'

Diane walked over to the window and looked out at the traffic on Thirty-fourth Street. Suddenly, her eyes widened and she gasped, 'Oh!'

Kelly rushed to her side. 'What is it? What did you see?'

Diane's throat was dry. 'A – a man walked by. He looked just like Richard. For a moment, I –' She turned away from the window.

Kelly said contemptuously, 'Would you like for me to send for the ghost catchers?'

Diane started to retort, but stopped. What's the use? We'll be out of here soon, she thought.

Kelly looked at Diane, wishing: Why don't you shut up and go paint something.

Flint was speaking on his mobile phone to a furious Tanner. 'I'm sorry, Mr Kingsley. They weren't in their room at the Mandarin. They were gone. They must have known I was coming.'

Tanner was apoplectic. 'Those bitches want to play mind games with *me*? With *me*? I'll call you back.' He slammed down the receiver.

Andrew was lying on the sofa in his office, and his mind drifted to the huge stage of the Stockholm Concert Hall. The audience was cheering enthusiastically.

'Andrew! Andrew!'

The crowd was shouting. The hall echoed with the sound of his name. He could hear the audience applauding as he walked across the stage to receive his award from King Carl XVI Gustav of Sweden. As he reached for the Nobel Prize, someone started cursing him.

'Andrew, you son of a bitch – get in here.'

The Stockholm Concert Hall shimmered away, and Andrew was in his office. Tanner was calling him.

He needs me, Andrew thought happily. He slowly rose and walked into his brother's office.

'I'm here,' Andrew said.

'Yes, I see that.' Tanner snapped. 'Sit down.'

Andrew took a chair.

'I have a few things to teach you, big brother. Divide and conquer.' There was a note of arrogance in Tanner's voice. 'I have Diane Stevens thinking that the Mafia killed her husband, and Kelly Harris is worried about a nonexistent Olga. Understand?'

Andrew said vaguely, 'Yes, Tanner.'

Tanner patted his brother on the shoulder. 'You're a perfect sounding board for me, Andrew. There are things I want to talk about that I can't discuss with anyone else. But I can tell you anything, because you're too stupid to understand.' He looked into Andrew's vacant eyes. 'See no evil, hear no evil, speak no evil.' Tanner was suddenly all business. 'We have a problem to solve. Two women have disappeared. They know we're looking for them, to kill them, and they're trying to stay out of sight. Where would they go to hide, Andrew?'

Andrew looked at his brother for a moment. 'I – I don't know.'

'There are two ways to find out. First, we'll try the Cartesian method, logic, building our solution one step at a time. Let's reason it out.'

Andrew looked at him and said, vacuously, 'Whatever you say . . .'

Tanner began to pace. 'They won't return to the Stevens' apartment because that's too dangerous – we're having it watched. We know that Kelly Harris doesn't have any close friends in the States because she's lived in Paris for so long, so she wouldn't trust anyone here to protect her.' He looked at his brother. 'Are you following me?'

Andrew blinked. 'I – yes, Tanner.'

'Now, would Diane Stevens go to friends for help? I don't think so. It might jeopardise them. Another alternative is for them to go to the police with their story, but they know they would be laughed at. So, what could their next step be?' He closed his eyes for a few seconds, then went on. 'Obviously they would have considered the airports, train stations and bus depots, but they would know we're having them watched. So where does that leave us?'

'I – I – whatever you say, Tanner.'

'It leaves us with a hotel, Andrew. They need a hotel to hide in. But what kind of hotel? These are two terrified women running for their lives. You see, no matter which one they choose, they'll figure we might have connections there, and they'll be exposed. They won't feel safe. Do you remember Sonja Verbrugge in Berlin? We finessed her with that message on her computer. She went to the Artemisia Hotel because it was for women only, so she thought she would be safe. Well, I think Mesdames Stevens and Harris would feel the same way. So where would that leave us?'

He turned to look at his brother again. Andrew's eyes were closed. He was asleep. Furious, Tanner walked over to him and slapped him hard across his face.

Andrew jerked awake. 'What –?'

'Pay attention when I'm talking to you, you cretin.'

'I – I'm sorry, Tanner. I was just –'

Tanner turned to a computer. 'Now, let's see what women's hotels there are in Manhattan.'

Tanner did a quick search on the Internet and printed out the results. He read the names aloud. 'The El Carmelo Residence on West 14th Street . . . Centro Maria Residence on West 54th Street . . . The Parkside Evangeline on Gramercy South, and the Wilton Hotel for Women.' He looked up and smiled. 'That's where Cartesian logic tells us they might be, Andrew. Now let's see what technology tells us.'

Tanner walked over to a painting of a landscape on the wall, reached behind it and pressed a concealed button. A section of the wall slid open, revealing a television screen with a computerised map of Manhattan.

'Do you remember what this is, Andrew? You used to operate this equipment. In fact, you were so good at it, I was jealous of you. It's a global positioning system. With this, we can locate anyone in the world. Remember?'

Andrew nodded, fighting to stay awake.

'When the ladies left my office, I gave each of them my calling card. The cards have microdot computer chips about the size of a grain of sand embedded in them. That signal is picked up by satellite, and when the global positioning system is activated, it pinpoints their exact location.' He turned to his brother. 'Do you understand?'

Andrew swallowed. 'I – I – yes, Tanner.'

Tanner turned back to the screen. He pressed a second button. A tiny light began to flash on the map and started downward. It slowed at a small area, then flowed ahead again. A moving pinpoint of red light swept along a street, going so slowly that the names of businesses were clearly visible.

Tanner pointed. 'That's West Fourteenth Street.' The red light kept moving. 'There's the Tequila Restaurant . . . a pharmacy . . . Saint Vincent's Hospital . . . Banana Republic . . . Our Lady of Guadalupe Church.' The light stopped. A note of victory came into Tanner's voice. 'And there's the Wilton Hotel for Women. That confirms my logic. I was right, you see.'

Andrew licked his lips. 'Yes. You were right . . .'

Tanner looked at Andrew. 'You may go now.' He picked up his mobile phone and dialled. 'Mr Flint, they're at the Wilton Hotel on West Thirty-fourth Street.' He turned off the phone. He looked up and saw Andrew standing in the doorway. 'What is it?' Tanner asked impatiently.

'Will I be going to – you know – Sweden, to pick up my Nobel Prize they just gave me?'

'No, Andrew. That was seven years ago.'

'Oh.' Andrew turned and shuffled back to his office.

Tanner started thinking about his urgent trip to Switzerland, three years earlier . . .

Tanner had been involved in a complicated logistics mishap when his secretary's voice came over the intercom. 'Zurich is on the line for you, Mr Kingsley.'

'I'm too busy for – never mind. I'll talk to them.' He picked up the phone. 'Yes?' As Tanner listened, his face became grim. He said impatiently, 'I see . . . are you sure? . . . No, never mind. I'll handle this myself.'

He pressed down the intercom button. 'Miss Ordonez, tell the pilot to have the Challenger ready. We're flying to Zurich. There will be two passengers.'

Madeleine Smith was seated at a table at the Grand Veranda, one of the finest restaurants in Zurich. She was in her early thirties, a lovely oval face, bobbed hair, and a beautiful complexion. She was visibly pregnant.

Tanner walked over to the table, and Madeleine Smith stood up.

Tanner Kingsley held out his hand. 'Please, sit down.'

He sat down opposite her.

'I am happy to meet you.' She had a lilting Swiss accent. 'At first, when I got the call, I thought it was a joke.'

'Why?'

'Well, you are such an important man and when they

said you were coming to Zurich just to see me, I could not imagine –'

Tanner smiled. 'I'll tell you why I'm here. Because I've heard that you are a brilliant scientist, Madeleine. May I call you Madeleine?'

'Oh, please, Mr Kingsley.'

'At KIG, we treasure talent. You're the kind of person who should be working for us, Madeleine. How long have you been with the Tokyo First Industrial Group?'

'Seven years.'

'Well, seven is your lucky number, because I'm offering you a job at KIG at twice what you're making now, and you'll be in charge of your own department and –'

'Oh, Mr Kingsley!' She was beaming.

'Are you interested, Madeleine?'

'Oh, yes! I am very interested. Of course I could not start right now.'

Tanner's expression changed. 'What do you mean?'

'Well, I am having a baby and getting married . . .'

Tanner smiled. 'That's no problem. We'll handle everything.'

Madeleine Smith said, 'But there is another reason I cannot leave right now. I am working on a project at our laboratory and we are just getting – we are almost at the end of it.'

'Madeleine, I don't know what your project is and I don't care. But the fact is that the offer I just made must be accepted immediately. In fact, I was hoping to fly you and your fiancé –' he smiled '– or should I say your future husband – back to America with me.'

'I could come as soon as the project is finished. Six months, maybe a year.'

Tanner was silent for a moment. 'Are you sure there is no way you can come now?'

'No. I am in charge of this project. It would be unfair for me to walk out.' She brightened. 'Next year –?'

Tanner smiled. 'Absolutely.'

'I am so sorry that you had to make this journey for nothing.'

Tanner said warmly, 'It wasn't for nothing, Madeleine. I got to meet you.'

She blushed. 'You are very kind.'

'Oh, by the way, I brought you a gift. My associate will bring it to your apartment tonight at six o'clock. His name is Harry Flint.'

The following morning, the body of Madeleine Smith was found on her kitchen floor. The oven had been left on and the apartment was filled with gas.

Tanner's thoughts came back to the present. Flint never failed him. In a little while, Diane Stevens and Kelly Harris would be disposed of, and with them out of the way, the project could continue.

TWENTY-SIX

Harry Flint walked up to the reception desk of the Wilton Hotel. 'Hello.'

'Hello.' The receptionist noticed the smile on his face. 'Can I help you?'

'Yes. My wife, Diane Stevens, and her friend checked in here a little while ago. I want to go up and surprise them. What's their room number?'

The receptionist said, 'I'm sorry. This is a hotel for women, sir. Men are not allowed upstairs. If you'd like to phone –'

Flint glanced around the lobby. Unfortunately, it was crowded. 'Never mind,' he said. 'I'm sure they'll be down soon.'

Flint walked outside and dialled a number on his mobile phone. 'They're upstairs in their room, Mr Kingsley. I can't go up.'

Tanner was still for a moment, concentrating. 'Mr

Flint, logic tells me that they will decide to separate. I'm sending Carballo over to help you. Here's my plan . . .'

Upstairs in their suite, Kelly turned the radio on to a pop station and the room was suddenly filled with loud rap music.

'How can you listen to that?' Diane asked, irritably.

'You don't like rap music?'

'That's not music. That's noise.'

'You don't like Eminem? And what about LLCoolJ and R Kelly and Ludacris?'

'Is that all you listen to?'

'No,' Kelly said tartly. 'I enjoy Berlioz's *Symphonie Fantastique*, Chopin's *Etudes*, and Handel's *Almira*. I'm particularly fond of –'

Kelly watched Diane walk over to the radio and turn it off. 'What are we going to do when we run out of hotels, Mrs Stevens? Do you know anyone who can help us?'

Diane shook her head. 'Most of Richard's friends worked at KIG, and our other friends – I can't get any of them involved in this.' She looked at Kelly. 'What about you?'

Kelly shrugged. 'Mark and I lived in Paris for the past three years. I don't know anyone here except the people at the model agency, and I have a feeling they wouldn't be a lot of help.'

'Did Mark say why he was going to Washington?'

'No.'

'Neither did Richard. I have a feeling that somehow that's the key to why they were murdered.'

'Great. We have the key. Where's the door?'

'We'll find it.' Diane was thoughtful for a moment, then her face lit up. 'Wait a minute! I know someone who might be able to help us.' She went over to the phone.

'Who are you calling?'

'Richard's secretary. She'll know what's been going on.'

A voice at the other end of the phone said, 'KIG.'

'I'd like to speak to Betty Barker, please.'

In his office, Tanner watched the voice identification blue light flash on. He pressed a switch and heard the operator say, 'Miss Barker is not at her desk right now.'

'Can you tell me how to reach her?'

'I'm sorry. If you'll give me your name and phone number, I'll have her –'

'Never mind.' Diane replaced the receiver.

The blue light went out.

Diane turned to Kelly. 'I have a feeling Betty Barker might be the door we're looking for. I have to find a way to get to her.' She frowned. 'It's so strange.'

'What is?'

'A fortune teller predicted this. She told me she saw death around me, and –'

Kelly exclaimed, 'No! And you didn't report it to the FBI and the CIA?'

Diane glared at her. 'Never mind.' More and more, Kelly was getting on her nerves. 'Let's have dinner.'

Kelly said, 'I have to make a call first.' She picked up the telephone and dialled the hotel operator. 'I want to place a call to Paris.' She gave the operator a number, and waited. After a few minutes, Kelly's face brightened. 'Hello, Philippe. How are you? . . . Everything's fine here . . .' She glanced over at Diane. 'Yes . . . I should be home in a day or two . . . How is Angel? . . . Oh, that's wonderful. Does she miss me? . . . Would you put her on?' Her voice changed to the tone adults use when talking to a small child. 'Angel, how are you, darling? . . . It's your mama. Philippe says you miss me . . . I miss you, too. I'll be home soon, and I'll hold you and cuddle you, sweetheart.'

Diane had turned to listen, puzzled.

'Goodbye, baby . . . All right, Philippe . . . Thanks. I'll see you soon. *Au revoir.*'

Kelly saw Diane's bewildered expression. 'I was talking to my dog.'

'Right. What did he have to say?'

'*She*. She's a bitch.'

'That figures.'

As they were afraid to leave the safety of their room, they ordered something from Room Service for their dinner.

The talk was desultory. Diane tried to make conversation with Kelly, but it was hopeless.

'So, you've been living in Paris?'

'Yes.'

'Was Mark French?'

'No.'

'Were you married long?'

'No.'

'How did you two meet?'

None of your damned business, Kelly thought as she said, 'I don't really remember. I've met so many men.'

Diane studied Kelly. 'Why don't you get rid of that wall you've built around yourself?'

Kelly said tightly, 'Did anyone ever tell you that walls are to keep people out?'

'Sometimes they keep people locked in, and –'

'Look, Mrs Stevens, mind your own business. I was doing fine until I met you. Let's drop it.'

'Right.' Diane was stunned. She's the coldest person I've ever met, she thought.

When they had finished a silent dinner, Kelly announced, 'I'm going to take a shower.'

Diane did not respond.

In the bathroom, Kelly shed her clothes, stepped into the shower and turned it on. The warm water against her nakedness felt wonderful. She closed her eyes and let her mind drift . . .

She could hear Sam Meadows' words: 'You know he's madly in love with you. He wants to marry you. I hope he doesn't get hurt.' And Kelly knew that Sam Meadows was right. Kelly enjoyed being with Mark. He was fun, and thoughtful, and caring, and a great friend. That was the catch, she mused, I think of him only as a friend. That's not fair to him. I must stop seeing him.

Mark had called the morning after the banquet. 'Hello, Kelly. What would you like to do tonight?' Mark's voice was filled with anticipation. 'Dinner and the theatre? Or there are some stores open at night, and then there's –'

'I'm sorry, Mark. I'm – I'm busy tonight.'

There was a brief silence. 'Oh. I thought you and I had a –'

'Well, we don't.' And Kelly stood there, hating herself for what she was doing to him. It's my fault for letting it go this far, she said to herself.

'Oh, all right. I'll call you tomorrow.'

He called the next day. 'Kelly, if I've offended you in any way –'

And Kelly had to steel herself to say, 'I'm sorry, Mark. I've – I've fallen in love with someone.' She waited. The long silence was unbearable.

'Oh.' Mark's voice was shaky. 'I understand. I – I should have realised that we – con – congratulations. I really hope you'll be happy, Kelly. Please say good-bye to Angel for me.'

Mark hung up. Kelly stood there, holding the dead phone in her hand, feeling miserable. He'll forget me soon, Kelly thought, and find someone who can give him the happiness he deserves.

* * *

Kelly worked every day, smiling her way across runways, and hearing the applause of the crowds, but inside she was saddened. Life was not the same without her friend. She was constantly tempted to call him, but she resisted. I can't. I've hurt him enough, she told herself.

Several weeks had gone by, and Kelly had not heard from Mark. He's out of my life. He's probably found someone else by now. I'm glad, she thought, and she tried to mean it.

One Saturday afternoon, Kelly was working at a fashion show in an elegant room crowded with the élite of Paris. She walked out onto the runway, and as soon as she appeared, there was the usual acclaim. Kelly was following a model wearing an afternoon suit and carrying a pair of gloves. One of the gloves slipped out of her hand and dropped onto the runway. When Kelly saw it, it was too late. She tripped on it and plummeted to the floor, falling on her face. There was a gasp from the audience. Kelly lay there, humiliated. Steeling herself not to cry, she took a deep, shuddering breath, raised herself up and fled from the catwalk.

When Kelly reached the dressing room, the wardrobe mistress said, 'I have the evening gown ready for you. You had better –'

Kelly was sobbing. 'No. I – I can't go out there in front of those people. They'll laugh at me.' She was becoming hysterical. 'I'm through. I'm never going to go out there again. Never!'

'Of course you are.'

Kelly spun around. Mark was standing in the door-way. 'Mark! What – what are you doing here?'

'Oh, I – I've kind of been hanging around lately.'

'You – you saw – what happened out there?'

Mark smiled. 'It was wonderful. I'm glad it happened.'

Kelly was staring at him. 'What?'

He stepped close to her and took out a handkerchief to dry her tears. 'Kelly, before you walked out there, the audience thought you were just a beautiful, untouch-able dream, a fantasy, out of reach. When you tripped and fell, it showed them that you're human, and they adored you for it. Now you go back out there and make them happy.'

She looked into Mark's compassionate eyes, and that was the moment Kelly realised she was in love with him.

The wardrobe mistress was putting the evening gown back on a clothes rack.

'Give me that please,' Kelly said. She looked at Mark and smiled through her tears.

Five minutes later, when Kelly confidently walked out onto the cat walk, there was a wave of thunder-ous applause and a standing ovation from the audi-ence. Kelly stood there facing them, overwhelmed by emotion. It was so wonderful to have Mark in her life again. She remembered how nervous she had been in the beginning . . .

* * *

Kelly had been tense, waiting for Mark to make a pass at her, but he was always the perfect gentleman. His shyness made her feel more confident. It was Kelly who began most of the conversations, and no matter what the subject was, she found that Mark was knowledgeable and amusing.

One evening, Kelly said, 'Mark, there's a great symphony orchestra opening tomorrow night. Do you like classical music?'

He nodded. 'I grew up with it.'

'Good. We'll go.'

The concert was brilliant and the audience enthusiastic.

As they reached Kelly's apartment, Mark said, 'Kelly, I – I lied to you.'

I should have known, Kelly thought. He's just like the rest of them. It's over. She steeled herself for his answer. 'Did you?'

'Yes. I – I don't really like classical music.'

Kelly bit her lip to keep from bursting out laughing.

On their next date, Kelly said, 'I want to thank you for Angel. She's great company.' And so are you, Kelly thought. Mark had the brightest blue eyes she had ever seen, and an endearing, crooked, little smile. She enjoyed his company tremendously and . . .

The water was getting cold. Kelly turned off the shower, towelled herself off, put on a dressing gown and went into the living room.

'It's all yours.'

'Thanks.'

Diane got up and stepped into the bathroom. It looked like a storm had struck. Water had spilled onto the floor and towels were strewn all over the place.

Angrily, Diane walked back into the bedroom. 'The bathroom is a mess. Are you used to having people pick up after you?'

Kelly smiled sweetly. 'Yes, Mrs Stevens. As a matter of fact, I grew up with a lot of maids taking care of me.'

'Well, I'm not one of them.'

You wouldn't be qualified for the job, thought Kelly angrily.

Diane took a deep breath. 'I think it would be better if we –'

'There's no "we", Mrs Stevens. There's you and there's me.'

They stared at each other for a long moment. Then, without another word, Diane turned and went back into the bathroom. Fifteen minutes later, when she emerged, Kelly was in bed. Diane reached for the switch to turn off the overhead light.

'No, don't touch that!' It was a scream.

Diane looked at Kelly, startled. 'What?'

'Leave the lights on.'

Diane asked, scornfully, 'Are you afraid of the dark?'

'Yes. I'm – I'm afraid of the dark.' Ever since Mark died.

Diane said, patronisingly, 'Why? Did your parents

tell you scary bogie-man stories when you were a little girl?'

There was a long silence. 'That's it.'

Diane went to her own bed. She lay there for a minute, then closed her eyes. Thoughts of Richard overwhelmed her: Richard, darling, I never believed that someone could die of a broken heart. I believe it now. I need you so much. I need you to guide me. I need your warmth and your love. You're here somewhere, I know you are. I can feel you. You're a gift that God loaned me, but not for long enough. Good night, my guardian angel. Please don't ever leave me. Please.

In her bed, Kelly could hear Diane quietly sobbing. Kelly's lips tightened, as she thought: Shut up. Shut up. Shut up. And tears began to roll down her cheeks.

TWENTY-SEVEN

When Diane woke up in the morning, Kelly was sitting in a chair, facing the wall.

'Morning,' Diane said. 'Did you get some sleep?'

There was no response.

'We have to figure out what our next move is. We can't stay here for ever.'

No response.

Exasperated, Diane said loudly, 'Kelly, can you hear me?'

Kelly spun around in her chair. 'Do you *mind*? I'm in the middle of a mantra.'

'Oh, sorry. I didn't –'

'Forget it.' Kelly rose. 'Did anyone ever tell you you snore?'

Diane felt a small shock. She could hear Richard's voice saying, on the first night they had slept together, 'Darling, did you know you snore? Let me put it another way. It's not really a snore. Your nose sings delicious little melodies through the night like the music of angels.' And he had taken her in his arms and –

'Well, you do,' Kelly said. She walked over to the television set and turned it on. 'Let's see what's happening in the world.' She began to channel surf and suddenly stopped. A news show was on the air and the host was Ben Roberts. 'It's Ben!' Kelly exclaimed.

'Who's Ben?' Diane asked, indifferently.

'Ben Roberts. He does the news, and interview shows. He's the only interviewer I really enjoy. He and Mark became great friends. One day –' She suddenly stopped.

Ben Roberts was saying:

'. . . and in a bulletin just in, Anthony Altieri, the purported Mafia head, who was recently acquitted in his murder trial, died this morning, of cancer. He was . . .'

Kelly turned to Diane. 'Did you hear that? Altieri's dead.'

Diane felt nothing. It was news from another world, another time.

Diane looked at Kelly and said, 'I think it would be better if you and I split up. The two of us together are too easy to spot.'

'Right,' Kelly said drily, 'We're the same height.'

'I meant –'

'I know what you meant. But I could put on a white face and –'

244

Diane was looking at her, puzzled. 'What?'

'Just kidding,' Kelly said. 'Splitting up is a great idea. It's almost a plan, isn't it?'

'Kelly –'

'It's certainly been interesting knowing you, Mrs Stevens.'

Diane said curtly, 'Let's check out of here.'

The lobby was crowded with a convention of women checking in, and half a dozen guests checking out. Kelly and Diane waited in the queue.

Out on the street, looking into the lobby, Harry Flint saw them, and moved out of sight. He picked up his mobile phone. 'They just came down to the lobby.'

'Good. Did Carballo get there, Mr Flint?'

'Yes.'

'Do exactly as I told you. Cover the entrance to the hotel from both corners, so that no matter which way they go, they're trapped. I want them to disappear without a trace.'

Kelly and Diane had finally reached the reception desk.

The woman behind the desk smiled. 'I hope you've had a pleasant stay here.'

'Very pleasant, thank you,' Diane said, thinking, we're still alive.

As they walked to the main entrance, Kelly asked, 'Do you know where you're going now, Mrs Stevens?'

'No. I just want to get away from Manhattan. What about you?'

I just want to get away from you, Kelly thought. 'Back to Paris.'

The two of them stepped outside and carefully looked around. There was the usual pedestrian traffic, and everything seemed normal.

'Goodbye, Mrs Stevens,' Kelly said, a note of relief in her voice.

'Goodbye, Kelly.'

Kelly turned to the left and started walking towards the corner. Diane looked after her for a moment, then turned to the right and began walking in the other direction. They had taken no more than half a dozen steps when Harry Flint and Vince Carballo suddenly appeared at opposite ends of the block. The expression on Carballo's face was vicious. Flint's lips were turned up in a half-smile.

The two men began closing in on the women, pushing their way through the pedestrians. Diane and Kelly turned to look at each other, panicky. They had been ambushed. They both hurried back towards the entrance of the hotel, but the doorway was so crowded, that there was no way for them to get back inside. There was nowhere to go. The two men were getting closer.

Kelly turned to Diane, and as she watched, stunned, Diane smiled and waved cheerily at Flint, and then at Carballo.

'Have you gone crazy?' Kelly whispered.

Diane, still smiling, took out her mobile phone and spoke into it rapidly. 'We're in front of the hotel now . . . oh, good. You're around the corner?' She grinned and gave a victory sign to Kelly. 'They'll be here in a minute,' she said loudly. She looked at Flint and Carballo and said into the phone, 'No, there are only two of them.' Diane listened and then laughed. 'Right . . . They're here? OK.'

As Kelly and the two men looked on, Diane stepped off the kerb into the street, scanning the oncoming cars. Diane started signalling to an approaching car in the distance, and excitedly waved it over. Flint and Carballo had stopped, puzzled by what was happening.

Diane pointed to the two men. 'Over here,' she shouted into the oncoming traffic, waving wildly. 'Over here.'

Flint and Carballo looked at each other and made a quick decision. They turned back to where they had come from, and disappeared around the corners.

Kelly was staring at Diane, her heart pounding wildly. 'They're gone,' she said. 'Who – who were you talking to?'

Diane took a deep breath to steady herself. 'Nobody. My battery is dead.'

TWENTY-EIGHT

Kelly was staring at Diane, dumbfounded. 'That was great. I wish I had thought of that.'

Diane said drily, 'You will next time.'

'What are you going to do now?'

'Get out of Manhattan.'

'How?' Kelly asked. 'They're going to be watching all the train stations, airports, bus stations, car rental –'

Diane thought for a moment. 'We can go to Brooklyn. They won't be looking there.'

'Fine,' Kelly said. 'Go ahead.'

'What?'

'I'm not going with you.'

Diane started to say something and then changed her mind. 'Are you sure?'

'Yes, Mrs Stevens.'

Diane said, 'Well, then, we – goodbye.'

'Goodbye.'

Kelly watched as Diane hailed a taxi and started to get into it. Kelly stood there, hesitant, trying to make a decision. She was standing alone on an unfamiliar street, with nowhere to go, and no one to go to. The taxi door closed, and the cab started to move.

'Wait!' Kelly shouted.

The taxi stopped. Kelly hurried up to it.

Diane opened the door, and Kelly stepped in and settled back in her seat.

'What made you change your mind?'

'I just realised I've never seen Brooklyn!'

Diane looked at Kelly for a moment and then shook her head.

The driver asked, 'Where to?'

'Take us to Brooklyn, please,' Diane said.

The taxi started. 'Any place special?'

'Just drive around.'

Kelly looked at Diane increduously. 'You don't know where we're going?'

'I'll know when we get there.'

Why did I come back? Kelly was asking herself.

During the ride, the two of them sat silent, side by side. In twenty minutes, they were crossing the Brooklyn Bridge.

'We're looking for a hotel,' Diane told the driver. 'I'm not sure which –'

'You want a nice hotel, lady? I know just the one. It's called The Adams. You'll like it.'

*   *   *

The Adams Hotel was a five-storey brick building with a canopy in front, and a doorman in attendance.

When the taxi pulled up at the kerb, the driver asked, 'Does this look OK?'

Diane said, 'This looks fine.'

Kelly said nothing.

They got out of the taxi and the doorman greeted them. 'Good day, ladies. Are you checking in?'

Diane nodded. 'Yes.'

'Do you have luggage?'

Diane said glibly, 'The airline lost our bags. Is there any place around here where we can shop and pick up some clothes?'

'There's a very nice clothes shop at the end of the block. Perhaps you would like to check in here first. Then we can have your things sent directly to your room.'

'Fine. Are you sure they'll have a room for us here?'

'This time of the year, there's no problem.'

The receptionist behind the hotel desk proffered registration forms. As Kelly signed hers, she said aloud, 'Emily Brontë.'

Diane glanced at the receptionist to see if there was any recognition on his face. Nothing.

Diane wrote, 'Mary Cassatt'.

The receptionist took their registration cards. 'And do you wish to pay by credit card?'

'Yes, we –'

'No,' Diane interrupted quickly.

Kelly looked at her and reluctantly nodded.

'Luggage?'

'It's coming. We'll be back.'

'You'll have Suite 515.'

The receptionist watched them walk out of the door. Two real beauties. And alone. What a waste, he thought.

The *For Madame* shop was a cornucopia. There were women's clothes of every description, and a leather section with handbags and suitcases.

Kelly looked around and said, 'It looks like we've lucked out.'

A saleslady walked up to them. 'May I help you?'

'We're just browsing,' Diane told her.

The saleslady watched as they each took a shopping trolley and started walking through the store.

'Look!' said Kelly. 'Stockings.' She grabbed half a dozen pairs. Diane followed suit.

'Panty hose . . .'

'Bras . . .'

'Slips . . .'

Soon their trolleys were overflowing with lingerie.

The saleslady hurried over with two more. 'Let me help you.'

'Thank you.'

Diane and Kelly began to fill the new trolleys.

Kelly was examining a rack of trousers. She selected four pairs and turned to Diane. 'No telling when we're going to be able to shop again.'

Diane picked out some trousers as well and a striped summer dress.

'You can't wear that,' Kelly said. 'Stripes will make you look fat.'

Diane started to put it back, then looked at Kelly, and handed the dress to the saleslady. 'I'll take this.'

The saleswoman watched in amazement as Kelly and Diane went through the rest of the racks. By the time they had finished, their selections filled four suitcases.

Kelly looked at them and grinned, 'That should hold us for a while.'

When they went to the paying desk, the cashier asked, 'Will that be cash or credit card?'

'Credit –'

'Cash,' Diane said.

Kelly and Diane opened their purses and divided the bill. They both had the same thought: Cash is running low.

Kelly said to the cashier, 'We're staying at The Adams. I wonder if you could –'

'Have your things delivered? Certainly. Your names?'

Kelly hesitated for a moment. 'Charlotte Brontë.'

Diane looked at her and said quickly, '*Emily*. Emily Brontë.'

Kelly remembered. 'Right.'

The cashier was watching them, a confused expression on her face. She turned to Diane. 'And your name?'

'I – er –' Diane's mind was spinning. What name had

she signed? Georgia O'Keeffe . . . Frida Kahlo . . . Joan Mitchell?

'Her name is Mary Cassatt,' Kelly said.

The cashier swallowed. 'Of course.'

Next to the *For Madame* shop was a pharmacy. 'We're in luck again,' Diane smiled.

They hurried inside and began a second shopping spree.

'Mascara . . .'

'Blush . . .'

'Toothbrushes . . .'

'Toothpaste . . .'

'Tampons and panty liners . . .'

'Lipstick . . .'

'Hairclips . . .'

'Powder . . .'

By the time Diane and Kelly arrived back at their hotel, the four suitcases had already been delivered to their room.

Kelly stared at them. 'I wonder which are yours and which are mine?'

'It doesn't matter,' Diane assured her. 'We're going to be here for maybe a week, or more, so we might as well just put everything away.'

'I suppose so.'

They began busily hanging up dresses and trousers, putting their lingerie in drawers and placing their toiletries in the bathroom.

When the suitcases were emptied and everything had been put in place, Diane took off her shoes and dress, and gratefully sank down on one of the beds.

'This feels wonderful.' She sighed contentedly. 'I don't know about you, but I'm having dinner in bed. Then I'm going to take a nice, long, hot bath. I'm not moving from here.'

A pleasant-faced, uniformed maid knocked and came into the suite, carrying an armful of fresh towels.

Two minutes later, she emerged from the bathroom. 'If there's anything you need, please ring for me. Have a good evening.'

'Thank you.' Kelly watched her leave.

Diane was browsing through the hotel brochure she had picked up at her bedside. 'Do you know what year this hotel was built?'

'Get dressed,' Kelly said. 'We're leaving.'

'It was built in –'

'Get dressed. We're getting out of here.'

Diane looked up at her. 'Is this some kind of joke?'

'No. Something terrible is going to happen.' There was panic in her voice.

Diane sat up, alarmed. 'What's going to happen?'

'I don't know. But we have to get out of here, or we're both going to die.'

Her fear was contagious, but it made no sense.

'Kelly, you're not being reasonable. If –'

'I'm begging you, Diane.'

Thinking about it later, Diane never knew whether

she gave in because of the urgency in Kelly's voice, or because it was the first time Kelly had called her Diane.

'All right.' Diane got up. 'We'll pack our clothes and –'

'No! Leave everything.'

Diane looked at Kelly in disbelief. '*Leave everything? We just bought* –'

'Hurry! *Now!*'

'All right.' As Diane was reluctantly dressing, she thought, I hope she knows what she's doing. If –

'Quick!' It was a strangled scream.

Diane hurriedly finished and followed Kelly out of the door. I must be as crazy as she is, Diane decided, resentfully.

When they reached the lobby, Diane found herself running to keep up with Kelly. 'Would you mind telling me where we're going?'

Outside, Kelly looked around. 'There's a park across the street from the hotel. I – I need to sit down.'

Exasperated, Diane followed Kelly into the park. They took seats on a bench.

Diane said, 'What are we doing here?'

At that instant, there was a tremendous explosion inside the hotel and from where they sat, Diane and Kelly could see windows being blown out of a fourth-floor room, with debris flying through the air.

In stunned disbelief, Diane watched what was happening. 'That – that was a bomb –' terror crept into her voice '– in our room.' She turned to Kelly. 'How – how did you know?'

'The maid.'

Diane looked at her, puzzled. 'What about her?'

Kelly said quietly, 'Hotel maids don't wear three-hundred-dollar Manolo Blahnik shoes.'

Diane was finding it difficult to breathe. 'How – how could they have found us?'

'I don't know,' Kelly said. 'But remember who we're dealing with.'

They both sat there, filled with dread.

'Did Tanner Kingsley give you anything when you were in his office?' Diane asked.

Kelly shook her head. 'No. Did he give you anything?'

'No.'

They realised it at the same instant. 'His card!'

They opened their bags and took out the cards Tanner Kingsley had given them.

Diane tried to break hers in half. It would not bend. 'There's some kind of chip inside,' Diane said, furious.

Kelly tried to bend her card. 'In mine, too. That's how the bastards have been tracking us.'

Diane took Kelly's card and said, angrily, 'Not any more.'

Kelly watched as Diane stepped out onto the road and threw the cards down on the street. Within minutes, they had been run over by a dozen cars and trucks.

In the distance, the sounds of approaching sirens were filling the air.

Kelly stood up. 'We'd better get away from here, Diane. Now that they can't track us any more, we'll be all right. I'm going back to Paris. What will you do?'

'Try to figure out why this is happening.'

'Be careful.'

'You, too.'

Diane hesitated for a moment. 'Kelly – thanks. You saved my life.'

Embarrassed, Kelly said, 'I feel bad about something. I lied to you.'

'You did?'

'You know what I said about your paintings?'

'Yes.'

'I really liked them – a lot. You're *good*.'

Diane smiled. 'Thanks. I'm afraid I've been pretty rude to you.'

'Diane?'

'Yes?'

'I never grew up with maids!'

Diane laughed, and the two of them embraced.

'I'm glad we met,' Diane said, warmly.

'So am I.'

They stood there, looking at each other, finding it difficult to say goodbye.

'I have an idea,' Diane said. 'If you need me, here's my phone number.' She wrote it on a piece of paper.

'Here's mine,' Kelly replied, and gave it to Diane.

'Well, goodbye again.'

Diane said, haltingly, 'Yeah. I – goodbye, Kelly.'

Diane watched Kelly walk away. At the corner, she turned and waved. Diane waved back. As Kelly disappeared, Diane looked up at the blackened hole that was to have been their tomb, and she felt a cold chill.

TWENTY-NINE

Kathy Ordonez walked into Tanner Kingsley's office with the morning newspapers and said, 'It's happening again.' She handed him the newspapers. They all had banner headlines: *Fog Disrupts Major German Cities*; *All German Airports Closed by Fog*; *Death Toll Rises from Fog in Germany*.

Kathy said, 'Shall I send this to Senator van Luven?'

'Yes. Right away,' Tanner said grimly.

Kathy hurried out of his office.

Tanner looked at his wristwatch and smiled, thinking: The bomb must have gone off by now. The two bitches have finally been disposed of.

His secretary's voice came over the intercom. 'Mr Kingsley, Senator van Luven is on the line for you. Do you wish to take it?'

'Yes.' Tanner picked up the phone. 'Tanner Kingsley.'

'Hello, Mr Kingsley. This is Senator van Luven.'

'Good afternoon, Senator.'

'My assistants and I happen to be near your head-quarters and I wondered if it would be convenient for you if we dropped in for a visit.'

'Absolutely,' Tanner said, enthusiastically. 'I would be very happy to show you around, Senator.'

'Fine. We'll be there shortly.'

Tanner pressed the intercom button. 'I'm expecting some visitors in a few minutes. Hold all my calls.'

He remembered the obituary he had seen in the news-papers a few weeks earlier. Senator van Luven's husband, Edmond Barclay, had died of a heart attack. I'll offer my condolences, he thought.

Fifteen minutes later, Senator van Luven and her two attractive young assistants arrived.

Tanner rose to greet them. 'I'm delighted you decided to come.'

Senator van Luven nodded. 'You met Corinne Murphy and Karolee Trost.'

Tanner smiled. 'Yes. It's nice to see you both again.' He turned to the Senator. 'I heard about your husband's passing away. I'm terribly sorry.'

Senator van Luven nodded. 'Thank you. He had been ill for a long time, and finally, a few weeks ago . . .' She forced a smile. 'By the way, the information on global warming that you've been sending me is very impressive.'

'Thank you.'

'Would you like to show us what you're doing here?'

'Of course. How much of a tour would you like? We have a five-day tour, a four-day tour, and an hour-and-a-half tour.'

Corinne Murphy grinned. 'It would be nice to take the four –'

Senator van Luven interrupted. 'We'll settle for the hour-and-a-half tour.'

'My pleasure.'

'How many people work at KIG?' Senator van Luven asked.

'Approximately 2,000. KIG has offices in a dozen major countries all over the world.'

Corinne Murphy and Karolee Trost looked impressed.

'We have 500 employees in these buildings. The staff members and the research fellows have separate quarters. Every scientist employed here has a minimum IQ of 160.'

Corinne Murphy gushed, 'They're geniuses.'

Senator van Luven gave her a disapproving look.

'Follow me, please,' Tanner said.

The Senator, and Murphy and Trost followed Tanner through a side door into one of the adjoining buildings. He led them into a room crammed with esoteric-looking equipment.

Senator van Luven walked up to one of the odd-looking machines and asked, 'What does this do?'

'That's a sound spectrograph, Senator. It converts the sound of a voice into a voiceprint. It can recognise thousands of different voices.'

Trost frowned, 'How does it do that?'

'Think of it this way. When a friend calls you on the telephone, you instantly recognise the voice because that sound pattern is etched in your brain. We program this machine the same way. An electronic filter allows only a certain band of frequencies to get through to the recorder, so that we have only the distinguishable features of each person's voice.'

The rest of the tour was a fascinating montage of giant machines and miniature electronic microscopes and chemical laboratories: rooms with blackboards filled with mysterious symbols, laboratories with a dozen scientists working together, and offices where a single scientist was absorbed in trying to solve some arcane problem.

They passed a redbrick building with a double set of locks on the door.

Senator van Luven asked, 'What's in there?'

'Some secret government research. Sorry, it's out of bounds, Senator.'

The tour took two hours. When it was over, Tanner escorted the three women back to his office.

'I hope you enjoyed it,' Tanner said.

Senator van Luven nodded. 'It was interesting.'

'*Very* interesting.' Corinne Murphy smiled. Her eyes were on Tanner.

'I loved it,' exclaimed Karolee Trost.

Tanner turned to Senator van Luven. 'By the way, have you had a chance to discuss with your colleagues the environmental problem we talked about?'

The Senator's voice was noncommittal. 'Yes.'

'Would you tell me what you think the chances are, Senator?'

'This is not a guessing game, Mr Kingsley. There will be more discussions. I'll let you know when it's been decided.'

Tanner managed a smile. 'Thank you. Thank you all for dropping by.'

He watched them leave.

As the door closed behind them, Kathy Ordonez's voice came over the intercom. 'Mr Kingsley, Saida Hernandez has been trying to reach you. She said it was urgent, but you told me to hold your calls.'

'Get her for me,' Tanner said.

Saida Hernandez was the woman he had sent to The Adams Hotel to plant the bomb.

'Line one.'

Tanner picked up the phone, anticipating the good news. 'All went well, Saida?'

'No. I'm sorry, Mr Kingsley.' He could hear the fear in her voice. 'They got away.'

Tanner's body went stiff. *'They what?'*

'Yes, sir. They left before the bomb went off. A bell-man saw them walk out of the hotel lobby.'

Tanner slammed the phone down. He buzzed his secretary. 'Send Flint and Carballo in here.'

A minute later, Harry Flint and Vince Carballo walked into Tanner's office.

Tanner turned to the two men. He was in a towering rage. 'The bitches got away again. That's the last time I will allow that to happen. Do you understand? I'm going to tell you where they are and you're going to take care of them. Any questions?'

Flint and Carballo looked at each other. 'No, sir.'

Tanner pressed a button that revealed the electronic city map. 'As long as they have the cards that I gave them, we can track them down . . .'

They watched the electronic lights appear on the television screen map. Tanner pressed a button. The lights did not move.

Tanner gritted his teeth. 'They've gotten rid of their cards.' His face got redder. He turned to Flint and Carballo. 'I want them killed today.'

Flint looked at Tanner, puzzled. 'If we don't know where they are, how can we –?'

Tanner cut in. 'Do you think I'd let a woman outwit me that easily? As long as they have their cell phones, they're not going anywhere without telling us.'

'You could get hold of their cell phone numbers?' Flint asked, surprised.

Tanner did not bother to reply. He was examining the map. 'By now, they've probably separated.' He pressed another switch. 'Let's try Diane Stevens first.' Tanner punched in a number.

The lights on the map started to move and began to slowly focus on Manhattan streets, panning across hotels, shops and malls. Finally, the moving lights stopped at a store front with a sign that read: 'The Mall for All'.

'Diane Stevens is in a shopping mall.' Tanner pressed

another button. 'Let's see where Kelly Harris is.' Tanner began to repeat the same procedure. The lights started moving again, this time focusing on a different part of the city.

The men watched as the lighted area narrowed down to a street with a clothing store, a restaurant, a pharmacy, and a bus station. The lights scanned the area and suddenly stopped in front of a large, open building.

'Kelly Harris is at a bus station.' Tanner's voice was grim. 'We've got to catch them both fast.'

'How?' Carballo asked. 'They're at opposite ends of town. By the time we get there, they'll be gone.'

Tanner turned, 'Come with me.' He headed for an adjoining room, Flint and Carballo close behind him. The room they entered had an array of monitors, computers and electronic keyboards with different colour-coded keys. On a shelf was a small, squat machine, with dozens of compact discs and DVDs. Tanner looked through them and slipped one labelled 'Diane Stevens' inside the machine.

He explained to the men: 'This is a voice synthesizer. The voices of Mrs Stevens and Mrs Harris were digitised earlier. The patterns of their speech have been recorded and analysed. With the press of a button, every word I say is calibrated to duplicate their voices.' Tanner picked up a mobile phone and pressed some numbers.

There was a cautious, 'Hello?' It was Kelly Harris's voice.

'Kelly! I'm so glad I found you.' It was Tanner speaking, but it was Diane Stevens' voice that they heard.

'Diane! You caught me just in time. I'm on my way out of here.'

Flint and Carballo were listening in wonder.

'Where are you going, Kelly?'

'To Chicago. Then I'm taking a plane home, out of O'Hare.'

'Kelly, you can't leave now.'

There was a moment of silence. 'Why?'

'Because I found out what's really happening. I know who killed our husbands and why.'

'Oh, my God! How did – are you sure?'

'Positive. I have all the proof we need.'

'Diane, that's – that's wonderful.'

'I have the proof with me. I'm at the Delmont Hotel, in Penthouse A. From here I'm going to the FBI. I wanted you to go with me, but if you have to go home, I understand . . .'

'No, no! I – I want to help finish what Mark was trying to do.'

Flint and Carballo were listening to every word, riveted. In the background, they could hear the station announcement for the bus to Chicago.

'I'll go with you, Diane. You said the Delmont Hotel?'

'Yes, on Eighty-sixth Street. Penthouse A.'

'I'm on my way. See you in a little while.'

The connection was broken.

Tanner turned to Flint and Carballo. 'Half the problem is solved. Now we'll take care of the other half.'

Flint and Carballo watched as Tanner inserted another compact disc labelled 'Kelly Harris' into the synthesizer. Tanner moved a switch on the phone and pressed some numbers.

Diane's voice came on almost immediately. 'Hello?'

Tanner spoke into the phone, but it was Kelly's voice they heard.

'Diane . . .'

'Kelly! Are you all right?'

'I'm wonderful. I have some exciting news. I found out who killed our husbands and why.'

'What? Who – who –?'

'We can't discuss this on the phone, Diane. I'm at the Delmont Hotel, on Eighty-sixth Street, Penthouse A. Can you meet me here?'

'Of course. I'll come right over.'

'Wonderful, Diane. I'll be waiting.'

Tanner clicked off the set and turned to Flint. '*You'll* be waiting.' He handed Flint a key. 'This is the key to Penthouse A. Get there right away and wait for them. I want you to kill them as soon as they walk in the door. I'll see to it that the bodies are taken care of.'

Carballo and Tanner watched Flint turn and hurry out of the door.

Carballo said, 'What would you like me to do, Mr Kingsley?'

'Take care of Saida Hernandez.'

Waiting inside Penthouse A, Flint was determined that this time nothing would go wrong. He had heard about

269

previous bunglers of whom Tanner had disposed. Not me, Flint thought. He took out his gun, checked the barrel, and screwed on the silencer. All he had to do now was wait.

In a taxi six blocks from the Delmont Hotel, Kelly Harris's mind was racing with excitement over what Diane had told her. Mark, I'm going to make them pay for what they did to you, she thought.

Diane was in a fever of impatience. The nightmare was at an end. Somehow Kelly had discovered who was behind the plot to kill them and she had proof.

I'm going to make you proud of me, Richard. I feel you near me, and – Diane's thoughts were interrupted by the taxi driver.

'We're here, lady. Delmont Hotel.'

THIRTY

As Diane walked through the Delmont Hotel lobby, toward the lifts, her heart began to beat faster. She could not wait to hear what Kelly had learned.

A lift door opened and the passengers moved out.

'Going up?'

'Yes.' Diane stepped inside. 'The Penthouse floor, please.' Her mind was racing. What project could our husbands have been working on that was so secret that they were murdered? And how has Kelly found the answer? she wondered.

People began to crowd in. The lift door closed and it started to rise. Diane had seen Kelly only a few hours ago, and to her surprise, she found that she missed her.

Finally, after half a dozen stops, the lift operator opened the door and said, 'Penthouse floor.'

*   *   *

Inside the living room of Penthouse A, Flint waited close to the door, trying to listen for sounds in the hallway. The problem was that the door was unusually thick and Flint knew why. It was not to keep sounds out. It was to keep them in.

Board meetings were held in the penthouse suite, but Flint liked to joke that no one was ever bored. Three times a year, Tanner invited KIG managers from a dozen countries. When the business meetings were adjourned, a bevy of beautiful girls was brought in to entertain the men. Flint had been a guard at several of the orgies, and now, as he stood there, thinking about the sea of naked, nubile bodies moaning and thrashing about the beds and couches, he began to get an erection. Flint grinned. The ladies would take care of it soon.

Harry Flint did not consider himself a necrophile. He had never killed a woman in order to have sex with her. But if she were already dead . . .

As Diane stepped out of the lift, she asked, 'Which way is Penthouse A?'

'It's to the left, at the end of the corridor. But there's no one there.'

Diane turned. 'What?'

'That penthouse is only used for board meetings, and the next one isn't until September.'

Diane smiled. 'I'm not going to a board meeting. I'm seeing a friend who's waiting for me.'

The lift operator watched as Diane turned left and

started walking towards Penthouse A. He shrugged, closed the lift door and started down.

As Diane was approaching the door to the penthouse, she began to walk faster, her excitement starting to build.

Inside Penthouse A, Flint was waiting for the knock on the door.

Which one of them will get here first – the blonde or the black chick? It doesn't matter. I'm not prejudiced – Flint's thoughts were interrupted as he heard someone approaching the door and he tightened his grip on the gun.

Kelly was fighting to control her impatience. Getting to the Delmont Hotel had been a series of delays: traffic . . . red lights . . . road repairs . . . She was late. She hurried through the lobby of the hotel and got into the lift. 'Penthouse, please.'

On the fiftieth floor, as Diane approached Penthouse A, the door to the neighbouring suite opened and a bellman came out, backing into the corridor, pulling a large cart filled with luggage, blocking Diane's passage.

'I'll have this out of your way in a minute,' he apologised.

The bellman returned to the suite and came out with two more suitcases. Diane tried to squeeze by, but there was no room.

The bellman said, 'All set. Sorry for the delay.' He moved the luggage cart out of the way.

Diane walked over to Penthouse A and raised her hand to knock on the door when a voice down the hall said, 'Diane!'

Diane turned. Kelly had just stepped out of the lift. 'Kelly –!'

Diane hurried back down the hall to meet her.

Inside the penthouse, Harry Flint was listening. Was someone out there? He could have opened the door to see, but that would have ruined the plan. 'Kill them as soon as they walk in the door,' his boss had said.

In the corridor, Kelly and Diane were hugging, delighted to see each other.

Kelly said, 'Sorry I'm late, Diane, but the traffic was terrible. You caught me just as my bus was leaving for Chicago.'

Diane looked at Kelly, puzzled. '*I* caught *you* –?'

'I was just getting on my bus when you called.'

There was a momentary silence. 'Kelly – I didn't call you. You called me. To tell me that you had the evidence we needed to –' She saw the stricken look on Kelly's face.

'I didn't –'

They both turned to look at Penthouse A.

Diane took a deep breath. 'Let's –'

'Right.'

They raced down one flight of stairs, got into a lift and were out of the hotel in three minutes.

Inside the penthouse, Harry Flint was looking at his watch, thinking, What's keeping the bitches?

Diane and Kelly were seated in a crowded subway carriage.

'I don't know how they did it,' Diane said. 'It was your voice.'

'And it was your voice. They're not going to stop until they kill us. They're like octopuses with a thousand bloody arms that they want to wrap around our necks.'

'They have to catch us before they can kill us,' Diane said.

'How could they have found us this time? We got rid of Kingsley's calling cards, and we have nothing else that they −'

They looked at each other, then looked at their mobile phones.

Kelly said wonderingly, 'But how could they have found out our phone numbers?'

'Remember who we're dealing with. Anyway, this is probably the safest place in New York. We can stay on the subway until −' Diane glanced across the aisle and her face paled. 'We're getting out of here,' she said, urgently. 'Next stop.'

'*What? You just said −?*'

Kelly followed Diane's eyes. On the strip that ran

through the car advertising different products was a photograph of a smiling Kelly, holding up a beautiful ladies' watch.

'Oh, my God!'

They rose and hurried to the door, waiting for the next stop. Two uniformed marines, seated nearby, were ogling them.

Kelly smiled at the men as she took Diane's mobile phone and her own, and handed one to each marine. 'Give us a call.'

And the women were gone.

In Penthouse A, the telephone rang. Flint snatched it up.

Tanner said, 'It's been over an hour. What's going on, Mr Flint?'

'They never showed up.'

'*What?*'

'I've been here all the time, waiting.'

'Get back to the office.' Tanner slammed the receiver down.

In the beginning, this had been a routine bit of business that Tanner had to dispose of. Now it had become personal. Tanner picked up his mobile phone and dialled Diane's number.

One of the marines to whom Kelly had given their phones, answered. 'There you are, baby. How would you two like to have a big treat tonight?'

The bitches have got rid of their phones, Tanner fumed.

*   *   *

276

It was a cheap-looking boarding house on a side street, on the west side. When the taxi started to pass it and Diane and Kelly saw the sign, 'Vacancy', Diane said, 'You can stop here, driver.'

The women got out and walked up to the front door of the house.

The landlady, who opened the door, was a pleasant, middle-aged woman named Alice Finley. 'I can give you a very nice room, for forty dollars a night, with breakfast.'

Diane said, 'That will be fine.' She looked at Kelly's expression. 'What's the matter?'

'Nothing.' Kelly closed her eyes for an instant. This boarding house had nothing to do with the boarding house she had been brought up in, cleaning toilets and cooking for strangers and listening to the sounds of her drunken stepfather beating her mother. She managed a smile. 'It's fine.'

The next morning, Tanner called a meeting with Flint and Carballo. 'They've disposed of my calling cards,' Tanner said, 'and they've got rid of their phones.'

Flint said, 'So, we've lost them.'

Tanner said, 'No, Mr Flint, not while I'm alive. We're not going after them. They're coming to us.'

The two men looked at each other, then back at Tanner.

'What?'

'Diane Stevens and Kelly Harris will be here at KIG Monday morning, at eleven-fifteen.'

THIRTY-ONE

Kelly and Diane woke up at the same time. Kelly sat up in bed, and looked over at Diane. 'Good morning. How did you sleep?'

'I had some crazy dreams.'

'So did I.' Diane hesitated. 'Kelly – when you got off the elevator at the hotel, just as I started to knock at the door of the penthouse – do you think that was a coincidence?'

'Of course. And lucky for both of us that –' Kelly looked at Diane's face. 'What do you mean?'

Diane said, carefully, 'We've been very lucky so far. I mean, *very* lucky. It's as though – as though some-one, or something, is helping us, guiding us.'

Kelly's eyes were fastened on her. 'You mean – like a guardian angel?'

'Yes.'

Kelly said, patiently, 'Diane, I know that you believe

279

in those things, but I don't. I *know* I don't have an angel on my shoulder.'

Diane said, 'You just don't see it yet.'

Kelly rolled her eyes. 'Right.'

'Let's get some breakfast,' Diane suggested. 'It's safe here. I think we're out of danger.'

Kelly grunted. 'If you think we're out of danger, you don't know anything about boarding-house breakfasts. Let's get dressed and eat out. I think I saw a diner at the corner.'

'All right. I have to make a call first.' Diane walked over to the telephone and called a number.

An operator came on. 'KIG.'

'I'd like to speak to Betty Barker.'

'Just a moment, please.'

Tanner had seen the blue light and was listening in on the conference line.

'Miss Barker is not at her desk. Can I take a message?'

'Oh. No, thanks.'

Tanner frowned. Too quick to put out a trace, he thought.

Diane turned to Kelly. 'Betty Barker is still working at KIG, so we'll just have to find a way to get to her.'

'Maybe her home number is listed in the telephone directory.'

Diane said, 'It could be, and the line could be tapped.' She picked up the directory next to the telephone and skimmed to the letter she was looking for. 'She *is* listed.'

280

Diane dialled the number, listened, and slowly replaced the receiver.

Kelly walked over to her. 'What's the matter?'

It took Diane a moment to answer. 'Her phone has been disconnected.'

Kelly took a deep breath. 'I think I want a shower.'

As Kelly finished her shower and started to leave the bathroom, she realised that she had left towels on the floor. She started to walk out, hesitated for a moment, then picked them up and put them neatly on the rail. She walked into the bedroom. 'All yours.'

Diane nodded absently. 'Thanks.'

The first thing Diane noticed when she walked into the bathroom was that all the used towels had been placed back on the rail. She smiled.

She stepped into the shower and let the warm water soothe her. She remembered how she used to shower with Richard and how good their bodies felt touching each other . . . Never again. But the memories would always be there. Always . . .

There were the flowers.

'They're beautiful, darling. Thank you. What are we celebrating?'

'Saint Swithin's Day.'

And more flowers.

'Washington Crossing the Delaware Day.' . . . 'National Parakeet Day.' . . . 'Celery Lovers' Day.' . . .

When the note with the roses said, 'Leaping Lizards'

Day', Diane had laughed and said, 'Sweetheart, lizards don't leap.'

And Richard had put his head in his hands and said, 'Damn it! I was misinformed.'

And he loved to write love poems to her. When Diane was getting dressed, she would find one in her shoes, or in a bra, or in a jacket . . .

And there was the time he had come home from work and she was standing inside the door, completely naked, except for a pair of high-heeled shoes. And she had said, 'Darling, do you like these shoes?'

And his clothes had dropped to the floor and dinner was delayed. They –

Kelly's voice called out, 'Are we going to have breakfast, or dinner?'

They were walking to the restaurant. The day was cool and clear, and the sky was a translucent blue.

'Blue skies,' Diane said. 'A good omen.'

Kelly bit her lip to keep from laughing. Somehow, Diane's superstitions seemed endearing.

A few doors from the diner, Diane and Kelly passed a small boutique. They looked at each other, grinned, and walked inside.

A saleslady approached them. 'May I help you?'

Kelly said enthusiastically, 'Yes.'

Diane warned, 'Let's take it easy. Remember what happened the last time.'

'Right. No spree.'

The two of them went through the store, picking out

a modest amount of necessities. They left their old clothes in the changing room.

'Don't you want to take these?' the saleslady asked.

Diane smiled. 'No. Give them to Goodwill.'

On the corner of the street was a convenience store. 'Look,' Kelly said, 'disposable cell phones.'

Kelly and Diane went inside and chose two of them, each equipped with a thousand pre-paid minutes.

Kelly said, 'Let's exchange phone numbers again.'

Diane smiled. 'Right.'

It only took a few seconds.

On their way out, as Diane was paying the cashier, she looked into her purse. 'I'm really beginning to run out of cash.'

'So am I,' Kelly said.

'We may have to start using our credit cards,' Diane said.

'Not until we find the magic rabbit hole.'

'What?'

'Never mind.'

When they were seated at a table in the diner, the waitress asked. 'What can I get you, ladies?'

Kelly turned to Diane. 'You first.'

'I'm going to have some orange juice, bacon and eggs, and toast and coffee.'

The waitress turned to Kelly. 'And you, miss?'

'Half a grapefruit.'

'That's it?' Diane asked.

'Yes.'

The waitress left.

'You can't live on half a grapefruit.'

'Habit. I've been on a strict diet for years. Some models eat Kleenex to curb their appetites.'

'Seriously?'

'Seriously. But it doesn't really matter any more. I'm never going to model again.'

Diane studied her for a moment. 'Why?'

'It's not important any more. Mark taught me what's really important, and –' She stopped, fighting tears. 'I wish you could have met him.'

'So do I. But you have to start your life again.'

Kelly said, 'What about you? Are you going to start painting again?'

There was a long silence. 'I tried . . . No.'

When Kelly and Diane had finished their breakfasts and were starting towards the door, Kelly noticed that the morning newspapers were being put into the news racks.

Diane started to walk on when Kelly said, 'Wait a minute.' She turned back and picked up one of the newspapers. 'Look!'

The story was an article at the top of the front page:

Kingsley International Group is holding a memorial service to honor all their employees whose recent deaths have been the cause of universal speculation. The tribute will take place at KIG headquarters, in Manhattan, on Monday, at 11:15 a.m.

'That's tomorrow.' Kelly looked at Diane for a moment. 'Why do you think they're doing this?'

'I think they're setting a trap for us.'

Kelly nodded. 'So do I. Does Kingsley believe we would be stupid enough to fall for –?' Kelly looked at Diane's expression and said, with dismay, 'We're going?'

Diane nodded.

'We can't!'

'We have to. I'm sure Betty Barker will be there. I must talk to her.'

'I don't want to be picky, but how do you expect to get out of there alive?'

'I'll think of a way.' She looked at Kelly and smiled. 'Trust me.'

Kelly shook her head. 'There's nothing that makes me more nervous than hearing someone say "Trust me".' She thought for a moment, and her face lit up. 'I have an idea. I know how to handle this.'

'What's your idea?'

'It's a surprise.'

Diane looked at Kelly, worried. 'You really think you can get us out of there?'

'Trust me.'

When they got back to the boarding house, Kelly made a telephone call.

*   *   *

285

They both slept badly that night. Kelly was lying in bed, worrying: If my plan fails, we're both going to die. As she was falling asleep, she seemed to see Tanner Kingsley's face looking down on her. He was grinning.

Diane was praying, her eyes tightly closed: Darling, this may be the last time I speak to you. I'm not sure whether to say goodbye or hello. Tomorrow, Kelly and I are going to KIG, to your memorial. I don't think our chances of getting away are very good, but I have to go, to try to help you. I just wanted to tell you once more, before it may be too late, that I love you. Good night, my dearest.

THIRTY-TWO

The memorial service was being held in KIG Park, an area that had been set aside at the back of the Kingsley International Group complex, as a recreation facility for its employees. There were a hundred people gathered in the park, which was accessible only through two gated paths leading in and out.

In the centre of the grounds, a dais had been erected, and half a dozen KIG executives were seated there. At the end of the row sat Richard Stevens' secretary, Betty Barker. She was an attractive patrician-looking woman, in her thirties.

Tanner was at the microphone. '. . . and this company was built by the dedication and loyalty of its employees. We appreciate and salute them. I have always liked to think of our company as a family, all working together toward the same objective.' As Tanner spoke, he was scanning the crowd. 'Here, at KIG, we have solved problems and executed ideas that have made the world a better place to live in, and there is no greater satisfaction than –'

At the far end of the park, Diane and Kelly had entered. Tanner glanced at his watch. It was eleven-forty. There was a satisfied smile on his face. He continued speaking. '. . . knowing that whatever success this company has had is due to you . . .'

Diane looked up at the platform and nudged Kelly, excitedly. 'There's Betty Barker. I have to speak to her.'

'Be careful.'

Diane glanced around and said, uneasily, 'This is too simple. I have a feeling we've been –' She turned to look back and gasped. Harry Flint and two of his men had appeared at one of the gates. Diane's eyes turned towards the second gate. It was blocked by Carballo and two more men.

'Look!' Diane's throat was dry.

Kelly turned to see the six men blocking the exits. 'Is there any other way out of here?'

'I don't think so.'

Tanner was saying, '. . . Regrettably, recent misfortunes have come to several members of our family. And when a tragedy befalls someone in the family, it affects us all. KIG is offering a five-million-dollar-reward to anyone who can prove who or what is behind all of this.'

'Five million dollars from one of his pockets into the other,' Kelly said softly.

Tanner looked out over the crowd at Kelly and Diane, and his eyes were cold. 'We have two bereaved members here today, Mrs Mark Harris and Mrs Richard Stevens. I'm going to ask them to please come up here on the podium.'

'We can't let him get us up there,' Kelly said, horrified. 'We have to stay with the crowd. What do we do now?'

Diane looked at Kelly, surprised. 'What do you mean? You're the one who's going to get us out of here, remember? Start your plan.'

Kelly swallowed. 'It didn't work.'

Diane said nervously, 'Then go to Plan B.'

'Diane . . .'

'Yes?'

'There is no Plan B.'

Diane's eyes widened. 'You mean you – you got us here with no way to get us out?'

'I thought –'

Tanner's voice boomed over the loudspeaker. 'Would Mrs Stevens and Mrs Harris come up here now, please?'

Kelly turned to Diane and said, 'I'm – I'm so sorry.'

'It's my fault. I should never have let us come.'

The people in the crowd were turning to watch them. They were trapped.

'Mrs Stevens and Mrs Harris . . .'

Kelly whispered, 'What are we going to do?'

Diane said, 'We have no choice. We're going up there.' She took a deep breath. 'Let's go.'

Reluctantly, the two women started slowly towards the podium.

Diane was looking up at Betty Barker, whose eyes were fastened on her, a panicky look on her face.

Diane and Kelly neared the podium, their hearts pounding.

Diane was thinking, Richard, darling, I tried. No matter what happens, I want you to know that I –

There was a sudden loud commotion at the back of the park. People were craning their necks to see what was happening.

Ben Roberts was making an entrance, accompanied by a large crew of cameramen and assistants.

The two women turned to look. Kelly grabbed Diane's arm, beaming. 'Plan A has arrived! Ben is here.'

And Diane looked up and said softly, 'Thank you, Richard.'

Kelly said, 'What?' She suddenly realised what Diane meant. She said, cynically, 'Right. Come on. Ben is waiting for us.'

Tanner was watching the scene, his face stiff. He called out, 'Excuse me. I'm sorry, Mr Roberts. This is a private memorial ceremony. I will have to ask you and your crew to leave.'

Ben Roberts said, 'Good morning, Mr Kingsley. My show is doing a television segment with Mrs Harris and Mrs Stevens at the studio, but while we were with them, I thought you might like to have us do a piece on the memorial service.'

Tanner shook his head. 'No, I can't permit you to stay here.'

'Too bad. Then I'll just take Mrs Harris and Mrs Stevens over to the studio now.'

'You can't,' Tanner said, harshly.

Ben looked at him. 'I can't what?'

Tanner was almost trembling with fury. 'I – I mean – you – nothing.'

The women had reached Ben.

He said, softly, 'Sorry I'm late. There was a breaking news story about a murder and –'

'There was almost a breaking news story about two more,' Kelly said. 'Let's get out of here.'

Tanner watched, frustrated, as Kelly, Diane, Ben Roberts and his crew pushed past Tanner's men and walked out of the park.

Harry Flint looked over to Tanner for instructions. As Tanner slowly shook his head, he was thinking, It's not over yet, bitches.

Diane and Kelly got into the car with Ben Roberts. His crew was following in two vans.

Roberts looked at Kelly. 'Now, can you tell me what that was all about?'

'I wish I could, Ben. But not yet. I will when I know what I'm talking about. I promise.'

'Kelly, I'm a reporter. I need to know –'

'Today you came as a friend.'

Roberts sighed. 'Right. Where would you like me to take you?'

Diane said, 'Would you drop us off at Forty-second Street and Times Square?'

'You've got it.'

Twenty minutes later, Kelly and Diane were getting out of the car.

Kelly kissed Ben Robets on the cheek. 'Thanks, Ben. I won't forget this. We'll stay in touch.'

'Be safe.'

They turned to wave as they walked away.

Kelly said, 'I feel naked.'

'Why?'

'Diane, we don't have any weapons, nothing. I wish we had a gun.'

'We have our brains.'

'I wish we had a gun. Why are we here? What are we going to do now?'

'We're going to stop running. From now on, we're on the offensive.'

Kelly looked at her curiously. 'What does that mean?'

'It means I'm sick and tired of us being the target of the day. We're going after them, Kelly.'

Kelly looked at Diane for a moment. '*We're* going after *KIG*?'

'That's right.'

'You've been reading too many mysteries. How do you think the two of us can bring down the biggest think-tank in the world?'

'We're going to start by getting the names of all their employees who have died in the past few weeks.'

'What makes you think there were more than Mark and Richard?'

'Because the newspaper announcement said *all* their employees, so there were more than two people.'

'Oh. And who's going to give us those names?'

'I'll show you,' Diane said.

The Easy Access Internet Café was a vast computer hall containing more than a dozen rows of cubicles equipped with 400 personal computers, nearly all of them in use. It was part of a chain that was springing up all over the world.

When they walked in, Diane went to a vending machine to purchase an hour of Internet access.

When she came back, Kelly said, 'Where do we start?'

'Let's ask the computer.'

They found an empty cubicle and sat down.

Kelly watched as Diane logged on to the Internet. 'What happens now?'

'First we do a "google" search to find the names of the other victims who were employees of KIG.'

Diane surfed the web to the search-engine site and typed in her search criteria: 'obituary' and 'KIG'.

A long list of search hits appeared. Diane looked specifically for items in newspapers that were available on-line and found several. She clicked on those links, which led her to a series of recent obituaries and other articles. One article led her to KIG Berlin, and she accessed its website.

'This is interesting . . . Franz Verbrugge.'

'Who's he?'

'The question is, *where* is he? He seems to have disappeared. He worked for KIG in Berlin, and his wife, Sonja, died mysteriously.'

Diane clicked onto another link. She hesitated and looked up at Kelly. 'In France – Mark Harris.'

Kelly took a deep breath and nodded. 'Go on.'

Diane pressed more keys. 'Denver, Gary Reynolds, and in Manhattan –' Diane's voice broke, '– Richard.' Diane stood up. 'That's it.'

Kelly said, 'What now?'

'We're going to figure out how to put all this together. Let's go.'

Half-way down the street, Kelly and Diane passed a computer store.

'Just a minute,' Kelly said.

Diane followed as Kelly walked into the store and approached the manager.

'Excuse me. My name is Kelly Harris. I'm Tanner Kingsley's assistant. We need three dozen of your very best and most expensive computers by this afternoon. Is that possible?'

The manager beamed. 'Why – why certainly, Mrs Harris. For Mr Kingsley, anything. We don't have them all here, of course, but we'll get them from our warehouses. I'll take care of it personally. Will that be cash or charge?'

'COD,' Kelly said.

As the manager hurried away, Diane said, 'I wish I had thought of that.'

Kelly grinned. 'You will.'

'I thought you would like to see these, Mr Kingsley.' Kathy Ordonez handed him several newspapers. The headlines told the story:

AUSTRALIA HAS FREAK TORNADO . . .
The first tornado ever to hit Australia has destroyed half a dozen villages. Death toll is unknown.
Meteorologists are baffled by new world weather patterns. Ozone layer blamed.

Tanner said, 'Send these to Senator van Luven with a note: *Dear Senator van Luven, I think time is running out. Best wishes, Tanner Kingsley.*'

'Yes, sir,' Kathy said as she left the room.

Tanner looked up at a computer screen when he heard the sound telling him he had received an alert from the security division of his Information Technology department.

Tanner had arranged for his IT department to have 'spiders' installed – high-tech software that constantly combed the Internet, searching for information. Tanner had privately set the 'spiders' to look for people searching for sensitive information, and he now stared with interest at the alert on the computer monitor.

He pressed a buzzer. 'Andrew, get in here.'

Andrew was in his office, daydreaming about his

accident, and remembering. He was in the dressing room, getting his space suit, the one the Army had sent. He started to take one from the rack, but Tanner was there, and Tanner handed him a suit and gas mask, saying, 'Wear this one. It will bring you luck.' Tanner was –

'Andrew! Get in here!'

Andrew heard the command, got up, and slowly walked into Tanner's office.

'Sit down.'

'Yes, Tanner . . .' He took a seat.

'The bitches just hit our website in Berlin. Do you know what that means?'

'Yes . . . I – no.'

Tanner's secretary buzzed. 'The computers are here, Mr Kingsley.'

'What computers?'

'The ones you ordered.'

Puzzled, Tanner rose, and walked out into the reception room. There were three dozen computers piled up on dollies. The store manager and three men in overalls were standing next to them.

The manager's face lit up when he saw Tanner approaching. 'I have just what you asked for, Mr Kingsley. State of the art. And we'll be happy to help you with any more –'

Tanner was staring at the pile of computers. 'Who ordered these?'

'Your assistant, Kelly Harris. She said you needed them right away, so –'

'Take them back,' Tanner said softly. 'Where she's going, they won't be needed.'

Tanner turned and walked back into his office. 'Andrew, do you have any idea why they accessed our website? Well, I'll tell you. They're going to try to track down the victims, and look for the motives behind their deaths.' Tanner sat down. 'To do that, they would have to go to Europe. Only they're not going to get there.'

Andrew said sleepily, 'No . . .'

'How are we going to stop them, Andrew?'

Andrew nodded. 'Stop them . . .'

Tanner looked at his brother and said, contemptuously, 'I wish there was someone with a brain that I could talk to around here.'

Andrew watched as Tanner walked over to a computer and began typing. 'We're going to start by wiping out all their assets. We have their Social Security numbers.' He kept typing as he talked. 'Diane Stevens . . .' he mused. With his sophisticated, high-tech software, Tanner could access and amend anyone's personal financial details.

'Look, all her bank account information, an IRA retirement account, her line of credit at the bank. See?'

Andrew swallowed. 'Yes, Tanner. Yes.'

Tanner turned back to the computer. 'We'll enter her credit cards as stolen . . . Now we're going to do the same with Kelly Harris . . . Our next step is going to Diane's bank's website.' He accessed the bank's website, and then clicked onto a link that said 'Manage your Accounts'.

Next, Tanner entered Diane Stevens' account number and the last four digits of her Social Security number and was granted access. Once inside, he transferred all her balance to the line of credit, then returned to the credit data base and cancelled her line of credit under, 'In collection'.

'Andrew –'

'Yes, Tanner?'

'Do you see what I've done? I've transferred all of Diane Stevens' assets as debts to be collected by their collection department.' His tone was filled with self-satisfaction. 'Now we'll do the same thing for Kelly Harris.'

When Tanner was through, he got up and walked over to Andrew. 'It's done. They have no money and no credit. There's no way they can get out of the country. We have them trapped. What do you think of your kid brother?'

Andrew nodded. 'On television last night, I saw a movie about a –'

Furious, Tanner clenched his fist and slammed it into his brother's face so hard that Andrew fell out of the chair and crashed into a wall, making a loud noise. 'You son of a bitch! Listen to me when I'm talking to you.'

The door flew open and Tanner's secretary, Kathy Ordonez, rushed in. 'Is everything all right, Mr Kingsley?'

Tanner turned to her. 'Yes. Poor Andrew fell down.'

'Oh, dear.'

The two of them lifted Andrew to his feet.

'Did I fall down?'

Tanner said gently, 'Yes, Andrew, but you're all right now.'

Kathy Ordonez whispered, 'Mr Kingsley, don't you think your brother might be better off in a home?'

'Of course he would,' Tanner answered. 'But it would break his heart. This is his real home, and I can take care of him here.'

Kathy Ordonez looked at Tanner admiringly. 'You're a wonderful man, Mr Kingsley.'

He shrugged, modestly. 'We all have to do what we can.'

Ten minutes later, Tanner's secretary was back in his office.

'Good news, Mr Kingsley. This fax just came in from Senator van Luven's office.'

'Let me see it.' Tanner snatched it from her hand.

Dear Mr Kingsley, this is to inform you that the Senate Select Committee on the Environment has decided to appropriate funds to immediately increase our investigation of global warming and how to combat it. Sincerely, Senator van Luven.

THIRTY-THREE

'Do you have your passport?' Diane asked.

'I always carry it with me in a strange country.' And Kelly added, 'And lately this has become one hell of a strange country.'

Diane nodded. 'My passport is in a bank vault. I'll get it. And we'll need some money.'

When they entered the bank, Diane went downstairs to her vault, and opened her safety deposit box. She removed her passport, put it in her bag and walked back upstairs to the cashier's desk.

'I would like to close my account.'

'Certainly. Your name, please?'

'Diane Stevens.'

The cashier nodded. 'Just a moment, please.' He walked back to a row of filing cabinets, opened a drawer and started rifling through the cards. He pulled one out,

301

looked at it for a moment, then walked back to Diane. 'Your account has already been closed, Mrs Stevens.'

Diane shook her head. 'No. There must be some mistake. I have –'

The cashier put the card in front of Diane. It read: 'Account closed. Reason: Deceased'.

Diane stared at it unbelievingly, and then looked up at the cashier. 'Do I look like I'm deceased?'

'Of course not. I'm sorry. If you'd like me to call the manager, I can –'

'No!' She had suddenly realised what had happened, and felt a small shiver. 'No, thanks.'

Diane hurried over to the entrance where Kelly was waiting.

'Is everything OK?'

'I got the passport, but the bastards closed my bank account.'

'How could they –?'

'It's very simple. They're KIG and we're not.'

Diane was thoughtful for a moment. 'Oh, my God.'

'What now?'

'I have to make a quick phone call.' Diane hurried over to a telephone cubicle, dialled a number, and pulled out her credit card. A few moments later, she was saying, 'The account is under the name of Diane Stevens. It's a valid –'

'I'm sorry, Mrs Stevens. Our records show that your card has been reported stolen. If you want to make out a report, we can issue a new card to you in a day or two and –'

Diane said, 'Never mind.' She slammed down the receiver and walked back to Kelly. 'They've cancelled my credit cards.'

Kelly took a deep breath. 'Now I'd better make a call or two.'

Kelly was on the telephone for almost half an hour. When she came back to Diane, she was furious. 'The octopus strikes again. But I still have a bank account in Paris, so I can –'

'We don't have time for that, Kelly. We have to get out of here now. How much money do you have with you?'

'Enough to get us back to Brooklyn. What about you?'

'I could get us to New Jersey.'

'Then we're trapped. You know why they're doing this, don't you? To keep us from going to Europe and finding out the truth.'

'It looks like they've succeeded.'

Kelly said thoughtfully, 'No, they haven't. We're going.'

Diane said sceptically, 'How? My spaceship?'

'Mine.'

Joseph Berry, the manager of the Fifth Avenue jewellery store, watched Kelly and Diane approach, and gave them his best professional smile. 'May I help you?'

Kelly said, 'Yes. I'd like to sell my ring. It –'

His smile faded. 'I'm sorry. We don't buy jewellery.'

'Oh. That's too bad.'

Joseph Berry started to turn away. Kelly opened her hand. In it was a large emerald ring. 'This is a seven-carat emerald surrounded by three carats of diamonds, set in platinum.'

Joseph Berry stared at the ring, impressed. He picked up a jeweller's loupe and put it to his eye. 'It's really beautiful, but we have a firm rule here that –'

'I want twenty thousand dollars for it.'

'Did you say twenty thousand dollars?'

'Yes, in cash.'

Diane was staring at her. 'Kelly –'

Berry looked at the ring again and nodded. 'I – er – think we can arrange that. Just a moment.' He disappeared into the back office.

Diane said, 'Are you crazy? You're being *robbed*!'

'Am I? If we stay here, we'll be killed. Tell me how much our lives are worth.'

Diane had no answer.

Joseph Berry came out of the back office, smiling. 'I'll have someone go across the street to the bank and get the cash for you right away.'

Diane turned to Kelly. 'I wish you wouldn't do this.'

Kelly shrugged, 'It's only a piece of jewellery . . .' She closed her eyes. It's only a piece of jewellery . . . she thought.

It was her birthday. The phone rang.

'Good morning, darling.' It was Mark.

'Good morning.'

She waited for him to say 'Happy birthday'.

304

Instead he said, 'You're not working today. Do you like hiking?'

That was not what Kelly had expected to hear. She felt a small *frisson* of disappointment. They had talked about birthdays a week earlier. Mark had forgotten.

'Yes.'

'How would you like to go for a hike this morning?'

'All right.'

'I'll pick you up in half an hour.'

'I'll be ready.'

'Where are we going?' Kelly asked, when they were in the car.

They were both dressed in hiking outfits.

'There are some wonderful trails outside of Fontainebleau.'

'Oh? Do you go there often?'

'I used to go there, when I wanted to escape.'

Kelly looked at him, puzzled. 'Escape from what?'

He hesitated. 'Loneliness. I felt less lonely there.' He glanced at Kelly and smiled. 'I haven't been there since I met you.'

Fontainebleau is a magnificent royal palace, surrounded by sylvan forests, located to the south-east of Paris.

As the beautiful, regal estate loomed up in the distance, Mark said, 'A lot of kings called Louis have lived here, starting with Louis the IV.'

'Oh, really?' Kelly looked at him and thought, I wonder if they had birthday cards in those days. I wish he had given me a birthday card. I'm acting like a schoolgirl.

They had reached the palace grounds. Mark pulled into one of the car-parks.

As they got out of the car and headed for the woods Mark said, 'Can you handle a mile?'

Kelly laughed. 'I handle more than that every day on the runway.'

Mark took her hand. 'Good. Let's go.'

'I'm with you.'

They passed a series of majestic buildings and started into the woodland. They were completely alone, wrapped in a greenery of ancient fields and old trees. It was a sun-kissed summer day filled with itself. The wind was warm and caressing, and there was a cloudless sky above.

'Isn't this beautiful?' Mark asked.

'It's lovely, Mark.'

'I'm glad you were free today.'

Kelly remembered something. 'Aren't you supposed to be working today?'

'I decided to take the day off.'

'Oh.'

They were walking deeper and deeper into the mysterious forest.

After fifteen minutes, Kelly asked, 'How far do you want to go?'

'There's a spot up ahead that I like. We're almost there.'

A few minutes later, they emerged into a glade with an enormous oak tree in the centre.

'Here we are,' Mark said.

'It's so peaceful –'

There seemed to be something lightly carved on the tree. Kelly went up to it. It read, 'Happy birthday, Kelly'.

She stared at Mark for a moment, speechless. 'Oh, Mark, darling. Thank you.'

So, he had not forgotten.

'I think there might be something in the tree.'

'In the tree?' Kelly moved closer to it. There was a hollow place at eyelevel. She put her hand inside and felt a small package, and pulled it out. It was a gift box. 'What –?'

'Open it.'

Kelly opened it and her eyes widened. In the box was a beautiful emerald ring, surrounded by diamonds, set in platinum. Kelly stared at it, unbelievingly. She turned and threw her arms around Mark. 'This is much too generous.'

'I would give you the moon if you asked for it. Kelly, I'm in love with you.'

She held him close, lost in a euphoria she had never known. And then she said something that she thought she would never, ever say. 'I'm in love with you too, darling.'

He was beaming. 'Let's get married right away. We –'

'No.' Her voice was harsh.

Mark was looking at her in surprise. 'Why?'

'We can't.'

'Kelly – don't you believe that I'm in love with you?'

'Yes.'

'Are you in love with me?'

'Yes.'

'But you don't want to marry me?'

'I do want to – but I – I can't.'

'I don't understand. What is it?'

He was studying her, confused. And Kelly knew that the moment she told Mark about the traumatic experience she had had, he would never want to see her again. 'I – I could never be a real wife to you.'

'What do you mean?'

This was the most difficult thing Kelly had ever had to say. 'Mark, we could never have sex together. When I was eight years old, I was raped.' She was looking out at the uncaring trees, telling her sordid story to the first man she had ever loved. 'I'm not interested in sex. I'm disgusted by the idea of it. It frightens me. I'm – I'm half a woman. I'm a freak.' She was breathing hard, trying not to cry.

Kelly felt Mark's hand on hers. 'I'm so sorry, Kelly. That must have been devastating.'

Kelly was silent.

'Sex is very important in a marriage,' Mark said.

Kelly nodded, biting her lip. She knew what he was going to say next. 'Of course. So I understand why you wouldn't want to –'

'But that's not what marriage is about. Marriage is about spending your life with someone you love – having someone to talk to, someone to share all the good times and the bad times.'

She was listening, stunned, afraid to believe what she was hearing.

'Sex finally goes away, Kelly, but real love doesn't. I love you for your heart and your soul. I want to spend the rest of my life with you. I can do without the sex.'

Kelly tried to keep her voice steady. 'No, Mark – I can't let you.'

'Why?'

'Because one day you would regret it. You'd fall in love with someone else who could give you . . . what I can't, and you would leave me . . . and that would break my heart.'

Mark reached out and took Kelly in his arms and held her close. 'Do you know why I could never leave you? Because you're the best part of me. We're getting married.'

Kelly looked into his eyes. 'Mark – do you realise what you're getting into?'

Mark smiled and said, 'I think you might rephrase that.'

Kelly laughed and hugged him. 'Oh, baby, are you sure you –?'

He was beaming. 'I'm sure. What do you say?'

She felt the tears on her cheeks. 'I say . . . yes.'

Mark slipped the emerald ring on her finger. They held each other for a long time.

Kelly said, 'I want to take you into the salon tomorrow to meet some of the models I work with.'

'I thought there was a rule against –'

'The rules have been changed.'

Mark was beaming. 'I'll arrange for a judge I know to marry us on Sunday.'

The next morning, when Kelly and Mark arrived at the salon, Kelly pointed up to the sky. 'It looks like it's going to rain. Everyone talks about the weather, but no one does anything about it.'

Mark turned and gave her a strange look.

Kelly saw the expression on Mark's face. 'Oh, I'm sorry. That's a cliché, isn't it?'

Mark did not answer.

There were half a dozen models in the dressing room when Kelly walked in.

'I have an announcement to make. I'm getting married on Sunday, and you're all invited.'

The room was instantly filled with chatter.

'Is this the mysterious beau you wouldn't let us meet?'

'Do we know him?'

'What does he look like?'

Kelly said proudly, 'Like a young Cary Grant.'

'Ooh! When can we meet him?'

'Now. He's here.' Kelly opened the door wide. 'Come in, darling.'

Mark stepped in through the door and the room became instantly quiet. One of the models looked at Mark and said under her breath, 'Is this some kind of joke?'

'It must be.'

Mark Harris was a foot shorter than Kelly, a plain, ordinary-looking man, with a thinning mop of grey hair.

When the first shock was over, the models stepped up to congratulate the soon-to-be bride and groom.

'That's wonderful news.'

'We're thrilled for you.'

'I'm sure you'll be very happy together.'

When the congratulations were over, Kelly and Mark left. As they were walking down the hall, Mark asked, 'Do you think they liked me?'

Kelly smiled. 'Of course they did. How could anyone not like you?' She stopped. 'Oh!'

'What is it?'

'I'm on the cover of a fashion magazine that just came in. I want you to see it. Be right back.'

Kelly started towards the models' dressing room. As she reached the door, she heard a voice say, 'Is Kelly really marrying him?'

Kelly stopped and listened.

'She must have gone crazy.'

'I've seen her turn down some of the handsomest men in the world, and the richest. What does she see in him?'

One of the models who had been quiet spoke up. 'It's very simple,' she said.

'What is?'

'You'll laugh.' She hesitated.

'Go ahead.'

'Did you ever hear the phrase "seeing someone through the eyes of love"?'

No one laughed.

The wedding took place at the Ministry of Justice, in Paris, and all of Kelly's model friends were there as bridesmaids. Outside on the street, there was a large crowd that had heard about the marriage of the model Kelly. The paparazzi were there in full force.

Sam Meadows was Mark's best man. 'Where are you going on your honeymoon?' he asked.

Mark and Kelly looked at each other. They had not even thought about a honeymoon.

Mark said, 'Er –' he picked a place at random, 'St Moritz.'

Kelly smiled uneasily. 'St Moritz.'

Neither of them had been to St Moritz before, and the view was breathtaking, an endless vista of majestic mountains and lush valleys.

Badrutt's Palace Hotel nestled high on a hill. Mark had called ahead to make reservations, and when they arrived, the manager welcomed them. 'Good afternoon, Mr and Mrs Harris. I have the honeymoon suite all ready for you.'

Mark stalled for a moment. 'Could – could we have twin beds put in the suite?'

The manager asked tonelessly, 'Twin beds?'

'Er – yes, please.'

'Why – certainly.'

'Thank you.' Mark turned to Kelly. 'There are a lot of interesting things to see here.' He pulled a list from his pocket. 'The Engadine Museum, the Druid Stone, St Mauritius fountain, the leaning tower . . .'

When Mark and Kelly were alone in their suite, Mark said, 'Darling, I don't want the situation to make you uncomfortable. We're just doing this to stop any gossip. We're going to spend the rest of our lives together. And what we're going to share is much more important than anything physical. I just want to be with you and I want you to be with me.'

Kelly threw her arms around him and hugged him. 'I – I don't know what to say.'

Mark smiled. 'You don't have to say anything.'

They had dinner downstairs and then went back to their suite. Twin beds had been put in the master bedroom.

'Should we toss a coin?'

Kelly smiled. 'No, you take whichever one you like.'

When Kelly came out of the bathroom fifteen minutes later, Mark was in bed.

Kelly walked over to him and sat on the edge of his bed. 'Mark, are you sure this is going to work for you?'

'I've never been more sure of anything in my life. Good-night, my beautiful darling.'

'Good-night.'

* * *

Kelly got into her bed and lay there, thinking. Reliving the night that had changed her life. 'Shhh! Don't make a sound . . . if you ever tell your mother about this . . . I'll kill her . . .' What that monster had done to her had taken over her whole life. He had killed something in her, and made her afraid of the dark . . . afraid of men . . . afraid of love. She had given him power over her. I'm not going to let him. Not any more, she thought. All the emotions she had repressed over the years, all the passion that had been building up in her exploded like a dam bursting. Kelly looked over at Mark and suddenly wanted him desperately. She threw back the covers and walked over to his bed. 'Move over,' she whispered.

Mark sat up, surprised. 'You said you – you didn't want me in your bed, and I –'

Kelly looked at him and said softly, 'But I didn't say I couldn't be in *your* bed.' She watched the look on his face as she took off her nightgown and slid into bed beside him. 'Make love to me,' she whispered.

'Oh, Kelly! Yes!'

He started softly and gently. *Too softly. Too gently.* The floodgates had opened and Kelly needed him urgently. She made violent love to him and she had never felt anything so wonderful in her life.

When they were lying in each other's arms, resting, Kelly said, 'You know that list you showed me?'

'Yes.'

She said softly, 'You can throw it away.'

Mark grinned.

'What a fool I've been,' Kelly said. She held Mark close, and they talked, and made love again, and finally they were both exhausted.

'I'll turn out the lights,' Mark said.

She tensed and squeezed her eyes shut. She started to say 'no', but as she felt his warm body close to her, protecting her, she said nothing.

When Mark turned out the lights, Kelly opened her eyes.

Kelly was no longer afraid of the dark. She –

'Kelly? *Kelly!*'

She was jolted out of her reverie. She looked up and she was back in the Fifth Avenue jewellery shop in New York, and Joseph Berry was holding out a thick envelope to her.

'Here you are. Twenty thousand dollars, in hundred dollars bills, just as you requested.'

It took Kelly a moment to get her bearings. 'Thank you.'

Kelly opened the envelope, extracted ten thousand dollars, and handed them to Diane.

Diane looked at her, puzzled. 'What's this?'

'This is your half.'

'For what? I can't –'

'You can pay me back later,' Kelly shrugged. 'If we're still around. If we're not around, I won't need it anyway. Now let's see if we can get out of here.'

THIRTY-FOUR

On Lexington Avenue, Diane hailed a cab.

'Where are we going?'

'To LaGuardia Airport.'

Kelly looked at Diane in surprise. 'Don't you know they'll be watching all the airports?'

'I hope so.'

'What are you –?' Kelly groaned. 'You have a plan, right?'

Diane patted Kelly's hand and smiled. 'Right.'

Inside LaGuardia terminal, Kelly followed Diane to the Alitalia Airlines counter.

The agent behind the counter said, 'Good morning. Can I help you?'

Diane smiled. 'Yes, we'd like two tickets to Los Angeles.'

'When would you like to leave?'

'On the first available flight. Our names are Diane Stevens and Kelly Harris.'

Kelly winced.

The ticket agent was consulting a schedule. 'The next plane will be boarding at two-fifteen.'

'Perfect.' Diane looked at Kelly.

Kelly managed a weak smile. 'Perfect.'

'Will that be cash or credit card?'

'Cash.' Diane handed him the money.

Kelly said, 'Why don't we just put up a neon sign telling Kingsley where we are?'

Diane said, 'You worry too much.'

As they started to pass the American Airlines booth, Diane stopped, and walked up to the ticket agent. 'We'd like two tickets to Miami on the next flight out of here.'

'Certainly.' The ticket agent checked the schedule. 'That flight will be boarding in three hours.'

'Fine. Our names are Diane Stevens and Kelly Harris.'

Kelly closed her eyes for an instant.

'Credit card or cash?'

'Cash.'

Diane paid the agent and he handed her their tickets.

As they walked away, Kelly said, 'Is this how we're going to outwit these geniuses? This wouldn't fool a ten-year-old.'

Diane started walking towards the airport exit.

Kelly hurried after her. 'Where are you going?'

'We're going to –'

'Never mind. I don't think I want to know.'

There was a row of taxis in front of the airport. When the two women walked out of the terminal, one of the taxis pulled out of line and drove up in front of the entrance. Kelly and Diane got into the cab.

'Where to, please?'

'Kennedy Airport.'

Kelly said, 'I don't know if *they're* going to be confused, but I sure am. I still wish we had some kind of weapon to protect ourselves.'

'I don't know where we could find a howitzer.'

The taxi went into gear. Diane leaned forward in her seat and looked at the license plaque on the dashboard. *Mario Silva.*

'Mr Silva, do you think that you can get us to Kennedy without being followed?'

They could see his grin in the mirror. 'You came to the right party.'

He pressed down on the accelerator and made a sudden U-turn. At the first corner, he drove half-way down the street, then sped into an alley.

The women looked through the rear window. There were no cars behind them.

Mario Silva's grin widened. 'OK?'

'OK,' Kelly said.

For the next thirty minutes, Mario Silva kept making unexpected turns and going through small side streets, to make sure no one could follow them. Finally, the taxi pulled up in front of the main entrance to Kennedy Airport.

'We're here,' Mario Silva announced, triumphantly.

Diane took some bills from her purse. 'There's something extra for you.'

The driver took the money and smiled. 'Thanks, lady.' He sat in his cab, watching his two passengers walk into the Kennedy terminal. When they were out of sight, he picked up his mobile phone.

'Tanner Kingsley please.'

At the Delta Airlines counter, the ticket agent glanced up at the board. 'Yes, we do have two tickets available on the flight you want. It leaves at five-fifty p.m. There's a one-hour layover in Madrid, and the plane arrives in Barcelona at nine-twenty a.m.'

'That will be fine,' Diane said.

'Will that be credit card or cash?'

'Cash.'

Diane handed the ticket agent the money and turned to Kelly.

'Let's wait in the lounge.'

Thirty minutes later, Harry Flint was on his mobile phone talking to Tanner.

'I got the information you asked for. They're flying Delta to Barcelona. Their plane leaves Kennedy at five fifty-five this evening, with a one-hour layover in Madrid. They'll arrive in Barcelona at nine-twenty in the morning.'

'Good. You'll take a company jet to Barcelona, Mr Flint, and meet them there when they arrive. I'm counting on you to give them a warm welcome.'

As Tanner hung up, Andrew walked in. He was wearing a boutonnière in his lapel. 'Here are the schedules for the –'

'What the hell is *that*?'

Andrew was confused. 'You asked me to bring –'

'I'm not talking about that. I'm talking about that stupid flower you have on.'

Andrew's face lit up. 'I'm wearing it to your wedding. I'm your best man.'

Kingsley frowned. 'What the hell are you –?' And the realisation suddenly struck him. 'That was seven years ago, you cretin, and there was no wedding. Now get your ass out of here!'

Andrew stood there, stunned, trying to understand what was happening.

'Out!'

Kingsley watched his brother leave the office. I should have put him away somewhere, he thought. The time is coming.

The take-off on the flight to Barcelona was smooth and uneventful.

Kelly looked out of the window at New York fading into the distance. 'Do you think we got away with it?'

Diane shook her head. 'No. Sooner or later they'll find a way to track us down. But at least we'll be over there.' She pulled the computer print-out from her bag and studied it. 'Sonja Verbrugge, in Berlin, who's dead and whose husband is missing . . . Gary

Reynolds, in Denver . . .' She hesitated. 'Mark and Richard . . .'

Kelly looked at the print-out. 'So, we're going to Paris, Berlin, Denver, and back to New York?'

'Right. We'll cross the border into France at San Sebastián.'

Kelly was looking forward to getting back to Paris. She wanted to talk to Sam Meadows. She had a feeling he was going to be helpful. And Angel would be waiting for her.

'Have you ever been to Spain?' Diane asked.

'Mark took me there once. It was the most –' Kelly was silent for a long time. 'Do you know the problem I'm going to have for the rest of my life, Diane? There's no one in the whole wide world like Mark. You know, when you're a kid, you read about people falling in love and suddenly the world's a magical place. That's the kind of marriage Mark and I had.' She looked at Diane. 'You probably felt that way about Richard.'

Diane said softly, 'Yes.' Then she asked, 'What was Mark like?'

Kelly smiled. 'There was something wonderfully child-like about him. I always felt that he had the mind of a child and the brain of a genius.' She gave a little chuckle.

'What?'

'The way he used to dress. On our first date, he wore a badly-fitting grey suit, with brown shoes, a green

322

shirt, and a bright red tie. After we were married, I saw to it that he was dressed properly.' She was silent. When she spoke, her voice was choked. 'Do you know something? I would give anything to see Mark again, wearing that grey suit, with brown shoes, a green shirt, and a bright red tie.' When she turned to Diane, her eyes were moist. 'Mark enjoyed surprising me with gifts. But his greatest gift was that he taught me how to love.' She dried her eyes with a handkerchief. 'Tell me about Richard.'

Diane smiled. 'He was a romantic. When we got into bed at night, he would say, "Press my secret button," and I would laugh and say, "I'm glad no one is taping this."' She looked at Kelly and said, 'His secret button was the "do not disturb" key on the telephone. Richard told me that we were in a castle, all alone, and the key on the phone was the moat that kept the world at bay.' Diane thought of something and smiled. 'He was a brilliant scientist and he enjoyed repairing things around the house. He would fix leaky faucets or electrical shorts, and I always had to call experts in to fix what Richard had repaired. I never told him.'

They talked until almost midnight.

Diane realised that it was the first time they had spoken about their husbands. It was as though some invisible barrier between them had evaporated.

Kelly yawned, 'We'd better get some sleep. I have a feeling tomorrow's going to be an exciting day.'

She had no idea how exciting.

* * *

Harry Flint elbowed his way through the crowd at El Prat Airport in Barcelona, and walked up to the large picture window that overlooked the runway. He turned his head to scan the board that listed the arrivals and departures. The plane from New York was on schedule, due to arrive in thirty minutes. Everything was moving according to plan. Flint sat down and waited.

Thirty minutes later, the passengers from the New York flight began to disembark. They all seemed excited – a typical plane-load of carefree tourists, travelling sales-men, children, and couples on their honeymoons. Flint was careful to stay out of sight of the exit ramp as he watched the stream of travellers pour into the termi-nal, and then finally trickle to a stop. He frowned. There was no sign of Diane or Kelly. Flint waited another five minutes, then started to go through the boarding gate.

'Sir, you can't go through here.'

Flint snapped, 'FAA. We have national security infor-mation about a package that is hidden in the lavatory of this plane. I was ordered to inspect it immediately.'

Flint was already moving towards the Tarmac. As he reached the plane, the crew was beginning to depart.

A flight attendant asked, 'May I help you?'

'FAA inspection,' Flint said.

He walked up the steps, into the plane. There were no passengers in sight.

The flight attendant asked, 'Is there a problem?'

'Yes. A possible bomb.'

She watched as Flint strode to the end of the cabin and pulled opened the lavatory doors. The rooms were empty.

The women had disappeared.

'They weren't on the plane, Mr Kingsley.'

Tanner's voice was dangerously soft. 'Mr Flint, did you see them board the plane?'

'Yes, sir.'

'And were they still aboard when the plane took off?'

'Yes, sir.'

'Then I think we can safely reason that they either jumped out in the middle of the Atlantic Ocean without parachutes, or that they disembarked in Madrid. Do you agree with that?'

'Of course, Mr Kingsley. But –'

'Thank you. So, that means they intend to go from Madrid to France.' He paused. 'They have four choices: they can take a different flight to Barcelona, or get there by train, bus, or car.' Tanner was thoughtful for a moment. 'They will probably feel that buses, planes and trains are too confining. Logic tells me that they will drive to the San Sebastián border to get into France.'

'If –'

'Do not interrupt me, Mr Flint. It should take them about five hours to drive from Madrid to San Sebastián. Here's what I want you to do. Fly back to Madrid. Check all the airport car rental places. Find out what kind of car they rented – colour, make, everything.'

'Yes, sir.'

'Then I want you to fly back to San Sebastián and rent a car – a large one. Lie in wait for them along the highway. I don't want them to reach San Sebastián. And Mr Flint –'

'Yes, sir?'

'Remember – make it look like an accident.'

THIRTY-FIVE

Diane and Kelly were at Barajas, the Madrid airport. They had their choice of renting a car from Hertz, Europcar, Avis and others, but they chose Alesa, a more obscure rental agency.

'What is the quickest way to get to San Sebastián?' Diane asked.

'It is very simple, *Señora*. Take the N-1 to the French border at Hondarribia, then right to San Sebastián. It is just a four- or five-hour drive.'

'*Gracias.*'

And Kelly and Diane were on their way.

When the KIG private jet arrived in Madrid, one hour later, Harry Flint hurried from one rental car booth to another.

'I was supposed to meet my sister and her girlfriend here – the girlfriend is a stunning African-American –

327

and I missed them. They arrived on the Delta nine-twenty from New York. Did they rent a car here?' he asked at each booth.

'No, *señor* . . .'

'No, *señor* . . .'

'No, *señor* . . .'

At the Alesa booth, Flint was in luck.

'Oh, yes, *señor*. I remember them well. They –'

'Do you remember what they rented?'

'It was a Peugeot.'

'What colour?'

'Red. It was our only –'

'Do you have the number of the license plate?'

'Of course. Just a moment.'

Flint watched the clerk open a book to look it up. He gave Flint the number. 'I hope you find them.'

'I will.'

Ten minutes later, Flint was flying back to Barcelona. He would rent a car, follow them to a place in the road where there was no traffic, run them off the road, and make certain that they were dead.

Diane and Kelly were only thirty minutes away from Barcelona, driving along in a comfortable silence. The highway was uncrowded and they were making good time. The countryside was beautiful. Ripe fields and orchards filled the air with the smells of pomegranate, apricot and orange trees, and off the road were old houses, with walls covered with jasmine vines. A few minutes out of the little medieval town of Burgos, the scenery began to erupt into the foothills of the Pyrenees.

'We're almost there,' Diane said. She looked ahead, frowned, and started to slam on the brakes. Two hundred feet in front of them was a burning car with a crowd gathered around it. The road was blocked by men in uniform.

Diane was puzzled. 'What's going on?'

'We're in Basque country,' Kelly said. 'It's a war zone. The Basques have been fighting the Spanish government for the last fifty years.'

A man in a green uniform with gold and red trim and a black belt, black shoes and black beret, stepped onto the highway in front of the car and held up his hand. He pointed to the side of the road.

Kelly said under her breath, 'It's the ETA. We can't stop, because God knows how long they'll keep us here.'

The officer walked to the side of the car and approached them. 'I am Captain Iradi. You will please get out of the car.'

Diane looked at him and smiled. 'I really would love to help you with your war, but we're busy fighting our own,' and she slammed her foot down on the accelerator, drove around the burning car and sped ahead, weaving the car through the screaming crowd.

Kelly's eyes were closed. 'Are we there yet?'

'We're fine.'

As Kelly opened her eyes, she looked in the side-view mirror and froze. A black Citroën Berlingo was behind them and she could see who was at the wheel.

'It's Godzilla!' Kelly gasped. 'He's in the car behind us.'

'*What?* How could he have found us so quickly?' Diane pressed the accelerator all the way to the floor. The Citroën was gaining on them. Diane looked at the double-faced speedometer. One dial read: 175 kilometres an hour. The other read: 110 miles an hour.

Nervously, Kelly said, 'I'll bet you're too fast to drive at the Indianapolis race track.'

A mile ahead Diane saw the customs checkpoint between Spain and France.

'Hit me,' Diane said.

Kelly laughed. 'I was only kidding, I just –'

'Hit me.' Diane's voice was urgent.

The Citroën was getting closer.

'What are you –?'

'Do it *now*!'

Reluctantly, Kelly slapped Diane across the face.

'No. Punch me *hard*.'

There were now only two cars between them and the Citroën.

'Hurry,' Diane shouted.

Wincing, Kelly punched Diane on the cheek.

'Harder.'

Kelly hit her again. This time, her diamond wedding ring made a gash in Diane's cheek and blood started flowing out.

Kelly was looking at Diane, horrified. 'I'm so sorry, Diane. I didn't mean to –'

They had reached the customs checkpoint. Diane braked to a stop.

The border guard approached the car. 'Good afternoon, ladies.'

'Good afternoon.' Diane turned her head so that the guard could see the blood running down her cheek.

He looked at it, aghast. '*Señora*, what happened?'

Diane bit her lip. 'It's my ex-husband. He enjoys hitting me. I got a restraining order against him, but I – I can't stop him. He keeps following me. He's back there now. I know there's no use asking for your help. No one can stop him.'

The guard turned around to scan the line of approaching cars and his face was grim. 'Which car is he in?'

'The black Citroën, two cars back. I think he plans to kill me.'

'He does, does he?' The guard growled. 'You ladies go on. You won't have to worry about him any more.'

Diane looked at him and said, 'Oh, thank you. Thank you.'

A moment later, they had crossed the border and were driving into France.

'Diane –'

'Yes?'

Kelly put her hand on Diane's shoulder. 'I'm so sorry about –' She pointed to Diane's cheek.

Diane grinned. 'It got rid of Godzilla, didn't it?' She glanced at Kelly. 'You're crying.'

'No, I'm not,' Kelly sniffed. 'It's the damn mascara. What you did was – you're not just a pretty face, are you?' Kelly asked, as she dabbed at Diane's wound with a tissue.

Diane looked in the rear-view mirror and grimaced. 'Not any more, I'm not.'

When Harry Flint reached the border checkpoint, the patrol guard was waiting. 'Step out of the car, please.'

'I haven't time for that,' Flint said. 'I'm in a hurry. I have to –'

'Step out of the car.'

Flint looked at him. 'Why? What's the problem?'

'We have a report that a car with this license number has been smuggling drugs. We're going to have to take the car apart.'

Flint glared at him. 'Are you crazy? I told you, I'm in a hurry. Drugs were never smuggled –?' He stopped and smiled. 'I get it.' He reached in his pocket and handed the guard a hundred-dollar bill. 'Here you are. Take this and forget about it.'

The border guard called out, 'José!'

A uniformed captain approached. The border guard handed him the hundred-dollar bill. 'This is an attempted bribe.'

The captain said to Flint, 'Remove yourself from the car. You are under arrest for bribery. Pull over to that space –'

'No. You can't arrest me now. I'm in the middle of –'

'And resisting arrest.' He turned to the guard. 'Call for a back-up.'

Flint took a deep breath and looked ahead at the highway. The Peugeot was out of sight.

Flint turned to the captain. 'I have to make a phone call.'

As Diane and Kelly sped through the French countryside, Diane spoke. 'You said you had a friend in Paris?'

'Yes. Sam Meadows. He worked with Mark. I have a feeling he can help us.' Kelly reached into her bag and took out her new mobile phone and dialled a number in Paris.

An operator said, 'KIG.'

'Could I speak to Sam Meadows, please?'

A minute later, Kelly heard his voice.

'Hello.'

'Sam, it's Kelly. I'm back in France.'

'My God! I've been worried sick about you. Are you all right?'

Kelly hesitated. 'I think so.'

'This is a nightmare,' Sam Meadows said. 'I still can't believe it.'

Neither can I, Kelly thought. 'Sam, I have to tell you something. I believe Mark was murdered.'

Sam Meadows' answer sent a chill through her. 'So do I.'

Kelly was finding it difficult to speak. 'I have to know what happened. Can you help me?'

'I don't think it's something we should discuss on the phone, Kelly.' He was trying to make his voice sound very casual.

'I – I understand.'

'Why don't we talk about it tonight? We can have dinner at my place.'

'Fine.'

'Seven o'clock?'

'I'll be there,' Kelly said.

Kelly turned off the phone. 'I'm going to get some of the answers tonight.'

'While you're doing that, I'm going to fly to Berlin and talk to people who worked with Franz Verbrugge.'

Kelly was suddenly silent.

Diane glanced at her. 'What's the matter?'

'Nothing. It's just that we're – we're such a great team. I hate for us to split up. Why don't we go to Paris together and then –?'

Diane smiled. 'We're not splitting up, Kelly. When you're through talking to Sam Meadows, you call me. We can meet in Berlin. I should have some information by then. We have our phones. We can stay in touch. I'm eager to hear what you're going to learn tonight.'

They reached Paris.

Diane looked in the rear-view mirror. 'No Citroën. We've finally lost them. Where do you want me to take you?'

Kelly looked out of the window. They were nearing La Place de la Concorde.

'Diane, why don't you turn the car in and be on your way? I can get a taxi here.'

'Are you sure, partner?'

'I'm sure, partner.'

'Be careful.'

'You, too.'

Two minutes later, Kelly was in a taxi, on the way to her apartment, eagerly looking forward to going home again. In a short while, she would meet Sam Meadows at his apartment for dinner.

When the taxi pulled up in front of Kelly's apartment building, she felt a deep sense of relief. She was home. The doorman opened the door.

Kelly looked up and started to say, 'I'm back, Martin –' and stopped. The doorman was a complete stranger.

'Good afternoon, Madame.'

'Good afternoon. Where is Martin?'

'Martin no longer works here. He left.'

Kelly was taken aback. 'Oh. I'm sorry.'

'Please, Madame, allow me to introduce myself. I am Jérôme Malo.'

Kelly nodded.

She walked into the lobby. A tall, thin stranger was standing behind the reception desk, next to Nicole Paradis, who was busily operating the switchboard.

The stranger smiled. 'Good evening, Madame Harris. We have been expecting you. I am Alphonse Girouard, the building superintendent.'

Kelly looked around, puzzled. 'Where's Philippe Cendre?'

'Ah. Philippe and his family moved to somewhere in

Spain.' He shrugged. 'Some business deal, I believe.'

Kelly felt a growing sense of alarm. 'And their daughter?'

'She left with them.'

Kelly remembered Philippe's proud words: 'Did I tell you that my daughter has been accepted at La Sorbonne? It's a dream come true.' And Kelly tried to keep her voice steady. 'When did they leave?'

'A few days ago, but please, do not worry, Madame. You will be taken good care of. Your apartment is all ready for you.'

Nicole Paradis, at the switchboard, looked up. 'Welcome home.' But her eyes were saying something else.

'Where is Angel?'

'Oh, your little dog? Philippe took her with him.'

Kelly was fighting a wave of panic. She was having trouble breathing.

'Shall we go now, Madame? We have a little surprise for you in your apartment.'

I'll bet you have, Kelly's mind was racing. 'Yes, just one minute,' Kelly said. 'There's something I forgot to pick up.'

Before Girouard could say anything, Kelly was outside, hurrying down the street.

Jérôme Malo and Alphonse Girouard stood on the pavement, looking after her. Caught off-guard, it was too late to stop her. They watched her get into a taxi.

My God! What have they done with Philippe and his family, and with Angel? Kelly wondered.

'Where to, *Mademoiselle*?'

'Just drive!' Tonight I'm going to get some answers from Sam, Kelly thought. Meanwhile, I have four hours to kill . . .

In his apartment, Sam Meadows was finishing a phone conversation. '. . . Yes, I understand how important it is. It will be taken care of . . . I'm expecting her in a few minutes for dinner . . . yes . . . I've already arranged for someone to dispose of her body . . . Thank you . . . That's very generous of you, Mr Kingsley.'

As Sam Meadows replaced the receiver, he looked at his watch. His dinner guest was due to arrive soon.

THIRTY-SIX

Berlin, Germany
When Diane arrived in Berlin at the Tempelhof Airport, there was a fifteen-minute waiting line for a taxi. Finally, it was Diane's turn.

The driver smiled. '*Wohin?*'

'Do you speak English?'

'Of course, *Fräulein.*'

'Kempinski Hotel, please.'

'*Ja wohl.*'

Twenty-five minutes later, Diane was checking into the hotel.

'I would like to hire a car and driver.'

'Certainly, *Fräulein.*' He looked down. 'Your baggage?'

'It's coming.'

*   *   *

When the car arrived, the driver asked, 'Where do you wish to go, *Fräulein*?'

She needed time to think. 'Just drive around for a while, please.'

'Good. There is much to see in Berlin.'

Berlin was a surprise to Diane. She knew that it had been bombed almost out of existence in World War II, but what she saw now was a bustling city with attractive, modern buildings and a brisk air of success.

The street names seemed so odd to her: *Windscheidstrasse, Regensburgerstrasse, Lützowufer* . . .

As they drove, the driver explained the history of the parks and buildings, but Diane was not listening. She had to speak to the people where Frau Verbrugge had worked, and find out what they knew. According to the Internet, Franz Verbrugge's wife had been murdered and Franz had disappeared.

Diane leaned forward and said to the driver, 'Do you know where the Cyberlin computer café is?'

'Certainly, *Fräulein*.'

'Would you take me there, please?'

'It is excellent. Very popular. You can get any information you want there.'

I hope so, Diane thought.

The Cyberlin Café was not as large as the one in Manhattan, but it seemed just as busy.

As Diane walked in through the door, a woman came

from behind the desk. 'We will have a computer available in ten minutes.'

'I want to speak to the manager,' Diane said.

'I am the manager.'

'Oh.'

'And what did you want to see me about?'

'I wanted to talk to you about Sonja Verbrugge.'

The woman shook her head. 'Frau Verbrugge is not here.'

'I know,' Diane said. 'She's dead. I'm trying to find out how she died.'

The woman was regarding Diane intently. 'It was an accident. When the police confiscated her computer, they found –' a sly expression came over her face. 'If you will wait right here, *Fräulein*, I will call someone who can help you. I will return quickly.'

Diane watched her hurry around the back, and as soon as she was out of sight, Diane walked outside and got into the car. There was going to be no help there. I have to talk to Franz Verbrugge's secretary, she thought.

At a telephone kiosk, Diane got the number of KIG and dialled.

'KIG Berlin.'

Diane said, 'Could I speak to Franz Verbrugge's secretary, please?'

'Who is calling?'

'This is Susan Stratford.'

'One moment, please.'

Manhattan, New York

In Tanner's office, the blue light had flashed on. Tanner smiled at his brother. 'That's Diane Stevens calling. Let's see if we can help her.' He put the call on the loudspeaker.

The voice of the KIG operator said, 'His secretary is not here. Would you like to speak to his assistant?'

'Yes, please.'

'Just a moment.'

A female voice came on. 'This is Heidi Fronk. May I help you?'

Diane hesitated. 'This is Susan Stratford. I'm a reporter with the *Wall Street Journal*. We're doing a story on the recent tragedies that have happened to some employees at KIG. I wonder if I could do an interview with you?'

'I don't know –'

'Just for some background information.'

Tanner was listening intently.

'What about lunch? Are you free today?'

'I'm sorry, no.'

'Dinner, then.'

There was hesitation in her voice. 'Yes, I suppose I could do that.'

'Where would you like to meet?'

'There is a fine restaurant called Rockendorf's. We could meet there.'

'Thank you.'

'Eight-thirty?'

'Eight-thirty.'

Tanner turned to Andrew, 'I've decided to do what I should have done in the first place. I'm calling Greg Holliday to handle the matter. He's never failed me.' He looked at Andrew. 'He has an inflated ego. He charges an arm and a leg but –' he smiled thinly '– he'll deliver an arm and a leg.'

THIRTY-SEVEN

Paris, France
As Kelly approached the door of Sam Meadows' apartment at 14 rue du Bourg-Tibourg, in the Fourth Arrondissement, she hesitated. Now that the chase was drawing to a conclusion, she was finally going to get some answers. She found herself drawing back, afraid to hear them.

Kelly rang the doorbell. The moment the door opened and she saw Sam Meadows, her fears went away. All she felt was pleasure and relief at seeing this man who had been so close to Mark.

'Kelly!' He cradled her in a warm bear hug.

'Oh, Sam.'

He took her hand. 'Come on in.'

Kelly stepped inside. It was a charming two-bedroom apartment, in a building that had once belonged to a member of the French nobility.

The drawing room was spacious and luxuriously appointed with French furniture, and in a small alcove, there was a curiously carved oak bar. On the wall was a Man Ray, and Adolf Wolfi drawings.

'I can't tell you how devastated I am about Mark,' Sam said awkwardly.

Kelly patted his arm. 'I know,' she whispered.

'It's unbelievable.'

'I'm trying to find out what happened,' Kelly said. 'That's why I'm here. I hope you can help me.'

She took a seat on the sofa, filled with a sense of anticipation and apprehension.

Sam's face darkened. 'No one seems to know the full story. Mark was working on a secret project. He was apparently collaborating with two or three other employees at KIG. They say he committed suicide.'

'I don't believe it,' Kelly said vehemently.

'I don't either.' His voice softened. 'And do you know the main reason? Because of you.'

Kelly looked at Sam, puzzled. 'I don't understand . . .'

'How could Mark ever leave someone as lovely as you?

How could *anyone* ever leave someone as lovely as you?' He was moving closer. 'What happened is a great tragedy, Kelly, but life has to go on, doesn't it?' He put her hand in his. 'We all need someone, don't we? He's gone, but I'm here. Your kind of woman needs a man.'

'My kind of –?'

'Mark told me how passionate you are. He says you love it.'

Kelly turned to him in surprise. Mark would never have said that. He would never have discussed her like that with anyone.

Sam put one arm around her shoulder. 'Yes. Mark told me you really had to have it. He used to tell me how great you were in bed.'

Kelly was filled with a quick sense of alarm.

Sam said, 'And Kelly, if it makes you feel any better, Mark didn't suffer at all.'

And she looked into Sam Meadow's eyes and she knew.

'We'll be having dinner in a few minutes,' Sam said. 'Why don't we work up an appetite in bed?'

Kelly felt suddenly faint. She managed to force a smile. 'That sounds great.' Her mind was working furiously. He was too big for her to fight, and she had nothing to fight him with. He began fondling her. 'You know you've got a great ass, baby. I go for that.'

Kelly smiled. 'Do you?' She sniffed. 'I'm hungry. Something smells good.'

'Our dinner.'

Before he could stop her, Kelly got up and moved towards the kitchen. As she passed the dinner table, she got a shock. The table had been set for one.

Kelly turned. In the drawing room, Sam was walking over to the door and turning the key in the lock.

She watched him put the key in the drawer of an armoire.

Kelly looked around the kitchen for a weapon. She had no way of knowing which drawer held the knives. On the counter was a box of angel hair pasta. On the stove was a pot of boiling water and next to it, a smaller pot with a red sauce that was cooking.

Sam walked into the kitchen and put his arms around Kelly.

She pretended not to pay any attention. She looked at the sauce on the stove. 'Looks wonderful.'

He was stroking her body. 'It is. What do you like to do in bed, baby?'

Kelly's mind was racing. She said softly, 'Everything. I used to do something kinky to Mark that drove him crazy.'

Sam's face lit up. 'What was that?'

'I would take a warm, wet washcloth and –' She spotted a soft cloth by the sink. 'I'll show you. Drop your pants.'

Sam Meadows grinned, 'Yeah.' He loosened his trousers and dropped them to the floor. He was wearing boxer shorts.

'Now your shorts.'

He dropped his shorts, revealing his engorged organ.

Kelly said admiringly, 'My, my . . .' She picked up the soft cloth with her left hand and moved towards him. With her right hand, she picked up the pot of boiling water and hurled the contents onto his genitals.

Kelly could still hear his screams as she took the key out of the armoire, unlocked the door and fled.

THIRTY-EIGHT

Berlin, Germany
Rockendorf's is one of the outstanding restaurants in Germany, its art nouveau décor long serving as a symbol of Berlin's prosperity.

When Diane walked in, she was greeted by the maitre d'. 'May I help you?'

'I have a reservation. Stevens. Miss Fronk is going to meet me here.'

'This way, please.'

The maitre d' seated her at a corner table. Diane looked around carefully. There were about forty customers in the restaurant, most of them businessmen. Across from Diane's table, an attractive well-dressed man was dining alone.

Diane sat there, thinking about her conversation with Heidi Fronk. How much would she know?

The waiter handed Diane a menu. '*Bitte.*'

'Thank you.'

Diane glanced at the menu. *Leberkäs*, *Kanödel*, *Haxen*, *Labskaus* . . . She had no idea what any of the dishes were. Heidi Fronk could explain them.

Diane glanced at her watch. Heidi was twenty minutes late.

The waiter came to the table. 'Would you like to order now, *Fräulein*?'

'No. I'll wait for my guest. Thank you.'

The minutes were ticking by. Diane was beginning to wonder whether something had gone wrong.

Fifteen minutes later, the waiter came back to the table. 'May I bring you anything?'

'No, thanks. My guest should be here any minute.'

At nine o'clock, Heidi Fronk had still not appeared. With a sinking feeling, Diane realised that she was not coming.

As Diane glanced up, she saw two men sitting down at a table near the entrance. They were ill-dressed and mean-looking, and the word that came to Diane's mind was 'thugs'. She watched as the waiter went to their table and they rudely waved him away. They were not interested in food. They turned back to stare at Diane, and with a feeling of dismay, she realised she had walked into a trap. Heidi Fronk had set her up.

Diane's heart began to beat so rapidly, that she felt she was going to faint. She looked around for a means of escape. There was none. She could keep sitting there, but eventually she was going to have to leave, and they would grab her. She thought about using her mobile phone, but there was no one who could help her.

Diane thought, desperately, I've got to get out of here, but how?

As she looked around the room, her gaze fell on the attractive man sitting alone at the table across from hers. He was sipping his coffee.

Diane smiled at him and said, 'Good evening.'

He looked up, surprised, and said pleasantly, 'Good evening.'

Diane gave him a warm, inviting smile. 'I see we're both alone.'

'Yes.'

'Would you like to join me?'

He hesitated for a moment and smiled. 'Certainly.' He rose and walked over to Diane's table.

'It's no fun eating alone, is it?' Diane said lightly.

'You're quite right. It's not.'

She held out a hand. 'I'm Diane Stevens.'

'Greg Holliday.'

Paris, France

Kelly Harris had been stunned by her terrifying experience with Sam Meadows. After her escape, she had spent the night walking the streets of Montmartre, constantly looking behind her, in fear that she was being followed. But I can't leave Paris without finding out what's going on, Kelly thought.

At dawn, she stopped at a small café and had a cup of coffee. The answer to her problem came to her unexpectedly. Mark's secretary. She had adored Mark. Kelly was sure she would do anything to be helpful.

At nine o'clock, Kelly made the call from a telephone kiosk. She dialled the familiar number and a female operator with a heavy French accent said, 'Kingsley International Group.'

'I'd like to talk to Yvonne Renais.'

'*Un moment, s'il vous plaît.*'

A moment later, Kelly heard Yvonne's voice.

'Yvonne Renais. May I help you?'

'Yvonne, this is Kelly Harris.'

There was a startled exclamation. 'Oh! Mrs Harris –'

Manhattan, New York

In Tanner Kingsley's office a blue light had flashed.

Tanner Kingsley picked up the telephone and listened to the conversation taking place in Paris.

'I'm so sorry about what happened to Mr Harris. It was so awful.'

'Thank you, Yvonne. I need to talk to you. Can we meet somewhere? Are you free for lunch?'

'Yes.'

'Some place public.'

'Do you know Le Ciel de Paris? It is in La Tour Montparnasse.'

'Yes.'

Tanner Kingsley made a mental note.

'Twelve o'clock?'

'That's fine. I'll see you there.'

Tanner Kingsley's lips puckered into a thin smile.

Enjoy your last lunch, he thought. He unlocked a drawer, opened it, and picked up the gold telephone.

A voice at the other end answered. 'Morning, Tanner.'

'Good news. It's over. We have them both.'

He listened for a moment, then nodded. 'I know. It took a little longer than we expected, but we're ready to go forward now . . . I feel the same way . . . Goodbye.'

Paris, France

La Tour Montparnasse is a 690-foot tower, built of steel and glass. The building was abuzz with activity, filled with busy offices.

Kelly was the first to arrive on the fifty-sixth floor, where the bar and restaurant were located. Yvonne came in fifteen minutes later, filled with apology.

Kelly had only met her a few times, but she remembered her well. Yvonne was a tiny, sweet-faced lady. Mark had often told Kelly how efficient she was.

'Thank you for coming,' Kelly said.

'I would do anything I could to – Mr Harris was such a wonderful man. Everyone at the office adored him. None of us could believe what – what happened.'

'That's what I wanted to talk to you about, Yvonne. You were with my husband for five years?'

'Yes.'

'So you got to know him pretty well?'

'Oh, yes.'

'Did you notice anything in the last few months that

seemed strange? I mean, any change in the way he acted or what he said?'

Yvonne avoided her eyes. 'I'm not sure . . . I mean . . .'

Kelly said earnestly, 'Whatever you say now can't hurt him. And it might help me understand what happened.' Kelly steeled herself to ask the next question. 'Did he ever talk about Olga?'

Yvonne looked at her, puzzled. 'Olga? No.'

'You don't know who she was?'

'I have no idea.'

Kelly felt a sense of relief. She leaned forward. 'Yvonne, is there something you're not telling me?'

'Well . . .'

The waiter came up to their table. '*Bonjour, Mesdames. Bienvenue au Ciel de Paris. Je m'appelle Jacques Brion. Notre chef de cuisine a préparé quelques spécialités pour le déjeuner aujourd'hui. Avez-vous fait vos choix?*'

'*Oui, Monsieur. Nous avons choisi le Châteaubriand pour deux.*'

When the waiter left, Kelly looked at Yvonne. 'You were saying . . . ?'

'Well, in the last few days before – before he died, Mr Harris seemed very nervous. He asked me to get him a plane ticket to Washington, DC.'

'I know about that. I thought it was just a routine business trip.'

'No. I think it was something very unusual – something urgent.'

'Do you have any idea what it was about?'

'No. Everything suddenly became very secret. That's all I know.'

Kelly quizzed Yvonne for the next hour, but there was nothing Yvonne could add except a remark about some phone calls Mark had received.

When they had finished their lunch, Kelly said, 'I would like you to keep this meeting confidential, Yvonne.'

'You don't have to worry about that, Mrs Harris. I won't tell a soul.' Yvonne stood up. 'I have to get back to work.' Her lips trembled. 'But it won't ever be the same . . .'

'Thank you, Yvonne.'

Who was Mark going to see in Washington? Kelly wondered. And there had been the strange phone calls from Germany and Denver and New York.

Kelly took the lift down to the lobby.

I'll give Diane a call and see what she's found out. Maybe – her thoughts were interrupted. As Kelly reached the front entrance of the building, she saw them. There were two large men, one on each side of the door. They looked at her, then grinned at each other. As far as Kelly knew, there was no other nearby exit. Could Yvonne have betrayed me? she thought.

The men started moving towards Kelly, roughly pushing past the people coming in and out of the building.

Kelly looked around frantically and pressed against the wall. Her arm was bumping something hard. She looked at it, and, as the two men moved closer, Kelly picked up the little hammer attached to the fire alarm unit on the wall, broke the glass, and the fire alarm clanged through the building.

Kelly yelled 'Fire! Fire!'

There was instant panic. People came running out of offices, shops and restaurants, heading for the door. Within seconds, the hall was jammed, with everyone fighting to get out. The two men were trying to find Kelly in the crowd. When they finally got to where they had last seen her, Kelly had disappeared.

Berlin, Germany

'I was waiting for a friend,' Diane explained to Greg Holliday. 'It looks like she wasn't able to make it.'

'Too bad. Are you in Berlin on a visit?'

'Yes.'

'It is a beautiful city. I am a happily married man, or I would offer to be your escort! But there are some excellent tours in Berlin that I can recommend.'

'That would be nice,' Diane said absently. She glanced towards the entrance. The two men were walking out of the door. They would be waiting for her outside. It was time to make her move.

'As a matter of fact,' Diane said, 'I'm here with a group.' She looked at her watch. 'They're waiting for me now. If you wouldn't mind walking me out to a taxi –'

'Not at all.'

A few moments later, they were heading out through the door.

Diane felt a deep sense of relief. The two men might attack her alone, but she did not think they would attack her with a man at her side. It would attract too much attention.

When Diane and Greg Holliday stepped outside, the two men were nowhere in sight. A taxi was in front of the restaurant, a Mercedes parked behind it.

Diane said, 'It was nice meeting you, Mr Holliday. I hope –'

Holliday smiled and took her arm, and gripped it so tightly that Diane felt an agonising pain.

She looked at him, startled. 'What –?'

'Why don't we take the car?' he said softly, as he pulled Diane towards the Mercedes. His grip tightened.

'No, I don't want to –'

As they reached the car, Diane saw the men from the restaurant sitting inside, on the front seat. Horrified, Diane suddenly understood what had happened, and she was filled with an overwhelming terror.

'Please,' she said, 'don't. I –' She felt herself being shoved into the car.

Greg Holliday moved in beside Diane and closed the door.

'*Schnell!*'

As the car pulled into the heavy traffic, Diane found herself becoming hysterical. 'Please –'

Greg Holliday turned to her and smiled reassuringly. 'You can relax. I am not going to hurt you. I promise you that by tomorrow, you will be on your way home.'

He reached into a cloth pocket attached to the back of the driver's seat and took out a hypodermic needle.

'I'm going to give you an injection. It's harmless. It will put you to sleep for an hour or two.'

He reached for Diane's wrist.

'*Scheisse!*' the driver yelled. A pedestrian had suddenly darted in front of the Mercedes and the driver had to jam on the brakes to avoid hitting him, catching his passengers unaware. Holliday's head had slammed against the metal framework of the headrest.

He tried to sit up, groggy. He yelled at the driver, 'What –?'

Instinctively, Diane grabbed Holliday's hand which was holding the hypodermic needle, twisted his wrist and plunged the needle into his flesh.

Holliday turned to her in shock. 'No!' It was a scream.

With growing horror, Diane watched Holliday's body go into spasm and then stiffen and collapse. He was dead within seconds. The two men in the front turned to see what was happening. Diane was out of the door and seconds later in a taxi, headed in the opposite direction.

THIRTY-NINE

The sound of her mobile phone startled Kelly. She picked it up cautiously. 'Hello?'

'Hi, Kelly.'

'Diane! Where are you?'

'In Munich. Where are you?'

'On the ferry, crossing the English Channel to Dover.'

'How did your meeting with Sam Meadows go?'

Kelly could still hear his screams. 'I'll tell you about it when we meet. Did you get any information?'

'Not much. We have to decide what to do next. We're running out of options. Gary Reynolds' plane crashed near Denver. I think we have to go there. Maybe it's our last chance.'

'All right.'

'The obituary said that Reynolds has a sister living in Denver. She might know something. Why don't we meet in Denver at the Brown Palace Hotel. I'm flying out of Schoenfeld Airport, in Berlin, in an hour.'

'I'll get a plane out of Heathrow.'

'Good. The room will be booked under the name of "Harriet Beecher Stowe".'

'Kelly –'

'Yes.'

'Just . . . you know.'

'I know. You, too . . .'

Tanner was alone in his office, talking on the gold phone. '. . . and they managed to escape . . . Sam Meadows is not a happy man and Greg Holliday is dead.' He was silent for a moment, thinking. 'Logically, the only place left for them is Denver. In fact, that's probably their last option . . . It looks as though I'm going to have to handle this personally. They've won my respect, so it's only fitting that I take care of them properly . . .' He listened, then laughed. 'Of course . . . Goodbye.'

Andrew was seated in his office, his mind floating, creating hazy visions . . . He was lying in a hospital bed and Tanner was saying, 'You surprised me, Andrew. You were supposed to die. Now the doctors tell me you can get out of here in a few days. I'm giving you an office at KIG. I want you to see how I'm saving your ass. You just wouldn't learn, would you, you imbecile? Well, I'm turning your penny-ante operation into a gold mine, and you can sit there and watch how

362

I do it. By the way, the first thing I did was to cancel all the bullshit do-good projects you started, Andrew . . . Andrew . . . Andrew . . .'

The voice was getting louder. 'Andrew! Are you deaf?'

Tanner was calling him. Andrew pulled himself to his feet and walked into his brother's office.

Tanner looked up. 'I hope I'm not interfering with your work,' Tanner said, sarcastically.

'No, I was just . . .'

Tanner studied his brother for a moment. 'You're really not good for anything, are you, Andrew? You don't reap, neither do you sow. It's good for me to have someone to talk to, but I don't know how much longer I want to keep you around . . .'

Denver, Colorado

Kelly arrived in Denver ahead of Diane, and she registered at the venerable Brown Palace Hotel.

'A friend of mine will be arriving this afternoon.'

'Would you like two rooms?'

'No, a double.'

When Diane's plane landed at Denver International Airport, she took a taxi to the hotel. She gave her name to the receptionist.

'Oh, yes, Mrs Stevens. Mrs Stowe is expecting you. She's in Room 638.'

It was a relief to hear.

Kelly was waiting. The two of them exchanged a warm hug.

'I've missed you.'

'I've missed *you*. How was your trip?' Kelly asked.

'Uneventful. Thank God.'

Diane looked at her and said, 'What happened to you in Paris?'

Kelly took a deep breath. 'Tanner Kingsley . . . What happened in Berlin?'

Diane said tonelessly, 'Tanner Kingsley . . .'

Kelly walked over to a table, picked up a telephone directory and brought it back to Diane. 'Gary's sister, Lois Reynolds, is still listed in the telephone book. She lives on Marion Street.'

'Good.' Diane looked at her watch. 'It's too late to do anything tonight. We'll go there first thing in the morning.'

They had dinner in their room and talked until midnight, then got ready for bed.

Diane said, 'Good-night.' She reached for the light switch and the bedroom was plunged into darkness.

Kelly screamed. 'No! Turn on the lights.'

Diane quickly turned them back on. 'I'm so sorry, Kelly. I forgot.'

Kelly was hyperventilating, fighting to control her panic. When she could speak, she said, 'I wish I could get over this.'

'Don't worry about it. When you're feeling very secure, you will.'

* * *

The following morning, when Diane and Kelly walked out of the hotel, there was a line of taxis in front of the entrance. The two women got into one, and Kelly gave the driver the number of Lois Reynolds' house on Marion Street.

Fifteen minutes later, the driver pulled up to the kerb. 'Here we are.'

Kelly and Diane stared out of the window, aghast. They were looking at the charred rubble of a house that had burned to the ground. There was nothing left but ashes, bits of burned wood and a crumbled concrete foundation.

Diane was finding it difficult to breathe.

'The bastards killed her,' Kelly said. She looked at Diane, despairingly, 'This is the end of the road.'

Diane was thinking. 'There's one last chance.'

Ray Fowler, the acerbic manager of Denver Airport, scowled at Kelly and Diane. 'Let's see if I have this straight. You two are investigating a plane crash, without any authority, and you want me to arrange for you to question the air-traffic controller who was on duty, so he can give you some privileged information? Do I have that right?'

Diane and Kelly glanced at each other.

Kelly said, 'Well, we were hoping –'

'You were hoping what?'

'That you would help us.'

'Why would I do that?'

'Mister Fowler, we just want to make sure that what happened to Gary Reynolds really was an accident.'

Ray Fowler was studying them closely. 'It's interesting,' he said. He sat there, bemused, and then spoke. 'This has been on my mind a lot. Maybe you *should* discuss this with Howard Miller. He was the air-traffic controller on duty when the accident happened. Here's his address. I'll call him and tell him you're coming over.'

'Thank you. That's very kind of you,' Diane said.

Ray Fowler growled, 'The only reason I'm doing this is because I think the FAA crash report is bullshit. We found the remains of the plane, but interestingly enough, the black box was missing. It had just disappeared.'

Howard Miller lived in a neat stucco house six miles from the airport. Miller was a small, energetic man in his forties. He opened the door for Diane and Kelly. 'Come in. Ray Fowler told me you were coming. What is it I can do for you?'

'We'd like to talk to you, Mr Miller.'

'Sit down,' he welcomed them in. 'Like some coffee?'

'No, thanks.'

'You're here about the Gary Reynolds crash?'

'Yes. Was it an accident or –?'

Howard Miller shrugged. 'I honestly don't know. I've never experienced anything like it in all the years I've been working here. Everything was going according to protocol. Gary Reynolds radioed for permission to land and we cleared him. The next thing I know, he was only two miles away, reporting a hurricane. A hurricane! Our weather monitors were clear. Later, I checked with the weather bureau. There was no wind at that time. To tell you the truth, I thought he was drunk or on drugs. The next thing we all knew, he crashed into the side of a mountain.'

Kelly said, 'I understand that the black box hasn't been found.'

'That's another thing,' Howard Miller commented, thoughtfully. 'We found everything else. What happened to the black box? The damned FAA came in and thought we had our records wrong. They didn't believe us when we told them what had happened. You know when you can feel something is not right?'

'Yes . . .'

'I feel that something is not right, but I can't tell you what. I am sorry I can't be of more help.'

Diane and Kelly rose, frustrated. 'Well, thank you very much, Mr Miller. We appreciate your time.'

'Not at all.'

As Miller started to lead the two women towards the door, he said, 'I hope Gary's sister will be all right.'

Kelly stopped. 'What?'

'She's in the hospital, you know. Poor thing. Her house burned down in the middle of the night. They don't know if she's going to make it or not.'

Diane froze. 'What happened?'

'The fire department thinks it was caused by an electrical short. Lois managed to crawl out of the front door, out onto the lawn, but by the time the firemen got to her, she was in pretty bad shape.'

Diane tried to keep her voice calm. 'What hospital is she in?'

'The University of Colorado Hospital. She's in the Burn Centre there. Three North.'

The nurse at the reception desk at Three North said, 'I'm sorry, Miss Reynolds is not allowed visitors.'

Kelly asked, 'Can you tell us what room she's in?'

'No, I'm afraid I can't.'

'This is an emergency,' Diane said. 'We have to see her and –'

'No one sees her without written authorisation.' There was a note of finality in her voice.

Diane and Kelly looked at each other.

'Well, thank you.'

The two women walked away. 'What are we going to do?' Kelly asked. 'This is our last chance.'

'I have a plan.'

A uniformed messenger carrying a large, beribboned parcel approached the reception desk. 'I have a package here for Lois Reynolds.'

'I'll sign for it,' the nurse said.

The messenger shook his head. 'Sorry. My orders are to deliver it to her personally. It's very valuable.'

The nurse hesitated. 'Then I'll have to go with you.'

'That's fine.'

He followed the nurse to the end of the hall. When

they reached Room 391, the nurse started to open the door and the messenger handed her the package. 'You can take it in to her,' he said.

One flight down stairs, the messenger walked over to the bench where Diane and Kelly were waiting.

'Room 391,' he told them.

'Thanks,' Diane said, gratefully. She handed him some money.

The two women took the stairs to the third floor, stepped into the corridor and waited until the nurse was on the telephone, and her back was turned to them. They quickly started down the hall and entered Room 391.

Lois Reynolds was lying in bed with a spider web of tubes and wires attached to her body. She was heavily bandaged. Her eyes were closed as Kelly and Diane approached the bed.

Diane said softly, 'Miss Reynolds, I'm Diane Stevens and this is Kelly Harris. Our husbands worked for KIG . . .'

Lois Reynolds' eyes slowly opened and tried to focus. When she spoke, her voice was a shadow of a whisper. 'What?'

Kelly said, 'Our husbands worked for KIG. They were both killed. We thought that because of what happened to your brother, you might be able to help us.'

Lois Reynolds tried to shake her head. 'I can't help you . . . Gary is dead.' Her eyes welled up with tears.

Diane leaned close. 'Did your brother say anything to you before the accident?'

'Gary was a wonderful man.' Her voice was slow and pained. 'He was killed in a plane crash.'

Diane said patiently, 'Did he say anything to you that might help us find out what happened?'

Lois Reynolds closed her eyes.

'Miss Reynolds, please don't go to sleep yet. Please. This is very important. Did your brother say anything to you that might help us?'

Lois Reynolds opened her eyes again and looked at Diane, puzzled. 'Who are you?'

Diane said, 'We think your brother was murdered.'

Lois Reynolds murmured, 'I know . . .'

Diane and Kelly felt a cold chill.

'Why?' Kelly asked.

'Prima . . .' It was a whisper.

Kelly leaned closer. 'Prima?'

'Gary told . . . told me about it a few . . . a few days before he was killed. Their machine that can control . . . control weather. Poor Gary. He . . . he never got to Washington.'

Diane said, 'Washington?'

'Yes . . . They were all going to . . . all going to see some senator about . . . about Prima . . . Gary said Prima was bad . . .'

Kelly asked, 'Do you remember the senator's name?'

'No.'

'Please think.'

Lois Reynolds was mumbling. 'Senator somebody . . .'

'Senator who?' Kelly asked.

'Levin – Luven – van Luven. He was going to see her. He was going to meet –'

The door flew open, and a doctor wearing a white jacket, with a stethoscope draped around his neck, strode into the room. He looked at Diane and Kelly, furious. 'Didn't anyone tell you no visitors were allowed in here?'

Kelly said, 'I'm sorry. We had to – speak to –'

'Leave, please.'

The two women looked at Lois Reynolds. 'Goodbye. Get well.'

The man watched them leave the room. When the door closed, he moved to the bed, stood over Lois Reynolds, and picked up a pillow.

FORTY

Kelly and Diane made their way down to the main lobby of the hospital.

Diane said, 'That's why Richard and Mark were going to Washington, to see Senator van Luven.'

'How do we get hold of her?'

'Simple.' Diane took out her mobile phone.

Kelly held up a hand to stop her. 'No. Let's use a pay phone.'

They got the telephone number of the Senate office building from Information and Diane called.

'Senator van Luven's office.'

'I'd like to speak to the Senator, please.'

'May I say who's calling?'

Diane said, 'It's a personal matter.'

'Your name, please?'

'I can't – just tell her it's very important.'

'I'm sorry, I can't do that.' The line was disconnected.

Diane turned to Kelly. 'We can't use our names.' Diane called the number again.

'Senator van Luven's office.'

'Please, listen to me. This is not a crank call. I need to speak to the Senator and I can't give you my name.'

'Then I'm afraid I can't put you through.' The call was disconnected.

Diane called again.

'Senator van Luven's office.'

'Please don't hang up. I know you're doing your job, but this is a matter of life and death. I'm calling from a pay phone. I'm going to give you the number. Please have the Senator call me.' She gave the secretary the number and heard her slam the phone down.

Kelly said, 'What do we do now?'

'We wait.'

They waited for two hours and finally, Diane said, 'It's not going to work. Let's –'

The phone rang. Diane took a deep breath and rushed to pick it up. 'Hello?'

An annoyed female voice said, 'This is Senator van Luven. Who is this?'

Diane held the phone towards Kelly, so that they could both hear what the Senator was saying. Diane was so choked up, she could hardly speak. 'Senator, my name is Diane Stevens. I'm here with Kelly Harris. Do you know who we are?'

'No, I don't, and I'm afraid I –'

'Our husbands were murdered on their way to meet with you.'

There was a gasp. 'Oh, my God. Richard Stevens and Mark Harris.'

'Yes.'

'Your husbands made an appointment to meet with me, but my secretary received a call saying that they had changed their plans. Then they – died.'

'That call was not from them, Senator,' Diane said. 'They were murdered to stop them from seeing you.'

'*What*?' She sounded shocked. 'Why would anyone –?'

'They were killed to prevent them from talking to you. Kelly and I would like to come to Washington to talk to you about what our husbands were trying to tell you.'

There was a brief hesitation. 'I'll meet with you, but not in my office. It's too public. If what you're saying is true, it could be dangerous. I have a home in Southampton, Long Island. I can meet you there. Where are you calling from?'

'Denver.'

'Just a moment.'

Three minutes later, the Senator came back on the line. 'The next flight out of Denver to New York is a red-eye. It's a United flight, nonstop to LaGuardia. It leaves at 12.25 a.m. and arrives in New York at 6.09 a.m. If the flight is full, there's one –'

'We'll be on that flight.'

Kelly looked at Diane, surprised. 'Diane, what if we can't get –?'

Diane held up a reassuring hand. 'We'll be on it.'

'When you get to the airport, a grey Lincoln Town

Car will be waiting for you. Go right to the car. The driver is Asian. His name is Kunio. He'll take you to my home. I'll be waiting for you there.'

'Thank you, Senator.'

Diane replaced the receiver and took a deep breath. She turned to Kelly. 'We're all set.'

Kelly said, 'How do you know we can get on that flight?'

'I have a plan.'

The concierge at the hotel arranged a rental car, and in forty-five minutes, Diane and Kelly were on their way to the airport. Kelly said, 'I don't know whether I'm more excited or more frightened.'

'I don't think we have anything to be frightened about any more.'

'It looks like a lot of people tried to meet with the Senator, but none of them made it, Diane. They were all killed first.'

'Then we're going to be the first to make it.'

Kelly said, 'I wish we had –'

'I know. A weapon. You said that. We have our wits.'

'Yeah, but I wish we had a weapon.'

Kelly looked out of the car window. 'Pull over.'

Diane pulled over to the kerb. 'What is it?'

'There's something I have to do.'

They had stopped in front of a hairdresser's shop. Kelly opened the car door.

Diane said, 'Where are you going?'

'I'm going to get a new hairdo.'

Diane said, 'You're joking.'

'No, I'm not.'

'You're getting a new hairdo *now*? Kelly, we're on our way to the airport, to catch a plane, and there's no time to –'

'Diane, you never know what's going to happen. And in case I should die, I want to look pretty.'

Diane sat there, speechless, as Kelly walked into the hairdresser's.

Twenty minutes later, Kelly came out. She was wearing a black wig, styled in a luxurious upswept hairdo, piled high at the back.

'I'm ready,' Kelly said. 'Let's go kick some ass.'

FORTY-ONE

'There's a white Lexus following us,' Kelly said.

'I know. There are half a dozen men in it.'

'Can you lose them?'

'I don't have to.'

Kelly stared at her. '*What?*'

'Watch.'

They were approaching an airport gate with a sign that read: *Deliveries Only*. The guard behind the gate had opened it to admit their car.

The men in the Lexus watched as Kelly and Diane got out and stepped into an official airport car that started across the Tarmac.

When the Lexus reached the gate, the guard said, 'This is a private entrance.'

'But you let that other car in.'

'This is a private entrance.' The guard closed the gate.

The official airport car crossed the Tarmac and stopped at the side of a jumbo jet. As Diane and Kelly stepped out, Howard Miller was waiting. 'You got here all right?'

'Yes,' Diane said. 'Thanks so much for making the arrangements.'

'My pleasure.' His face became grim. 'I hope some good comes out of all this.'

Kelly said, 'Thank Lois Reynolds for us and tell her –'

Howard Miller's expression changed. 'Lois Reynolds passed away last night.'

The two women both felt a sense of shock. It took Kelly a moment to speak. 'I'm sorry.'

'What happened?' Diane asked.

'I guess her heart gave out.' Howard Miller looked over at the jet. 'They're ready to go. I've arranged seats for you near the door.'

'Thanks again.'

Miller watched as Kelly and Diane went up the ramp. Moments later, the flight attendant closed the door and the plane began to taxi.

Kelly turned to Diane and smiled. 'We've made it. We outsmarted all those brainiacs. What are you going to do after we talk to Senator van Luven?'

'I haven't really thought about it,' Diane said. 'Are you going back to Paris?'

'It depends. Do you think you'll be staying in New York?'

'Yes.'

Kelly said, 'Then maybe I'll stick around New York for a while.'

'Then we might go to Paris together.'

They sat there, smiling at each other.

Diane said, 'I was just thinking how proud Richard and Mark would be if they knew we're going to finish the job they started.'

'You bet.'

Diane looked out of the window and up at the sky, and said softly, 'Thank you, Richard.'

Kelly glanced at Diane, shook her head and said nothing.

Diane kept the rest of her thoughts to herself. *Richard, I know you can hear me, darling. We're going to finish what you started. We're going to avenge you and your friends. It won't bring you back, but it will help a little. Do you know what I miss most about you, my love? Everything . . .*

When the plane landed at LaGuardia Airport three and a half hours later, Diane and Kelly were the first passengers to disembark. Diane remembered Senator van Luven's words. 'When you get to the airport, a grey Lincoln Town Car will be waiting for you.'

The car was waiting at the terminal entrance. Standing next to it was an elderly Japanese man in a chauffeur's uniform. He stood up straight as Kelly and Diane approached him.

'Mrs Stevens? Mrs Harris?'

'Yes.'

'I'm Kunio.' He opened the door of the car and they stepped in.

Moments later, they were on their way to Southampton.

'It is a two-hour drive,' Kunio said. 'The scenery is very beautiful.'

The last thing they were interested in was scenery. Both were busily thinking about the quickest way to explain to the Senator what had happened.

Kelly said to Diane, 'Do you think the Senator will be in danger when we tell her what we know?'

'I'm sure she'll have protection. She'll know how to handle this.'

'I hope so.'

The Town Car drove up to a large, limestone, eighteenth-century English-style mansion with a slate roof, and tall, slender chimneys. There were large, manicured grounds, and they could see a separate house for the servant quarters and garage.

As the car stopped at the front door, Kunio said, 'I will be waiting for you, if you need me.'

'Thank you.'

The door was opened by a butler. 'Good morning. Come in, please. The Senator is expecting you.'

The two women entered. The entrance hall was elegant, yet casual, furnished with an eclectic assortment of antiques and comfortable-looking sofas and chairs. On the wall, above a large fireplace with a baroque mantle, were mirrored candle sconces.

The butler said, 'This way, please.'

Kelly and Diane followed the butler into a large drawing room.

Senator van Luven was waiting for them. She was wearing a light-blue, silk suit and blouse, and her hair was hanging loosely. She was more feminine-looking than Diane had expected.

'I'm Pauline van Luven.'

'Diane Stevens.'

'Kelly Harris.'

'I'm glad to see you both. It's taken much too long.'

Kelly looked at Senator van Luven, puzzled. 'I'm sorry?'

Tanner Kingsley's voice behind them said, 'She means you have been very lucky, but your luck has just run out.'

Diane and Kelly turned. Tanner Kingsley and Harry Flint had come into the room.

Tanner said, 'Now, Mr Flint.'

Harry Flint raised a pistol. Without a word, he aimed at the women and fired twice. Pauline van Luven and Tanner Kingsley watched as Kelly's and Diane's bodies tumbled backwards and fell to the floor.

Tanner walked over to Senator van Luven and hugged her. 'It's finally over, Princess.'

FORTY-TWO

Flint asked, 'What do you want me to do with the bodies?'

Tanner did not hesitate. 'Tie some weights around their ankles, have them flown out about two hundred miles, and drop them into the Atlantic.'

'No problem.' Flint left the room.

Tanner turned to Senator van Luven. 'That ends it, Princess. We can be on our way.'

She moved up to him and kissed him. 'I've missed you so much, baby.'

'I've missed you, too.'

'Those once-a-month rendezvous were frustrating because I knew you had to leave.'

Tanner held her close. 'From now on, we're together. We'll wait a respectable three or four months as a homage to your dear departed husband, and then we'll get married.'

She smiled and said, 'Let's make it a month.'

He nodded. 'Sounds good.'

'I resigned from the Senate yesterday. They were very understanding about my grief over my husband's death.'

'Wonderful. Now we can be seen together freely. I want you to see something at KIG that I couldn't show you before.'

Tanner and Pauline reached the redbrick building. Tanner walked up to the solid steel door. There was a recess in the centre of it. He was wearing a heavy cameo ring with the face of a Greek warrior on it.

Pauline watched as Tanner pressed the ring hard into the recess and the door began to open. The room was enormous, filled with huge computers and television screens. At a far wall were generators and electronics, all linked together with a control panel in the centre.

Tanner said, 'This is ground zero. What you and I have here is something that's going to change lives for ever. This room is the command centre of a satellite system that can control the weather in any area of the world. We can cause storms anywhere. We can create famines by stopping rain. We can fog-in every airport in the world. We can manufacture hurricanes and cyclones that would stop the world's economy.' He smiled. 'I've already demonstrated some of our power. A lot of countries have been working on weather control, but none of them has solved it yet.'

Tanner pressed a button and a large television screen lit up. 'What you're seeing here is an advance that the

Army *wishes* it had.' He turned to Pauline and smiled. 'The only thing that prevented Prima from giving me perfect control was the greenhouse effect, and you took care of that beautifully.' He sighed. 'Do you know who created this project? Andrew. He really was a genius.'

Pauline was staring at the mass of equipment. 'I don't understand how this can control the weather.'

'Well, the simple version is that warm air rises toward colder air, and if there is moisture in –'

'Don't patronise me, darling.'

'Sorry, but the longer version is a bit complicated,' Tanner said.

'I'm listening.'

'It's a little technical, so bear with me. Microwave lasers, created with the nano-technology my brother produced, when fired into the earth's atmosphere, make free-forming oxygen that bonds with hydrogen, thus producing ozone and water. Free oxygen in the atmosphere pairs up – that's why it's called O_2 – and my brother discovered that firing a laser from space into the atmosphere made the oxygen bond with two hydrogen atoms into ozone – O_3, and water – H_2O.'

'I still don't understand how that would –'

'The weather is driven by water. Andrew found in larger-scale tests that so much water was created as a by-product of his experiments, that winds shifted. More lasers, more wind. Control the water and the wind, and you control all weather.'

He was thoughtful for a moment. 'When I found out that Akira Iso in Tokyo, and later, Madeleine Smith in

Zurich, were close to solving the problem, I offered them jobs. But they turned me down. I told you that I had four of my top meteorologists working on the project with me.'

'Yes.'

'They were good, too. Franz Verbrugge in Berlin, Mark Harris in Paris, Gary Reynolds in Vancouver, and Richard Stevens in New York. I had each of them trying to solve a different facet of weather control, and I thought that because they were working in different countries, they would never put the pieces together and find out what the ultimate purpose of the project was. But somehow they did. They came to me, to ask me what plans I had for it. When I told them I didn't intend to offer it to our government, they objected and decided to go to Washington, to talk to someone, to tell them about Prima. It wouldn't have mattered who they chose because I would have had them taken care of before they got there, but they chose you, because you were head of the Senate Select Committee on the Environment. Now watch this.'

On a computer screen, a map of the world appeared, dotted with lines and symbols. As Tanner spoke, he moved a switch and the focus of the map kept shifting until it highlighted Portugal.

'The agricultural valleys in Portugal are supplied by rivers that flow to the Atlantic from Spain. Just imagine what would happen to Portugal if it continued to rain until the valleys were drowned out.'

Tanner pressed a button and on a huge screen, a

picture appeared of a massive pink palace with ceremonial guards standing watch while its lush, beautiful gardens glimmered in the bright sunlight.

'That's the presidential palace.'

The picture switched to a dining room inside, where a family was having breakfast.

'That's the President of Portugal and his wife and two children. When they speak, it's going to be in Portuguese, but you'll hear it in English. I have dozens of nano-cameras and microphones set up in the palace. The President doesn't know it, but his head security guard works for me.'

An aide was saying to the President, 'At eleven o'clock this morning, you have a meeting at the Embassy and a labour union speech. At one p.m., luncheon at the museum. This evening, we're having a state dinner.'

The phone rang at the breakfast table. The President picked it up. 'Hello.'

Then Tanner's voice, instantaneously translated from English to Portuguese as he spoke, said 'Mr President?'

The President looked startled. 'Who is this?' he asked, as his voice was immediately translated from Portuguese to English for Tanner.

'I'm a friend.'

'Who – how did you get my private number?'

'That's not important. I want you to listen very carefully. I love your country and I would not want to see it destroyed. If you don't want terrible storms to wipe it off the map, you must send me two billion dollars in gold. If you're not interested now, I'll call you back in three days.'

On the screen, they watched the President slam the phone down. He said to his wife, 'Some crazy man got my phone number. Sounds like he escaped from an asylum.'

Tanner turned to Pauline. 'That was recorded three days ago. Now let me show you the conversation we had yesterday.'

A picture of the massive pink palace and its beautiful gardens flashed on again, but this time heavy rains were pouring down, and the sky was filled with thunder and ablaze with lightning.

Tanner pressed a button and the scene on television moved into the President's office. He was seated at a conference table, with half a dozen assistants all talking at once. The President's face was grim.

The telephone on his desk rang.

'Now watch,' Tanner grinned.

The President picked up the telephone apprehensively. 'Hello.'

'Good morning, Mr President. How –?'

'You are destroying my country! You have ruined the crops. The fields are flooded. The villages are being –' He stopped and took a deep breath. 'How long is this going to go on?' There was hysteria in the President's voice.

'Until I receive the two billion dollars.'

They watched the President grit his teeth and close

his eyes for a moment. 'And you will stop the storms, then?'

'Yes.'

'How do you want the money delivered?'

Tanner turned off the television set. 'You see how easy it is, Princess? We already have the money. Let me show you what else Prima can do. These are our earlier tests.'

He pressed another button and a picture of a raging hurricane appeared on the screen. 'This is taking place in Japan,' Tanner said. 'Real time. And this season for them is always calm weather.'

He pressed a different button and pictures of a violent hailstorm appeared, battering a grove of citrus fruit. 'This is live from Florida. The temperature there now is near zero – in June. The crops are being wiped out.'

He activated another button and on the giant screen was a scene of a tornado tearing down buildings. 'This is what's happening in Brazil. As you see,' Tanner said proudly, 'Prima can do anything.'

Pauline moved closer to him and said, softly, 'Like its papa.'

Tanner turned off the television set. He picked up three DVDs and showed them to her. 'These are three more interesting conversations that I had – with Peru, Mexico and Italy. Do you know how the gold is delivered? We send trucks to their banks and they fill them. And then there's the Catch Twenty-two. If they make any attempt to find out where the gold is going, I promise them that the storm will begin again and never stop.'

Pauline looked at him, worried. 'Tanner, is there any way they can trace your calls?'

Tanner laughed. 'I hope they do. If someone tries to trace them, they'll reach a relay in a church, then a second relay takes them to a school. The third relay will set up storms they'll wish they had never seen. And the fourth time it ends up at the Oval Office of the White House.'

Pauline laughed.

The door opened and Andrew walked in.

Tanner turned. 'Here's my brother.'

Andrew was staring at Pauline, a puzzled expression on his face. 'Don't I know you?' He looked at her for almost a minute, as he concentrated, and then his face lit up. 'You – you and Tanner were – going to get married. I was the best man. You're – you're Princess.'

Pauline said, 'Very good, Andrew.'

'But you – you went away. You didn't love Tanner.'

Tanner spoke up. 'Let me straighten you out. She went away because she *did* love me.' He took Pauline's hand. 'She telephoned me the day after her wedding. She married a very rich, influential man so she could use her husband's influence to get important clients for KIG. That's why we were able to grow so fast.' Tanner gave Pauline a hug. 'We arranged to meet secretly every month.' He said proudly, 'And then she got interested in politics and became a senator.'

Andrew frowned. 'But – but Sebastiana – Sebastiana –'

'Sebastiana Cortez.' Tanner laughed. 'She was a decoy,

to throw everyone off the track. I made sure that everyone at the office knew about her. Princess and I couldn't afford to let anyone become suspicious.'

Andrew said vaguely, 'Oh, I see.'

'Come over here, Andrew.' Tanner led him to the control centre. They stood in front of Prima.

Tanner said, 'Do you remember this? You helped develop it. Now it's finished.'

Andrew's eyes widened. 'Prima . . .'

Tanner pointed to a button and said, 'Yes. Weather control.' He pointed to another button, 'Location.' He looked at his brother. 'See how simple we made it?'

Andrew said, under his breath, 'I remember . . .'

Tanner turned to Pauline. 'This is only the beginning, Princess.' Tanner took her in his arms. 'I'm researching thirty more countries. You got what you wanted. Power and money.'

Pauline said happily, 'A computer like that could be worth –'

'*Two* computers like that,' Tanner said. 'I have a surprise for you. Have you ever heard of Tamoa Island, in the South Pacific?'

'No.'

'We just bought it. It's sixty square miles and unbelievably beautiful. It's in the French Polynesian islands, and it has a landing strip and a yacht harbour. It has everything, including –' he paused dramatically, '– Prima II.'

Pauline said, 'You mean there's another –?'

Tanner nodded. 'That's right. It's underground, where no one can ever find it. Now that those two nosy bitches are finally out of the way, the world is ours.'

FORTY-THREE

Kelly was the first to open her eyes. She was lying on her back, naked, on the bare floor of a concrete basement, her hands handcuffed to eight-inch chains fastened to the wall, just above the floor. There was a small, barred window at the far end of the room, and one heavy, closed door.

Kelly turned to see Diane next to her, also naked and handcuffed. Their clothing had been thrown into a corner.

Diane said groggily, 'Where are we?'

'We're in hell, partner.'

Kelly tested the handcuffs. They were tight and firm around her wrists. She could lift her arm four or five inches, but that was it. 'We walked right into their trap,' Kelly said bitterly.

'You know what I hate most about this?'

Kelly looked around the bare room, and said, 'I can't imagine.'

'They won. We know why they killed our husbands, and why they're going to kill us, but there's no way we can ever tell the world. They've gotten away with it. Kingsley was right. Our luck has finally run out.'

'No, it hasn't.' The door had opened and Harry Flint was standing in the room. His smile widened. He locked the door behind him and put the key in his pocket. 'I shot you with Xylocaine bullets. I was supposed to kill you, but I thought we'd all have a little fun first.' He moved closer.

The two women exchanged a terrified look. They watched Flint, grinning, take off his shirt and trousers. 'Look what I have for you,' he said. He dropped his shorts. His member was stiff and turgid. Flint looked at the two of them and moved towards Diane. 'Why don't I start with you, baby, and then –'

Kelly interrupted. 'Wait a minute, handsome. How about taking me first? I feel horny.'

Diane looked at her, stunned. 'Kelly –'

Flint turned to Kelly and smirked. 'Sure, baby. You're going to love this.'

Flint reached down and started to stretch out on top of Kelly's naked body.

'Oh, yes,' Kelly moaned. 'I've really missed this.'

Diane had closed her eyes. She could not bear to watch.

Kelly stretched her legs apart and as Flint started to enter her, Kelly raised her right arm a few inches, and reached into her upswept hairdo. When her hand came down, there was a rat-tailed comb with a steel tip five inches long in it. In one quick motion, she slammed the steel tail into the back of Harry Flint's neck, pushing the blade all the way through.

Flint tried to scream, but all that came out was a loud gurgle. Blood was pouring out of his neck. Diane opened her eyes, stunned.

Kelly looked over at Diane. 'You – you can relax now.' She pushed away the limp figure on top of her. 'He's dead.'

Diane's heart was beating so fast, it felt as though it was going to leap from her chest. Her face was ghostly white.

Kelly was watching her, alarmed. 'Are you all right?'

'I was afraid he was going to –' Her mouth went dry. She looked at the bloody body of Harry Flint and shuddered. 'Why didn't you tell me about –?' She pointed to the rat-tail comb in his neck.

'Because if it hadn't worked . . . well, I didn't want you to think I'd failed you. Let's get out of here.'

'How?'

'I'll show you.' Kelly stretched out a long leg to where Flint had dropped his pants. Her toes reached out to grab his trousers. Two inches too far away. She shifted closer. One inch too short. Then finally, success.

Kelly grinned. '*Voilà!*' Her toes clutched the leg of the trousers and she slowly pulled them closer until they were near enough to grab with her hands. Kelly was going through his pockets, looking for the key to the handcuffs. She found it. A moment later, her hands were free. She hurried to free Diane.

'My God, you're a miracle,' Diane said.

'Thank my new hairdo. Let's get away from here.'

The two women picked up their clothes from the floor and quickly dressed. Kelly took the key to the door from Flint's pocket.

They walked over to the door and listened for a moment. Silence. Kelly opened the door. They were in a long, empty corridor.

'There must be a back way out of here,' Diane said.

Kelly nodded. 'All right. You go that way and I'll go the other way and –'

'No. Please. Let's stay together, Kelly.'

Kelly squeezed Diane's arm and nodded. 'Right, partner.'

Minutes later, the two women found themselves in a garage. There was a Jaguar and a Toyota in it.

'Take your choice,' Kelly said.

'The Jaguar is too noticeable. Let's take the Toyota.'

'I hope the key is –'

It was. Diane took the wheel.

'Do you have any idea where we're going?' Kelly asked.

'To Manhattan. I don't have a plan yet.'

'That's good news.' Kelly sighed.

'We need to find a place to sleep. When Kingsley finds out we've escaped, he's going to go crazy. We're not going to be safe anywhere.'

Kelly was thinking. 'Yes, we are.'
Diane glanced at her. 'What do you mean?'
Kelly said, proudly, 'I have a plan.'

FORTY-FOUR

As they drove into White Plains, a typical, peaceful little American town, twenty-five miles north of Manhattan, Diane said, 'This looks like a nice town. What are we doing here?'

'I have a friend here. She'll take care of us.'

'Tell me about her.'

Kelly said slowly, 'My mother was married to a drunk who enjoyed beating her. When I was able to afford to take care of my mother, I persuaded her to leave him. One of the models I knew had run away from an abusive boyfriend, and told me about this place. It's a boarding house run by an angel of a woman named Grace Seidel. I took my mother there to stay until I could find an apartment for her. I used to visit her at Grace's every day. My mother loved it, and became friends with some boarders. I finally found an apartment for mother and went to pick her up.' She stopped.

Diane looked at her. 'What happened?'

'She had gone back to her husband.'

They had reached the boarding house.

'We're here.'

Grace Seidel was in her fifties, a dynamic, motherly ball of energy. When she opened the door and saw Kelly, her face lit up.

'Kelly!' She threw her arms around her. 'I'm so glad to see you.'

Kelly said, 'This is my friend Diane.'

They exchanged hellos.

'Your room is all ready for you,' Grace said. 'As a matter of fact, it was your mother's room. I had an extra bed put in.'

As Grace Seidel walked them to their bedroom, they passed through a comfortable-looking living room where a dozen women were engaged in card games and various other activities.

'How long will you be staying?' Grace asked.

Kelly and Diane looked at each other. 'We're not sure.'

Grace Seidel smiled. 'No problem. The room is yours for as long as you want it.'

The room was lovely – neat and clean.

When Grace Seidel had left, Kelly said to Diane, 'We'll be safe here. And by the way, I think we made the Guinness Book of Records. Do you know how many times they've tried to kill us?'

'Yes.' Diane was standing by the window. Kelly heard her say, 'Thank you, Richard.'

Kelly started to speak, then thought, It's no use . . .

Andrew, dozing at his desk, dreamed that he was asleep in a hospital bed. Some voice in the room had awakened him. '. . . and luckily, I discovered this when we were decontaminating Andrew's safety equipment. I thought I should show it to you right away.'

'The goddamn Army told me it would be safe.'

A man was handing Tanner one of the gas masks from the Army experiment.

'I found a tiny hole at the base of the mask. It looks like someone cut it. That would be enough to have caused your brother's condition.'

Tanner looked at the mask and thundered. 'Whoever is responsible for this is going to pay.' He looked at the man and said, 'I'll look into this immediately. Thanks for bringing it to me.'

From his bed, Andrew groggily watched the man leave. Tanner looked at the mask for a moment and then walked over to a corner of the room where there was a large hospital cart filled with soiled linens.

Tanner reached down into the bottom of the cart and buried the gas mask under the linens.

Andrew tried to ask his brother what was happening, but he was too tired. He fell asleep.

* * *

Tanner, Andrew and Pauline had returned to Tanner's office.

Tanner had asked his secretary to bring in the morning newspapers. Tanner skimmed through the front pages. 'Look at these: "Scientists are baffled by freak storms in Guatemala, Peru, Mexico and Italy . . ."' He looked at Pauline, exultantly. 'And this is only the beginning. They're going to have a lot more to be baffled about.'

Vince Carballo came running into the room. 'Mr Kingsley –'

'I'm busy. What is it?'

'Flint is dead.'

Tanner's jaw dropped. '*What*? What are you talking about? What happened?'

'Stevens and Harris killed him.'

'That's impossible!'

'He's dead. They escaped and took off in the Senator's car. We've reported it stolen. The police have found it in White Plains.'

Tanner's voice was grim. 'Here's what I want you to do. I want you to take a dozen men and go to White Plains. Check every hotel, boarding house, and flophouse – any place where they could be hiding. I'm giving a 500,000 dollar reward to anyone who turns them in. Move it!'

'Yes, sir.'

Vince Carballo hurried out of the door.

In their room at Grace Seidel's boarding house, Diane said, 'I'm sorry about what happened when you got to Paris. Did they kill the superintendent?'

'I don't know. His family just disappeared.'

'What about your dog, Angel?'

Kelly said tightly. 'I don't want to talk about it.'

'I'm sorry. Do you know what's frustrating? We were so close. Now that we know what happened, there's no one we can tell it to. It would be our word against KIG's. They would put us in an asylum.'

Kelly nodded. 'You're right. There is no one left to go to.'

There was a momentary silence and Diane said, slowly, 'I think there is.'

Vince Carballo's men were spread out all over the town, checking every hotel, boarding house and flophouse. One of his men showed pictures of Diane and Kelly to the receptionist at the Esplanade Hotel.

'Have you seen either of these ladies? There's a half a million dollar reward for them.'

The receptionist shook his head. 'I wish I did know where they were.'

At the Renaissance Westchester Hotel, another man was holding up pictures of Diane and Kelly.

'A half million? I wish I could collect that.'

At the Crowne Plaza, the receptionist was saying, 'If I see them, I'll sure let you know, Mr.'

Vince Carballo himself knocked at the door of Grace Seidel's boarding house.

'Good morning.'

'Good morning. My name is Vince Carballo.' He

held up a picture of the two women. 'Have you seen these women? There's a half a million dollar reward for each of them.'

Grace Seidel's face lit up. 'Kelly!'

In Tanner's office, Kathy Ordonez was overwhelmed. Faxes were coming in faster than she could handle them and her E-mail inbox was inundated. She picked up a pile of the papers and walked into Tanner's office. Tanner and Pauline van Luven were seated on a sofa, talking.

Tanner looked up as his secretary came in. 'What is it?'

She smiled. 'Good news. You're going to have a very successful dinner party.'

He frowned. 'What are you talking about?'

She held up the papers. 'These are all acceptances. Everyone's coming.'

Tanner got up. 'Coming where? Let me see those.'

Kathy handed him the papers and went out to her desk.

Tanner read the first E-mail aloud. '"We would be delighted to come to dinner at KIG Headquarters on Friday to see the unveiling of Prima, your weather control machine." From the editor of *Time* magazine.'

His face turned white. He looked at the next one. '"Thank you for your invitation to see Prima, your weather control computer, at KIG Headquarters. We look forward to being there." It's signed by the editor of *Newsweek*.'

He skimmed the rest of the papers. 'CBS, NBC, CNN, *The Wall Street Journal*, the *Chicago Tribune*, and the *London Times*, all eager to see the unveiling of Prima.'

Pauline sat there, speechless.

Tanner was so furious, he could hardly speak. 'What the hell is going on –?' He stopped. 'Those bitches!'

At Irma's Internet Café, Diane was busily operating a computer. She looked up at Kelly. 'Have we left anyone out?'

Kelly said, '*Elle, Cosmopolitan, Vanity Fair, Mademoiselle, Readers Digest . . .*'

Diane laughed. 'I think this does it. I hope Kingsley has a good caterer. He's going to have a big party.'

Vince Carballo was looking at Grace Seidel, excitedly. 'You know Kelly?'

'Oh, yes,' Grace said. 'She's one of the most famous models in the world.'

Vince Carballo's face lit up. 'Where is she?'

Grace looked at him in surprise. 'I don't know. I've never met her.'

His face reddened. 'You said you knew her.'

'I mean – everybody knows her. She's very famous. Isn't she beautiful?'

'You have no idea where she is?'

Grace said thoughtfully, 'I do have kind of an idea, but I'd be amazed if it *was* her.'

'Where?'

'I saw a woman who looked like her get on a bus this morning, but someone that famous would be in a limousine, surely. She was travelling with someone –'

'What bus was it?'

'It was the bus to Vermont. You, don't think it was really her, do you?'

'No. Thanks.'

Vince Carballo hurried away.

Tanner threw the pile of faxes and E-mails to the floor, and turned to Pauline. 'Do you know what those bitches have done? We can't let anyone see Prima.' He was thoughtful for a long moment. 'I think Prima will have an accident the day before the party and blow up.'

Pauline looked at him for a moment and then smiled. 'Prima II.'

Tanner nodded. 'That's right. We can travel around the world and, any time we're ready, we'll go to Tamoa and start operating Prima II.'

Kathy Ordonez's voice came over the intercom. She sounded frantic. She buzzed into Tanner's office. 'Mr Kingsley, the phones are going crazy. I have *The New York Times*, *The Washington Post* and Larry King, all holding for you.'

'Tell them I'm in a meeting.' Tanner turned to Pauline. 'We have to get out of here.' He patted Andrew on the shoulder. 'Andrew, come with us.'

'Yes, Tanner.'

The three of them walked over to the redbrick

building. 'I have something very important for you to do, Andrew.'

'Anything you want,' Andrew said.

Tanner led the way into the redbrick building, and walked over to Prima. Tanner turned to Andrew. 'Here's what I want you to do. Princess and I have to leave now, but at six o'clock, I want you to turn this computer off. It's very simple.' He pointed. 'You see this big red button?'

Andrew nodded. 'I see it.'

'All you have to do is press it three times, at six o'clock. Three times. Can you remember that?'

Andrew said, 'Yes, Tanner. Six o'clock. Three times.'

'Right. See you later.'

Tanner and Pauline started to walk out.

Andrew looked after them. 'You're not taking me with you?'

'No. You stay here. Just remember: Six o'clock, three times.'

'I'll remember.'

As they walked outside, Pauline said, 'What if he doesn't remember?'

Tanner laughed. 'It doesn't matter. I'll set it to explode automatically at six o'clock. I just wanted to make sure he's there when it happens.'

FORTY-FIVE

It was a perfect day for flying. KIG's 757 was speeding over the Pacific Ocean, under a cerulean blue sky. Pauline and Tanner were snuggled together on a sofa in the main cabin.

Pauline said, 'Darling, do you know it's a shame that people will never know how brilliant you are?'

'If they ever found out, I'd be in big trouble.'

She looked at him and said, 'No problem. We could buy a country, and proclaim ourselves the rulers. Then they couldn't touch us.'

Tanner laughed.

Pauline stroked his hand. 'Did you know that I wanted you from the first time I saw you?'

'No. As I remember, you were very impertinent.'

'And it worked, didn't it? You had to see me again, to teach me a lesson.'

There was a long, erotic kiss.

Far away, lightning flashed.

Tanner said, 'You'll love Tamoa. We'll spend a week or two there and relax, and then we'll travel around the world. We're going to make up for all the lost years that we couldn't be together.'

She looked up and grinned impishly. 'You bet we will.'

'And every month or so, we'll come back to Tamoa and put Prima II to work. You and I can pick our targets together.'

Pauline said, 'Well, we could create a storm in England, but they wouldn't notice!'

Tanner laughed. 'We have the whole world to choose from.'

The steward approached. 'Is there anything I can get you?' he asked.

Tanner said, 'No. We have everything.' And he knew that it was true.

In the distant sky, there were more flashes of lightning.

'I hope there isn't going to be a storm,' Pauline said. 'I – I hate flying in rough weather.'

Tanner said reassuringly, 'Don't worry, darling. There's not a cloud in the sky.' He thought of something and smiled. 'We don't have to worry about the weather. We control it!' He looked at his watch. 'Prima blew up an hour ago and –'

Sudden drops of rain began to pound against the plane.

Tanner held Pauline closer. 'It's all right. It's just a bit of rain.'

As Tanner said this, the sky suddenly began to darken

412

and tremble with loud peals of thunder. The huge plane started to bounce up and down. Tanner was looking out of the window, puzzled by what was happening. The rain began to turn into large hailstones.

Tanner said, 'Look at –' The realisation suddenly hit him. 'Prima!' It was a cry of exultation, a look of glory in his eyes. 'We can –'

At that instant, a hurricane hit the plane, bouncing it around savagely.

Pauline was screaming.

In the redbrick building at KIG, Andrew Kingsley was operating Prima, his fingers flashing over the keys in remembrance. Watching his target on the screen, he could see an image of his brother's plane being buffeted by 300-mile-an-hour hurricane winds. He pressed another button.

At a dozen branch offices of the National Weather Service, from Anchorage, Alaska to Miami, Florida, meteorologists were staring at their computer screens in disbelief. What was happening seemed impossible, but it really was happening.

Working alone in the redbrick building, Andrew was grateful that there was still one thing he could do to help make the world a better place. He carefully guided an F-6 tornado he had created – up – up – higher and higher . . .

* * *

413

Tanner was looking out of the window of the wildly tossing plane and he heard the tell-tale freight train sound of the approaching tornado over the roar of the storm. Tanner's face was flushed and he was trembling with excitement, watching the tornado spinning up towards the plane. He was ecstatic. 'Look! There's never been a tornado this high. Never! I created it! It's a miracle! Only God and I could –'

In the redbrick building, Andrew moved a switch and watched the screen as the plane exploded and pieces of wreckage and bodies were hurled into the sky.

Then Andrew Kingsley pressed the red button three times.

FORTY-SIX

Kelly and Diane were finishing getting dressed when Grace Seidel knocked at their door. 'Breakfast is ready whenever you are.'

'Coming,' Kelly called out.

Diane said, 'I hope our little stunt worked. Let's see if Grace has a morning newspaper.'

They stepped out of their room, and went into the television and games room. A few people were gathered around the television set. As Kelly and Diane started to pass it, to go to the dining room, they heard the news anchorman saying . . .

. . . and according to reports, there were no survivors. Tanner Kingsley and Senator Pauline van Luven were on the plane, along with a pilot, co-pilot and a steward.

The two women froze. They looked at each other, turned, and walked up to the television set. On the screen were pictures of the exterior of KIG.

> *The Kingsley International Group constitutes the largest think-tank in the world, with offices in thirty countries. The weather bureau has reported that an unexpected electrical storm in the South Pacific area where Tanner Kingsley's private plane was headed . . .*

Diane and Kelly were listening, fascinated.

> *. . . and in another piece of the puzzle, there's a mystery here that the police are trying to solve. The press was invited to a dinner party, to visit Prima, a new weather control computer that KIG has been developing, but yesterday evening there was an explosion at KIG and Prima was completely destroyed. The fire department found the body of Andrew Kingsley in the wreckage and believe he was the only victim.*

Diane said, 'Tanner Kingsley is dead.'

'Say that again. Slowly.'

'Tanner Kingsley is dead.'

Kelly breathed a deep sigh of relief. She looked at Diane and smiled. 'Life is sure going to be dull after this.'

'I hope so,' Diane replied. 'How would you like to sleep at the Waldorf-Astoria Towers tonight?'

Kelly grinned. 'I wouldn't mind.'

As they said their goodbyes to Grace Seidel, she hugged Kelly and said, 'Any time.'

She never mentioned the money that she had been offered.

In the presidential suite in the Waldorf-Astoria Towers, a waiter was setting up a table for dinner. He turned to Diane. 'Did you say you wanted it set for four?'

'That's right.'

Kelly looked at her and said nothing.

Diane knew what she was thinking.

As they were sitting down at the table, Diane said, 'Kelly, I don't think we did this alone. I think we had a little help.' She raised her glass of champagne and said to the empty chair next to her, 'Thank you, Richard, darling. I love you.'

As Diane lifted the glass to her lips, Kelly said, 'Wait a minute.'

Diane turned to her.

Kelly picked up her glass of champagne and looked at the empty chair next to her. 'Mark, I love you so much. Thank you.'

They drank their toasts.

Kelly smiled and said, 'That felt good. Well, what's next?'

'I'm going to the FBI in Washington, to tell them what I know.'

Kelly corrected her. '*We're* going to Washington, to tell them what *we* know.'

Diane smiled. 'Right, partner.'

After dinner, they watched television and every channel was carrying the story of Tanner Kingsley's death. As Kelly watched, she said, thoughtfully, 'You know, when you cut off a snake's head, the rest of the snake dies.'

'What does that mean?'

'Let's find out.' Kelly walked over to the telephone. 'I want to place a call to Paris,' she told the hotel operator.

Five minutes later, she heard the voice of Nicole Paradis. 'Kelly! Kelly! Kelly! I'm so glad you called.'

Kelly's heart sank. She knew what she was going to hear next. They had killed the Cendre family, and Angel.

'I didn't know how to reach you.'

'You've heard the news?'

'The whole world has heard the news. Jérôme Malo and Alphonse Girouard packed their things and left in a hurry.'

Kelly was afraid to ask the next question. 'And the Cendres, and Angel –?'

'Philippe and his family are safe, and I have Angel in my apartment. Those thugs were planning to use her as bait in case you wouldn't co-operate.'

Kelly felt a sudden glow. 'Oh, that's wonderful!'

'What would you like me to do with her?'

'Put her on the next Air France flight to New York. Let me know when she'll arrive and I'll pick her up at the airport. You can call me here at the Waldorf–Astoria Towers.'

'I'll take care of it.'

'Thank you.' Kelly replaced the receiver.

Diane had been listening. 'Angel is all right?'

'Yes, and the Cendre family.'

'Oh, that's great!'

'Isn't it? I'm thrilled. By the way, what are you going to do with your half of the money?'

Diane looked at her. 'What?'

'KIG put up a five-million-dollar-reward. I think it's going to us.'

'But Kingsley's dead.'

'I know, but KIG isn't.'

They laughed.

Kelly asked, 'What's your plan after we go to Washington? Are you going to start painting again?'

Diane was thoughtful for a moment. 'No.'

Kelly was watching her. 'Really?'

'Well, there is a painting that I want to do. It's a picnic scene in Central Park.' Her voice broke. 'Two lovers having a picnic in the rain. Then . . . we'll see. What about you? Are you going back to modelling?'

'No, I don't think –'

Diane was looking at her.

'Well . . . maybe, because while I'm on the runway, I can imagine Mark watching me, and blowing kisses. Yes, I think he would want me to go back to work.'

Diane smiled. 'Good.'

They watched television for another hour and then Diane said, 'I think it's time for bed.'

Fifteen minutes later, they were undressed and in their queen beds, both reliving their recent adventures.

Kelly yawned. 'I'm sleepy, Diane. Let's turn out the lights.'

AFTERWORD

The old adage that everyone talks about the weather but no one does anything about it is no longer valid. Today, two countries have the ability to control weather around the world: the United States and Russia. Other countries are working feverishly to catch up.

The search for the mastery of the elements that began with Nikola Tesla in the late 1800s, involving the transmission of electrical energy through space, has become a reality.

The consequences are monumental. Weather can be used as a blessing or as a weapon.

All the necessary elements are in place.

In 1969, the US Patent Office granted a patent for 'a method of increasing the likelihood of precipitation by the artificial introduction of sea water vapor into the atmosphere'.

In 1971, a patent was issued to the Westinghouse Electric Corporation for a system for irradiation of planet surface areas.

In 1971, a patent was issued to the National Science Foundation for a weather modification method.

In 1978, the United States launched an experiment which created a downpour of rain over six counties of northern Wisconsin. The storm generated winds of 175 miles per hour and caused fifty million dollars in damages.

In 1995, the US Patent Office issued a patent for a satellite weather modification system.

Russia, meanwhile, has developed an 'elf' system – thirty huge transmitters that form high-pressure blocking systems that can change weather patterns around the world. 'Elf' waves started in the early 1980s and strange weather patterns began to occur, with unusual droughts, flooding and storms.

Weather is the most powerful force we know. Whoever controls the weather can disrupt world economies with perpetual rainstorms, wipe out crops in a drought, and unleash destruction on enemy battlefields.

The danger of a devastating confrontation between the United States and Russia became so great, that in 1977, a UN Treaty against weather modification for hostile purposes was signed by the United States and Russia.

In spite of signing the UN Treaty, the United States is in the process of building a huge weather experimental complex called HAARP, in a remote part of Alaska.

*   *   *

I would sleep better if a world leader said, 'Everyone talks about the weather, but no one does anything about it.'

And it were the truth.